From the Files of the Department of the Arcane:

Spring Blessings

As Revealed By:

S.C. Houff

405 Buchanan Street
Richlands, VA 24641
schouffauthor@gmail.com

Spring Blessings
©2014 S. C. Houff

Self published edition 2016

Grammar-mancer: Rebekah McGrady
Cover design: S. C. Houff
Cover Art: Rebekah McGrady, Mercenary Art Ninja
D. O. A. Logo: Oddite Delight Designs

ISBN 0615943721
ISBN-13: 978-0615943725

Printed by CreateSpace

Super Awesome Thanks Go To...

Evil Bekka, who slugged through editing to get to this point.

The Very Talented Summer Hogan McCoy who did the wonderful First Edition Cover Art.

My hella awesome family of my brothers Jeffery and David and my father, Vince.

Heather, Sarah, Miki, Jordan, Karin and too many others to name here -- thank you so much.

Hal, who has never EVER let me get away with quitting

This book is offered in tribute to the memory of Marilyn Banks Carroll,

Phyllis John Banks, and all the matriarchs who came before me and made me the woman I am today.

Sing to me, oh Muse,

and I will share your song with the world.

Tell me your stories

and I will carve them into the tree of history.

Dance with me

and I will walk down your path.

Guide my hands to craft words that reflect your wishes,

To represent my ancestors proudly

and bring hope to generations to come.

Grant me, oh Muse,

the ability to tell my story.

I. A Brief History of Gaiman Heights

Gaiman Heights was founded in 1670 in what would become the state of Massachusetts by Puritan leader Robert Goodchild. He led a group of fifteen families to the New World for whatever reason that Puritans came to the New World. I think it was something to do with religious freedom and junk. I don't think it was for the shopping. Shopping in the New World wasn't very good back then. And that would continue to be the case for some time. No, it was definitely religious freedom. The colony they called Harmony was settled in the Gaihaim --a Native American word for all manner of shit that be freaky -- Valley. The Puritans wanted to build that city on the hill. On the day that the first cabin went up, two representatives from the local Indian tribe stood on the high hill and looked down.

"I say, you think we should tell them, Nigel?" asked one of the noble savages.

"No, Winslow," Nigel replied. "They don't speak the civilized tongue. Besides, they'll find out soon enough."

With that, the two ambassadors of the New World left. At the same time, two more people came to watch the fledgling group with peaked interest. They were not indigenous to this land, nor were they European, although they had just arrived from Merry Old England. They had lent their names to a young poet for use while they were there. Maybe you've heard of them...

The two of them came from somewhere further away than the Old World. Their homeland lay beyond this world; in one that mortals rarely wandered into on their own -- a land that was only perceived in dreams and fevered delusions of mad men. Their home was surrounded by a high wall and a thorny Hedge that hid it away from our world. The two of them could not return home, no matter how much they wanted to do so. Well, they could but they would be ripped apart and their glittering blood would be spilled for the whole realm to see as an example. Such an act was a difficult feat that could only be achieved by their king. It would also shorten their very long lives.

The pink haired one stood on the edge of the ridge overlooking a winding river. His toes hung over the edge as he rocked back and forth with his arms outstretched, embracing an unseen light. His dark and sinister eyes twinkled excitedly in the cold New England sun. The man stepped back and then took a long look at his companion who was more interested in the book that he was reading than the group working to survive in this new land below. He then smiled wildly as he bit at the air. His companion rolled his handsome moss colored eyes. Part of their integration was developing a less otherworldly look as they roamed in our world. The pink haired man's companion chose to look more human while the pink haired man preferred to look like, if it was at all possible, a gay and inhuman Adam Ant.

"Do you smell that!?!" he exclaimed. "Puck, I can taste it!"

Puck took a long whiff of the untainted air. He sighed wistfully as a satisfied grin snuck across his face. He turned towards the pink haired man with an almost erotic sparkle in his eye.

"It's powerful," said Puck. "Whatever it is, I haven't felt something like that since we left home. Iago, whatever that is.....it's just cake. There is some power in it."

Puck squinted as he peered into the valley below.

"Iago," Puck said, "there are people down there."

Iago leaned down over the ridge and sniffed the air. He let his eyes widen with excitement as his mouth opened to a jagged grin that exposed rows of sharp teeth. He cracked his neck as deviousness flashed over his features.

"Puritans, Puck, they're Puritans," Iago hissed in an orgasmic release.

"They're mundane. They're average. They're human. Do you know what this means, Puck? We're the first ones here!"

"No, we aren't," Puck replied quietly as he squatted down next to a pair of tracks. Iago turned to Puck with a sneer. He had never liked being told that he was wrong. However, the tracks started out as human and slowly turned into that of a large dog. "There are lycans here too."

"Werewolves?" Iago asked with a jackal's growl. "Do we have to share the Puritans with werewolves?"

"Nah," said Puck. "They'll leave the Puritans alone if left alone in return. We'll see how long that lasts."

"Well, Puck," Iago said with a wistful sigh. "We might not have been the first, but we won't be the last. I say we take advantage while we can. Waddaya say, Puck?"

Puck leaned forward as he furrowed his brow in deep thought. He was looking down at the perfect opportunity to teach a lesson or two.

"We have a group of completely repressed and superstitious people," explained Iago, trying to drive his point home. He had always been a halfway decent salesman. "I say we raise a little hell while we can and eat whatever that thing is down there before someone stops us."

Puck mulled over Iago's arguments. How could he say no? Iago's proposition offered him an opportunity to create a form of amusement that they had been missing since their exile from the Dream. More importantly, it was a chance to find out whatever delicious power source was down there and torment Puritans, no less. Anyone who took themselves too seriously was a valid target for him. He nodded before grinning at Iago. That is how the village of Harmony got their first supernatural residents. And Iago was right; they weren't the last to arrive in the Valley.

Once the levee broke, the rest of the world came flooding in.

After the skin walkers and the fairies, George Trublood arrived in the New World. George came to Harmony in the dead of night escorted by two men whom he trusted dearly. He was looking to start a new life, so to speak, for himself in this strange new land. He was a pale, handsome man who lived in a dark wood cabin built into the deep forest away from the rest of the village. George was also the only one in the Gaihaim Valley who had servants, which branded him as very lazy and to not be trusted by the settlers of Harmony. He had three of them and they worshipped their master who had brought them with him over the ocean. He also had a pale blonde wife he called Temperance. She was pretty, but always looked lost during the day.

If it hadn't been for a simple psychic trick that most vampires know how to use, his neighbors wouldn't have thought he was lazy. They would have noticed the missing livestock. They would have burned down the Trublood estate and done unspeakable things to George and his family. George used this trick to mentally suggest that he was not living up to the Puritan work ethic and they should shun him. With age comes wisdom.

George Trublood was not his real name. George had chosen this name when he found Jesus. He was visited by a revelation about the Christ while feeding on a cloister of nuns. While draining the abbess, George had been visited by a vision of the risen Lord. The Prince of Peace stepped down from on high and calmly looked at George. He placed his pierced hand on George's shoulder, gently trying to calm the vampire's violent nature. Suddenly, George had felt the glory of divine love working into his unbeating heart.

"My son," said the Living Christ. "Why do you kill your brothers and sisters? My son, you can walk in my light by loving them as I care for you."

George took this advice to his unbeating heart and became the first Puritan vampire, but not the last.

An interesting side note is this; after the talk, Jesus met up with his friend at the pub. He put his hand on his friend's shoulder with a hard slap. His friend jumped with a sudden blink.

"Dude," said Jesus. "Did you see what I did there? Them being dead doesn't make them any smarter. Puck, this opens up a whole new level of awesome."

"Iago," responded Puck, "Pretending to be Jesus just to convince a vampire to convert to Christianity is pretty messed up, even for you. You know, Jesus is going to be mad when He comes back."

The only non-living resident of Harmony was left to his quiet self until the winter. That's when the sickness hit. There was nothing supernatural about the sickness that spread through the settlement. By all historical accounts, it was nothing more than a bad case of pneumonia. It was an epidemic brought on by being a displaced people without the benefits of modern medicine. In that situation, you have a tendency to believe bad things happen for evil reasons. For example, instead of blaming a sudden and horrific illness on poor sanitation or a brutal New England winter, you blame it on demons or witches. After deep study, Robert Goodchild blamed Harmony's hardships on his flock. Their lack of faith had let the evil into the village.

Well, he was half right. Humans are funny creatures. They aren't willing to blame themselves for something when they can blame someone or something else. Case in point, take a look at the man sitting to your left. Now, kick him really hard. Guaranteed, he'll blame you for that kick rather than himself for sitting beside you. You can imagine the path that one goes on in colonial America when an epidemic hits. This will be aggravated by the fact that you are obsessively religious. It is ten times worse when you have two fairies rolling around causing chaos.

Long before the trials in Salem, there were the witch riots of Harmony. This is ironic since the first recorded coven of Gaiman Heights didn't arrive until twenty years after the riots. The riots were never a trial but more of a violent paranoid blood bath that at the end left thirty-seven people dead, including George Trublood and his brood. The world's first Puritan Vampire met his final death because of an act of kindness.

George idolized Robert Goodchild as would anyone who found themselves devoted to a religious leader. So, when Robert's young daughter, Prudence, fell ill, George decided to give the Kiss to the girl. The mob found the pair just as George was sealing the deal with his own blood. The mob did what any superstitious and paranoid group would do when they find an adult feeding blood to a seemingly dead little girl: they dragged him to the center of town and tied him to a stake. Despite his pleas for mercy, they lit the pyre.

There was a flash of blue light and a low magma changing rumble as the ground shook, which is what happens when a vampire dies on a supernatural fault line. The townspeople congregated and congratulated each other by putting their hands up to the air and then slapping their partner's hand with a thunderous clap in praise of their Lord God. Browning Goodwin called it an exalted five.

"Finally," Browning Goodwin proclaimed. "The evil has been purged from this village."

From behind the crowd there was a low primal growl from an unearthly voice that halted the celebrations suddenly in an almost a clichéd horror movie fashion. Then, there was a rush of wind. Suddenly, there was Prudence Goodchild with newly-grown fangs firmly planted in Browning Goodwin's jugular. There was nothing but quiet from the townspeople watching in horror as Prudence drained the man of his blood. What they don't tell you in those stupid teenage vampire novels or soap opera TV shows is that a newly created vampire's birth comes with a twofold problem. They are both angry and hungry. They also feel the pain of anyone, human or otherwise, that they are bound to in blood. Now with the sudden and violent death of George Trublood, Prudence was in a world of hurt. The subsequent screams could be heard as far away as Boston.

Then, there was Puck and Iago. This wasn't Puck's typical style of mayhem. Puck had always been the more level headed of the two. Blind chaos confused and vexed him. More importantly, he was all about teaching lessons with his pranks. You can't teach someone if they are dead which was too often the end result of Iago's tricks. However, from the chaos came something that suited his more primal needs. Puck stood on top of a mountain of ash and bones with his mouth open. He took in air with hungry gasps. He felt the power of a bald nexus pulse through him. For the first time, in a long time, Puck felt almost normal.

Iago was having just as good a time as Puck.

This was the kind of chaos he was made for in the most literal sense of the word. He found a dark cloak and a pale horse. He leaned against the horse's neck as it trotted slowly through the flowers of carnage. To the outside observer, the pink haired man looked drunk. They would have been mostly correct. Iago was, like Puck, feeling the effects of the exposed nexus. For Iago, this was calming, leaving him in a more sedated state. He ran his fingers through the horse's mane singing in a low voice. A twisted smile played across his lips. This was perfect.

Well, perfect until the horse was stolen out from under him in the most literal use of the word. As Iago pulled himself out of the muck and the mire, he watched the young vampire gorge on horse blood. She ripped out the animal's throat and cupped the blood in her hands. She drank greedily as she violently shoveled the warm liquid into her mouth. Over her swallowing, she let out a hard growl. Iago felt his hands shake.

"By Zeus's station wagon!" Iago eloquently exclaimed, "What fresh hell is this?!?"

Prudence looked up with her dead eyes at the loudly obnoxious voice. Her blood stained fangs were bared as a furious hiss flowed out between them. She sniffed the air for a moment and then let out a predatory growl as she caught the scent of sweet blood. The new vampire dropped to her hands and knees and started a lupine run towards the fae. Vampires are fast and are twice as fast when they are in frenzy. Those who are in tune with their inner beasts, i.e. werewolves, vampires, and the like, can smell the blood that flows through their prey. The smell of fairy blood is intoxicating to blood drinkers due to the amount of magic that flows through the veins of the fairy. Prudence caught the scent of the fairy blood and decided in that moment that she wanted all of it. Fairies aren't faster than anything. In a foot race between a fae and a human, the fae and human will both be equally matched as per speed. The fae will still win largely because the fae will cheat: it is in their nature. Iago ripped a tiny hole in time and space. He, then, swan dove through the hole in an effort to cheat the vampire out of a meal. He found himself spat out on top of the nexus and, more specifically, right onto Puck, sending them both into the remains of the pyre.

"Iago," yelled Puck. "What is wrong with you?"

"Vampire brat!" Iago yelled back. "Mother of God and all the wacky cousins!"

That last was in response to Prudence appearing before them. The pair looked at each other. Puck picked up Iago. They disappeared in a cloud of purple-blue smoke or, as a certain mainstream comic would say, bamfed into another spot. Within seconds, they heard her screams and wails echoing through the Gaihaim Valley searching the forest for her prey. It would be only a matter of minutes before the frenzying vampire found them and their sun shining blood.

Sure, they could have run into the night screaming. They could have ported to the other side of the world. However, she had their scent. Once a hungry vampire has a scent, she will hunt that scent until it is found and God help anyone who got in her way. The two fae decided that the wisest thing to do was to catch the vampire. So, they built an elaborate trap for Prudence. They dug a deep hole and set a rosewood casket at the bottom of the hole. Puck opened his mouth to protest and then stopped. This, the sudden appearance of a casket, was better left unquestioned. There were things that Iago did that were better left unknown. Sometimes, his tricks and designs were sinister and downright evil. It just made Puck feel terrible when he knew about them. Iago's deep dark secrets were better not known. Puck placed his hands on the lid and softly whispered to the wood.

The world of the fae relies on a series of agreements. The act of breathing, for example, takes three such agreements; this is an agitation for the fae living in the mundane world trying to eke out an existence, but very useful when dealing with the supernatural world.

"Well," said Iago, "We need to set out some bait. Puck, give me your blood."

"What?" said Puck. "No, kiss off. Use your own blood! Iago, if you hadn't played your stupid prank, then we wouldn't be staring down the barrel of a frenzying vampire brat."

"I know!" Iago squealed. "I did all the hard work. You get to bleed."

Puck sighed before he picked up a shovel. He swung it at the back of Iago's bright pink head. You can't kill a fairy through merely natural means. The very nature of the fae is intangible. It would be like trying to kill the wind. That doesn't mean you can't hurt them. Of course, the only thing that can really hurt a fairy is cold iron, which is a fancy way of saying iron. However, the colder the piece is the more it'll hurt the fairy. So, when the shovel made of cold iron connected with the back of Iago's skull, it ripped his skin letting green black blood pour from the gash. Iago went down with a flailing scream. As Iago bled, Puck gently guided his head over the hole. Prudence let out a shrill call as she smelled fairy blood. Puck then threw the glittering shovel into the casket. He picked up Iago and disappeared in a puff of logic. The two of them took shelter in a high oak tree. Puck clamped his hand down over Iago's whimpering.

"Shut up, man," hissed Puck. "She'll hear you."

The trees shook as a wild-eyed Prudence entered the clearing. She sniffed the air before lunging towards the sweet smelling blood. She fell into the casket. The casket, as per its agreement with Puck, snapped its lid tightly on the vampire. Prudence screamed and wailed as her claws tore at the lid. The fair folk came down from their tree and shoveled dirt over the shaking, venom-spewing casket. They finished burying Prudence just before sunrise. Iago danced a little jig over her grave.

"Man," said Iago, "I feel bad for whoever is here when she wakes up. Hungry and tripping, what a combination."

"Well," Puck replied, "She's not getting out. Not by human hands anyway. Those bonds are the strongest I can invoke on this side of the Hedge. The only thing that could break that bond is either a high powered mage or a witch."

"And the likelihood of them coming to Puritan country?"

"If your little blood bath is an indication of things to come? I doubt it." said Puck with a soft head roll, "Besides, mages and witches don't leave their caves to migrate to the New World."

"So, what now?" asked Iago. "I say breakfast."

"Yes," agreed Puck. "Breakfast sounds good."

It was after the arrival of the third race of supernatural residents to the Gaihaim Valley that the fae became bored with the nexus. There were the ghosts now in the township of Harmony. Ghosts are hard to live with, not because they're scary but because they whine. This is the case with most intelligent hauntings. To the average human, this often looks like a desk moving or a light flickering. To the supernatural viewer, this is a great deal of whining about being dead. The fae put up with the ghostly droning for all of two hours before leaving for greener pastures. The settlement of Harmony stayed untouched for almost twenty years.

Then Mim arrived in the New World.

When Mim was born, she was already twenty years older than God. Mim had traveled the world for a number of years and had a collection of different names. She came to the New World because the Nexus beckoned her near. Years before her arrival, she'd had a dream about the nexus, a focal point of incredible magical power, being born on an altar of fire and bone. She had hoped that a sacrifice would not be offered to coax the being to show itself. However, those years had finally come to pass with the death of the Puritan vampire and as the Crone of several covens, she felt the need to watch it.

"I'll take it!" she said excitedly, as she stood on a hill overlooking the Gaihaim Valley.

"Splendid!" Nigel replied. "It's always marvelous to have new neighbors like you, madam. Would you like cream and sugar in your tea?"

"Cream, please." said Mim as Nigel poured the Earl Gray tea. "Now, I brought twelve beaver pelts and three blue glass beads. Is that going to be enough?"

"Yes, my good woman," said Nigel.

Nigel and Mim discussed their business quietly over tea until sundown. At that time, Mim started to set up her home. Nigel met up with Winslow to walks back to their village.

"These are jolly good pelts," Winslow said. "What do you suppose she is?"

"Witch," said Nigel. "We should inform Cyril. Witches never travel alone."

Sure enough, the Daughters of the Moon, the first coven of white witches in America, found its way to the Gahiaim Valley shortly after the Crone settled in the valley. It is very rare that a coven solely practices one type of magic. Saying one does x magic doesn't happen often since people are generally a collective of a few things, not just one type; although the two most common types of magic practitioners to say that they practice exclusively one type of magic would be white and black witches. However, the Crone had decreed their formation and arrival to the New World and no one said no to the Crone. They chose to build their sanctuary on the edge of the old settlement of Harmony. The first order of business for the coven was to dispel the bad energy and quiet the restless spirits of the village. With the nexus, however, firmly planted in the living rock, that was easier said than done. Then during the planting season, they found Prudence's screaming casket. After the hail stones shaped like male genitalia, the high priestess met with the matron of all witchcraft.

"I can't take it!" exclaimed the high priestess, "Skin walkers and ghosts are one thing. And, by the way, those ghosts are super mean and one of our sisters was raped at the last full moon. That is something I can cope with, but not on top of the vampire and whatever that thing is in the middle of town. And yesterday? You don't want to know what I saw yesterday."

"Well," said Mim, "Ghosts can be ignored and skin walkers just need their bellies rubbed. As for the other things? Don't worry your pretty little head about it."

It was around that time Doctor Duke arrived in Gaiman Heights. Doctor Duke was two things: enigmatic and old. He wasn't as old as Mim, but he was old. There had many a legend written about the traveling mage, as magi are wont to travel when they get bored of being locked away in their colleges studying. It only made sense that the man would come to the New World. Doctor Duke didn't so much immigrate to the New World as much as he appeared one day in Mim's drawing room. He and Mim had an odd relationship that neither one of them would ever admit to publicly. Despite her protests of business as usual, she had begged for him to show up after everything that had occurred since her arrival in the Valley. He propped his aged boots on the shaking casket as he leaned back in a chair. He wore a low brimmed hat that was dipped over his eyes as he waited for the Crone to address him. Mim gave him forty minutes to see if he'd try to move at some point. When he didn't, she too walked into her drawing room.

"So, dancing with the devil in the pale moonlight at the equinox just not cutting it?" He asked from the corner of his mouth in a jerky drawl. He took a draw from his long pipe.

"Die in a fire, mage." Mim said by way of greeting. "There is a lot more going on than my girls can handle. For example, that casket under your feet is going up to Brockton. That poor girl can't control her inner beast. As far as I can tell, though, she's only vampire in the valley."

"Then track down her creator." retorted Dr. Duke

"According to the ghosts, they burned her creator at the stake," Mim said flatly. "Purtians, what will they do next? Claudius, has his garrison up in Arkham. I figure he takes care of his own. If he can't help her, then he can deal with her in that way too. Duke, she's the least of our problems."

Doctor Duke arched a brow as pushed the brim of his hat up.

"When we came here," continued Mim, "to this valley, we were followed by a pair of fae. We couldn't figure who they are or why they were harassing my girls. Fairies generally stay away from other magic users, because you know, we call their bull shit. Then we came across something. Duke, you should see this, it'll make the nine-year-old vampire look tame."

They walked towards the ruins of the old village of Harmony. Doctor Duke watched as a group of elder witches formed a circle. Their naked bodies writhed in congress with the ground.

Doctor Duke flinched uncomfortably as their moan of ecstasy echoed off the trees. Mim rolled her eyes.

"You know, Mim," said Doctor Duke slowly. "Your rites...."

"Don't typically involve dry humping the air," finished Mim. "There are my most powerful girls. Now, before you start ranting about my girls being seduced into sex magic, just smell the air."

Doctor Duke didn't need to smell the air. The benefit of being one of the most powerful magi in existence meant that he could see the light or aura that radiated off a magical being or object. Doctor Duke's senses were overwhelmed by the faintly blue light of an indefinable nature. It took every ounce of restraint not to lick the nexus.

"How does a nexus end up appearing in the back of beyond of New England?" Doctor Duke said, astounded.

"It's a nexus," said Mim. "The last one showed up where it wanted and so will this one. They do what they want."

Doctor Duke nodded slowly as he walked around the nexus with his brow firmly quirked. He glanced back at Mim with slack jawed amazement as he completed his circuit.

"Not to worry Mim," he said finally. "My order will keep it in check. We have to do that. That thing is going to attract all kinds of supernatural parasites."

"Well, yes that is a problem. Merlin, the world is shrinking," Mim said. "I thought this new place would afford some hiding for us, but they'll be there just as quickly as we are. Our kind can only hide for so long before the mundane world finds us or even this place. You and I both know what kind of hell it is dealing with an unveiled human."

"Then, Mim, when they come, we protect them from us." Doctor Duke said while the wheels turned. "We put up the bounds and laws to keep our world in check. I think if we use the codex of the veil, we should be fine. We'll delegate a column from my order to police the more magical beings. Do you think that your coven can place a protection spell over the village?"

"Can I?" Mim was offended by this question. "Fuck you, Merlin. If you can do your job, I can do mine."

This was the start of the Department of the Arcane, long before it was incorporated by the United States government. What we know as the lesser known government branch started as a cross-discipline supernatural police force for the New World and a new understanding of co-habitation with the magical and the mundane. The mages settled in and built their fortress, the current headquarters of the Department, around the nexus much to the chagrin of the fae.

"Mages," said Iago dourly when the tower went up. "Why did it have to be mages?"

The Daughters of the Moon, with the help of the Monocle Indian tribes, invoked the bounds of the veil. By inscribing the true name of the valley on a piece of wormwood, they were able to prevent any mundane person from being unveiled by the nexus. Mundane people got to remain mundane by their own choice. They placed these bounds of the village on the signs facing in the cardinal directions. These bounds were disguised as welcome signs that declared Gaiman Heights a city of wonder and magic.

"Really, Mim, really?" asked Dr. Duke upon inspecting the boundary signs. He wasn't amused by this phrase.

Mim put her skeletal hands on her hips; she gave Doctor Duke a scowl that could and had killed before.

"Really, Duke," she said.

And as the mage and the Crone expected, they came to the

city in droves. They all passed through the academic halls of the Department like a paranormal Ellis Island. The mages, the witches, all manner of creatures both angelic and demonic flocked to Gaiman Heights and settled, they all came looking for that rare and pungent aroma. Then, twenty-seven years ago, the nexus suddenly and without provocation, disappeared.

And that, dear reader is where Asher Stone's story begins.

II. Our Hero

He sank to the shag carpet with a pained grunt, catching himself before he fainted. His long fingers gripped tightly like a vice around the hilt of the katana in his bloody hands. His white-knuckled grip made the vibrant red and black tattoos stamped in ancient words and elaborate patterns just under the skin of his knuckles and wrist show more noticeably. His chest rose harshly and fell with a deep breath. As the released breath left his body, he felt his brain return to an unusually sober state. His free hand shook with the violence of his recent attack. Slowly, his head lolled back to rest against the leather couch or, at least, what remained of the leather couch. The hole in the living room wall left him with a lovely view of the suburban street. Everything seemed so perfect and picturesque. The quiet split-level house bordered by Japanese maples around the yard had all the trappings of the average modern family. Brady, his step-father, had lined the walls of the now disheveled living and dining room with academic tomes he'd collected over his years of trying to be Indiana Jones. The photographs that trailed down the hallway depicting a peaceable suburban family hung akimbo on the wall. This was a perfect little house.

Well, except for the gaping hole in the wall and the twenty foot lion corpse in the dining room.

His hands shook again as he opened his cadet blue blazer. A spot of bright red blood pooled on the front of his neatly-pressed white shirt and soaked his pastel purple tie. He surveyed the barrage of damage to his person. He was missing a shoe which was, he suspected, in the gullet of the lion. His neatly-pressed thrift store pants were ripped and covered in plaster, dirt and blood. His almost translucent skin and tattoos that dotted his thighs and calves peeked through the jagged holes in his pants covered in a shivering layer of sweat. He loosened his tie, working his tightening jaw. His tongue flicked over his gashed lips as his stone gray eyes shifted through the carnage.

Suddenly a loud and tired laugh left his body.

A wave of pain rolled through his body, starting at his toes and ending at the split ends of what had been his perfectly coiffed pompadour. He still kept laughing out of a lack of understanding of what else he should do. The rush of adrenaline as well as the large jungle cat busting through a wall made of brick like it was a cardboard box left him with few sane reactions.

This was not what he had planned for his day off.

He coughed in the middle of his laugh. A hollow pain echoed through his chest. He made a face as an involuntary tear rolled down his cheek. Come on Asher, he told himself, think. You have to focus or you're going to bleed to death and mom is going to be mad at you for doing that. Internalize, damn it. What do I do first? Find Yoshi. No, get out of here and get help. Yes, that seems like a good idea. Asher, you're a genius.

Thank you, Doug.

Besides, Mom, Brady, and Jordan won't be back until August. Plenty of time to explain what happened.

He stabbed the katana into the carpet, putting his weight on the tempered steel for lack of a better way to stabilize himself on his feet. He let out a grunt as he pushed the weight of his battered body upright. If he thought he was in pain before now, standing and walking completely changed that thought. It was as if with every walking step, the pain pushed through his body as easily as the blood flowing in his veins and into neat spots on his vintage clothing. With determination reserved only for action heroes and firemen, he drug his feet in a zombie like fashion. He stumbled on the cobblestone steps that led to the street from the front door. He put his weight on the katana. His cool but makeshift cane clanked as the bladed edge pushed down on the sidewalk. It nicked the concrete and the clay beneath his feet with each limping step. Natalie had the car today. That was fine by him. It was his day off. Why would he need it? It wasn't like he was going to need to drive himself to the hospital after being attacked by a twenty foot lion thing.

Oh, wait.

Fifteen minutes and one block later, he had to rest. He leaned against a tree, taking the pressure off his body. His chest ached under labored breaths of what seemed like an incredibly difficult task. A pretty suburban wife slowed down her mid-morning jog when she saw the mangled hipster growing out of a tree. She blinked softly at him. He gave her his most charming, bloodied and bruised smile. She was a resident of Gaiman Heights. Normally, she would have chosen to ignore the weird much like the rest of the city. There was something about Asher that made that hard to do. Largely it was due to the fact that it was hard to look nonchalant when your liver is falling out of a large gash in your side.

"Hi, how are you?" he said weakly.

The housewife pulled out her ear buds and twisted her head slightly while looking at Asher, as if the bloody-extra-escaped-from-an-action-movie veneer was a trick of the sunlight. She walked slowly.

"Are you okay?" she asked, jaw agape.

"Yea," he said with a grunt, pulling himself up from the tree.

"Do you need me to do anything for you?"

"Yea," he said looking around. "Do you know where the bus stop is?"

"Sure," she looked at a direction and then pointed. "Two blocks that way. You know you don't have to take the bus. I can drive you to the hospital."

"Nah," he said. "It's okay. I'm not hurt that bad."

He put his weight back on the katana. He nodded at the housewife again before staggering down the street towards the bus stop. The housewife shook her head, blinked a few times, and went on with her run. In typical human fashion or, at least, typical fashion for a citizen of Gaiman Heights, she'd forgotten about the mangled hipster. This wasn't callousness on her part. This was how the typical resident of Gaiman Heights dealt with things that they couldn't explain. I'd elaborate but I touched on the reason for this phenomenon in the last chapter. I also plan on going into more detail later. You're going to just have to wait unless I forget about it and then well...sorry.

There had never been a moment of relief in Asher's life that felt better than sitting on the bus stop bench after struggling to walk four blocks with a hole in his abdomen well after being mauled by a large jungle cat. He delicately laid the dented, blood-stained katana to rest against the bench next to his shoeless foot. He leaned forward, burying his head in his hands as his body strained and groaned in exhausted pain. He straightened his back and raised his head up. Gradually, he leaned back with his head resting against the smog and urine covered Plexiglas shelter. He placed a hand on the chilling wet spot on his shirt. His convulsing fingers pressed down on the wound inspecting the amount of pain he was in at that moment. This wasn't a good development. There is a point when you stop feeling pain and a sense of tired claims your body. Asher was in that moment. What he felt was that his life was passing through a waking dream. His shoes, well shoe, felt like they were made of lead. He tried desperately to hold to a single thought but that passed away from him in like a fainting melody. Asher had a hard time convincing himself that he was still existing and was losing that battle. He felt like he did back in the days when he used to spend his better hours in an opium induced haze.

Man, he thought, I wish I could get high right now.

If there was ever a time to fall off the wagon it would be after being attacked by a twenty foot lion and waiting for the bus to take you to the hospital to get yourself sewn back together. He knew that the second he hit the ER that pain relief drugs would not be happening. It would be twice as bad if the bus went to Our Lady of the Angels as opposed to Gaiman General Hospital. Despite his track record at Gaiman General, he could at least get a naproxen at Gaiman General. At our Lady, he could get the same naproxen assuming that Natalie didn't swoop in as an avenging angel of sobriety.

On second thought, Natalie would beat him with her sensible shoe if he went to the hospital.

Asher sighed weakly as he looked to left. The elderly lady who had been sitting on the bench for twenty minutes before he'd sat down smiled sweetly at him. There wasn't anything supernatural about the old woman. She was a lonely old woman and was happy to have a stop buddy. He gave her a sideways glance and then smiled sheepishly. In his short life, Asher had realized that weird things happened to him on a daily basis. That and being embarrassed about not seeing the old woman made him leery of her. The old woman forgave his caution. After all, she was just happy to have a new friend. She smiled twice as hard at him to reassure him of her goodwill.

"This stop is en route to the hospital?" asked our hero, emboldened by the friendliness of the manic smile shining on him.

"Oh Honey, it sure is," said the nicest woman in the world, "I go to Our Lady of the Angels every Thursday for my kidney dialysis."

Damn it, he thought, *so much for pain relief. Maybe Natalie will be on a break for lunch off site when I get there.* He could at least then get help without her intense blue eyes staring him down violently.

"Those papists have the nicest hospital. So much nicer than Gaiman General. I took my neighbor, Arvelle, there last Spring before my eye sight got too bad to drive. And one of those street walkers was looking for drugs." The old woman shook her head. She then realized how badly her new friend was hurt. "Sweetheart, do you need me to call someone? My grandson got me this cellular telephone for my birthday in case of an emergency."

"What?" He looked down at his mangled suit. He started to laugh again as an old ache twisted through his body. With that laugh, he became even more numb to the pain. He didn't feel it as much as he heard it. It was as if there was a high pitched whine pulsing through his cells.

The old woman still smiled at him. He lofted an eyebrow at her and then regretted it. The coppery taste of blood should not be a side effect of a quizzical expression.

"Oh, no, no." Asher said. "It's just a paper cut."

"Oh, those can be nasty," said the old woman. "You should get one of those nice doctors to give you some of that antibiotic cream. You know, that's how my William died in the War. He got shot in the head and died from an infection. You seem like such a nice boy. I'd hate for you to die like that."

"I, I will take that under advisement." Asher didn't really want to die from a bullet to the head either. It was good advice.

He blinked quietly. The old woman dug into her purse unexpectedly. He felt his brow knit together in confusion at the old woman. Her sudden distraction made him think of Iggy. The man couldn't focus on anything for more than five minutes at one time. Why was he thinking so much about Iggy today? Probably because he was thinking about getting high; the two went hand in hand perfectly. He'd look up Iggy, but there were two major problems with that plan. One, Iggy being his former dealer, made sobriety difficult. Asher had been clean for nine months. He was starting to get his life turned around. Part of that success was that he was able to avoid triggers from his former life of debauchery which included Iggy. He knew that if was to meet up with his former best friend it would be two steps backwards for him. Iggy would insist on partying in a way that Asher wouldn't have a choice. He would have to get high and Asher didn't want anything to do with that former life.

Two, Iggy lived a nomadic life style. It was almost impossible to track him down except for four times a year. During then he could be found at Goodfellow Comics in Old Gaiman. Iggy had somewhat of an odd relationship with the owner, Robin Goodfellow and could be found sleeping on a couch there. In the between times, it was more difficult to pin down Iggy. He lived like a gypsy and never slept in the same place twice unless he could trick someone into letting him stay.

Asher leaned forward in his own human curiosity. His nose wrinkled at the all too familiar smell of almond lotion and cat urine. He had a pair of boots from his grandmother that perpetually smelled like that. The old woman dug through a layer of used tissue until her fingers curled around something at the bottom of her purse. She let out a triumphant "hah". He braved the suffering that came from his eyes going wide at that exclamation. His leeriness was starting to become a safer stance to maintain. He couldn't run if there was danger. After all he'd been through; the last thing that he needed was a reason to be mugged by an octogenarian. She pulled out a piece of candy wrapped in gold foil.

"No," he said. "I'm good."

The old woman held the piece of candy in front of his face. He stared at the candy with quiet panic. If he took the candy, knowing where it had been, he'd feel like a chump for not politely taking a gift from this woman. Yet, if he didn't take it, that would be rude. The old woman didn't care one way or another. She assumed that her new friend had had a rough day and was upset. When she was upset, hard candy made her feel better.

Thankfully, the bus arrived quickly, thus negating the need to decide on whether or not to take the candy. He waited until the old woman boarded the bus before he started the arduous task of standing up. He pushed the blade of the katana into the soft spring ground and slowly levered himself forward on tired feet. His feet dragged each other on their grueling path guiding his battle beaten body onto the bus. He propped himself up on the guardrail and fished in his coat pocket for his wallet. After a few minutes of digging, he presented a blood laced bill to the driver with sticking fingers.

"Do you have change for a twenty?" He asked the bus driver tiredly.

The bus driver looked at the twenty with the bright red stains and a hole in the middle of Andrew Jackson's face. He then inspected the Sanskrit and rune marked hand that clutched said twenty dollar bill. The driver's gold flecked eyes traveled over the wrecked body of the young man that leaned before him. Despite the apparently young age of the driver, he was quite ancient. In fact, the bus driver wasn't always a driver of buses but he took the job of driving the AM bus for a reason that made sense to him. He'd been driving from east to west for a very, very long time.

"No," he said, shaking out his long white blonde hair. "I'm afraid I don't."

"Oh," said Asher before digging into his wallet feverishly. He looked up at the driver.

In the time that Asher stood there, the bus driver's complexion had become lighter. No, that wasn't the right world. The driver looked younger and his skin was becoming brighter. Asher wondered if the rest of the patrons of the public transportation could see the solar display at the front of the bus.

The driver, on the other hand, recognized the feeling of power growing inside him. He knew that in a matter of minutes, he'd illuminate the whole bus. In an instant, the bus driver recognized Asher for what he was and the power he had. Inversely, the longer he and Asher were in the same spot, the more apparent it would be to the mundane people on the bus. They would know who he was and that would violate the terms of his residence in Gaiman Heights.

The identity of the bus driver is completely inconsequential to this story. I am sure, however, that you are very clever and can figure out the driver's identity. It's pretty obvious if I might say so myself.

The bus driver took a gamble.

"We aren't supposed to do this," he said conspiratorially. His voice was so soft that it reminded Asher of harp music. He was, of course, wrong. It was more like lute music. "But we'll get you to the hospital."

Asher blinked slowly as he weakly lumbered towards the back of the bus. As he struggled to gain his footing on the industrial rubber flooring, he collapsed into a seat. Asher felt his heart vibrate off his ear drums as his legs twitched. Slowly, he closed his eyes. He felt the weight of the attack pull him under like a lead balloon. He let out a relaxed sigh. It was the first time this morning that he felt safe.

Then, the pungent aroma of old woman lotion and cat urine hit his nose yet again. He cracked open a cold gray eye with utter disbelief. An inch away from his face was an elderly hand. Asher suppressed an agitated grunt as he opened his eyes fully. Sitting in the palm of the elderly hand was the piece of candy. His eyes traveled up the aged arm to the face of the old woman from the bus stop. The old woman took this as a sign from her dear and fluffy Lord. What sign you ask? I don't know. I should have interviewed her for her backstory more fully, but I didn't ask and that probably makes me a bad storyteller. Regardless, she was just so happy to receive this sign that Asher took the offered candy from her. Suddenly, he regretted not taking it sooner. Despite a lack of supernatural properties, the candy did make Asher feel better. The candy was surprisingly tasty. When things surprised him pleasantly, that made him happy. Asher smiled warmly at the old woman.

Quietly, having made her new friend happy by giving him the candy, the old woman clapped.

III. The Bachelor and the Psychic

It's a god damn shame, thought Karl Spangler as he watched his partner of three years pace like a hostile beast in a cage, that I'm not Norvita's type. She is stupidly hot when she's mad. It makes a man want to do bad things to get that kind of attention from her. Her jewel encrusted hands gripped tightly on her firmly sculpted hips just above the belt line of her low rise jeans. He watched enviously as her fingers pressed into warm brown skin. Her pillowy and lacquered lips pursed into a pouted scowl, smearing her blackberry-colored lipstick just a little under her lower lip. She threw her head back, shaking out her shiny black hair as her arched spine pushed her perfect breasts out, making them look larger than they were. However, the sexiest thing about an angry Norvita Patel was her eyes. When she was mad, her rich Harrapan eyes danced like Kali in the firelight of a funeral pyre. She can make the blood rush downward when her eyes sparked with malice. *No wonder she and Carson fought all the time.* Karl thought... *Even I want to throw something at her when she's this angry just to see if she'd rip me apart and...Oh no, can she hear me think this?*

"I don't understand what is wrong with you idiots!" yelled Norvita Patel in a distinct New England accent that ripped apart ear drums with piercing staccatos and made your heart beat that much faster. Their perpetrators huddled together in terror of the ninety pound girl. At least Karl was safe.

Karl ran his weather-beaten fingers over the stained, old and dog-eared copy of <u>Mages and Monsters</u>. This series of role play books were very popular in Gaiman Heights. This is largely due to its simplified combat system and its compatibility with other books put out by the same publisher which included <u>Forever Midnight</u> and <u>Hymn of the Lesser Gods</u>. It was also published by a local company which was a great source of pride for the geek community. Karl never quite understood the appeal of tabletop role play games. What was so wrong with a simple board game? Why did things have to have to be complicated with math and dice? Did people need to slip out of their human skin and into a shape of imagination? He didn't see the point in disappearing into another world with wizards and monsters. Real life, he thought, is so weird that disappearing into a fantasy world of monsters and magic didn't seem like much of an escape. Karl had been thrown into the unseen world against his own devices. If he could escape it, it would not be to the land of ten sided dice.

It's why he preferred P.D. James to Anne MacCaffery.

Karl and Norvita had worked the domestic unit of the Normalization Enforcement Squad of the Department of the Arcane for the last three years. Before that, Karl had been a detective with the Gaiman Heights Police Department. He came under the employ of the Department of the Arcane after the incident in the West Hills District of Gaiman Heights. The Incident cost Karl his gold shield and almost his life. I'd go into more detail, but that's a story for another time and probably another book.

Norvita didn't have a colorful back story like Karl's. Hers was more simple and typical ---she was your average psychic from Gaiman Heights. Norvita was a third generation psychic, having inherited the gift from her father. Her father had, in turn, inherited the gift from his father, the Legendary Swami Patel. Norvita put her hands on her temples as her eyes flickered with pain.

"I can feel something that was big, hungry, and super-magical escaped from here." Her legs shifted their weight viciously.

"Fess up, geniuses."

Karl looked up from his inspection of the role play tomes to watch Norvita's ham fisted interrogation of their suspects. She had far too much fun reveling in the terror of her quarry. Karl's face turned to a sick flat expression as his fingers danced over the oldest book in the pile. The feel of the soft tanned leather was all too familiar to his practiced fingers as he picked up the book. You know you've been doing the job too long when you can recognize human leather by touch.

And yet, this situation was getting old fast for Karl to the point of being boring. Every Thursday for the last year the magic sensors at the Department of the Arcane went off. That meant a potential exposure of magic to mundane world could have occurred which is a major problem for the Department of the Arcane. Exposure of magic is the leading cause of unveiling, to become aware of the supernatural world, of a mundane person. Every time this had happened during the meeting of the Seventh Street Guild, who were more than likely doing something foolish.

Norvita was getting more agitated the longer they stayed with them. Karl watched her as his jaw went slack. She slowly paced again and her shoulder blades rose and fell like a predatory cat. On days like these Karl felt like he was back in his beat cop days busting up illegal gambling games. Between the psychic partner and the Seventh Street Guild, he almost missed those days. He held up the human leather bound book up to eye level.

"You boys need to explain to me why there is an Assyrian Grimoire among the Mages and Monsters books," Karl stated in his slow farmer's drawl. He wasn't from Indiana but he did sound like it.

Karl rubbed his eyes. He felt tired like Richard Decker from

Blade Runner. The leader of the Seventh Street Guild lowered the hood of his Guild Cloak. He stared at them through thick glasses that he pushed back onto the bridge of his nose. Norvita cringed at his sheepish grin.

"It's not a grimoire…?" said the Guild Master.

"Then the book bound in human skin and sown with hair is what?" Karl flashed a steely glare over the rims of his bifocals that could have stopped a bus.

"T-T-Tuesdays with Morrie?" stuttered the guild member wearing the striped shirt and Viking helmet.

Norvita turned her head to one side, resting her chin on her shoulder. She stared at Karl out of the corner of her eye. When Norvita felt frustrated by a situation, she often broadcasted her feelings on a low telepathic level. She was never terribly aware that she was doing it. To people who didn't spend time with Norvita, like the Guild, this was often dismissed as a mild skin irritation and watery eyes. Karl, on the other hand, having spent more time with Norvita, was more perceptive. Paired with his own agitation, her broadcasting left Karl's skin prickling with irritation. His fingers curled into a tight fist. She turned back to the Guild.

"Karl," his name rattled around in his brain like a striking diamondback. Her voice dropped three octaves behind a telepathic hiss ripping at Karl's skin. The room grew darker as a psychic storm rolled into the room. "Let me hurt them."

Karl weighed his options. There was a chance that Norvita was bluffing. However, her voice had dropped to the Dune register. That was fantastic evidence in the opposite direction. This didn't end well.

"No, Norvita," Karl said reluctantly. He hated playing good cop to a nineteen-year-old bipolar psychic. This did nothing for his confidence. "But if people don't start talking to me, I will be unleashing you on them."

"And I will be starting with…" She lazily lifted her finger and pointed at them. She slowly moved it between the group of roleplayers. She stopped on the shortest one in the Guild. She liked his wig. "You."

The shortest one looked at her finger. His lower lip quivered and his knees shook. Beads of sweat formed on his brow. Karl was amused and strangely aroused by the amount of terror commanded by Norvita.

"It was Sam's idea!" blurted out the shortest one in a fit of terror.

"Way to go, Timmy!" yelled Sam defensively as his felt armor jiggled.

"Boys!" Karl raised his voice half a decibel. Karl never yelled. He was the father of two and knew that yelling had never, ever, yielded correct results. It never worked to quiet a group of people. The guild immediately hushed up. "What happened?"

"Well," said the Guild Master, picking at a pizza roll stain on the front of a T-shirt that had the logo of a popular super hero franchise. "The party approached the cave lair of Frente the black wizard. After doing a spot check, they heard enchanting lute music. The half-orc fighter rolled investigate and then poked the bush where he thought that the music came from. He then hit the bush with a stick."

"Which I still dispute." interrupted the half-orc fighter. "I have a plus six in investigation, Trevor."

"And a two in intelligence, Darren," said Trevor the Guild Master, "You don't have the wherewithal to use the scientific method. So, he provoked the manticore at the mouth of the cave."

"Manticores don't guard caves," said Karl after searching the wealth of his knowledge about the occult and the mythical world that resided in his brain. It was a helpful tool in his day to day job but made him a bore at dinner parties.

"That's what I said!" yelled Sam triumphantly.

"And I told you, stately paladin, that the manticore wasn't guarding the cave. He was living in the woods around cave after making a pact with the wizard to eat wayward travelers."

"And I said that made less sense." said the guild member with the guitar. "Manticores are aligned lawful evil. By your admission, Frente is chaotic evil. Why would that type of evil align with the other?"

"Which would you prefer?" asked Trevor, "An engaging story or some story that is so caught up in its own rules that it chokes your creativity?"

"Creativity is fine," retorted Sam. "But you aren't being creative. You just throw out random monsters because you can. Trevor, you do this every week!"

"Nerds!" Norvita called out, piercing their cerebellums on an esoteric level. Everyone got very quiet for one minute. "This doesn't explain why there is major structural damage to a colonial style home or why I just got a big whiff of fairy dust. Fess up, someone has been doing some unsanctioned magic."

"Well, the party made a successful saving roll to resist the seductive call of the manticore," continued Trevor the Guild Master, "So they decided to attack the beast. We rolled for attack order and the bard was up first. Since Zach rolled the bard, we all know what happened next."

"Oh, die in a fire, mage!" yelled Zach, as spit flew off his lips. The expression is an old insult used in mage circles. Karl never understood why that was the highest form of mage insult. Sure, dying in a fire was bad, but there were worse things to wish on someone.

"What happened?" Karl asked again impatiently.

"I rolled a one," Zach said meekly, his cheeks flushed with embarrassment.

Norvita quirked a perfectly-groomed eyebrow in confusion. For a moment the irritation ceased. Karl unclenched his fists as she calmed down.

"Karl," she whispered, "What does that mean?"

"In a standard table top roleplay game, a botched roll is a one."

For someone who didn't like role play games, Karl knew a great deal about them. That's either a little inconsistent and hypocritical of him or bad storytelling. Since I don't want to take the blame for it, I'm going to blame it on Karl's hypocrisy. "In a combat roll, it's considered an epic fail. Not only did Zach fail, but he failed tremendously."

"Boltair the Sage Bard of Willshire tried to lull the manticore into slumber. Instead, the manticore heard a battle cry calling his mother a hippogriff," Trevor summarized. "The manticore was not only threatened but also insulted. So, it impaled Boltair with its scorpion-like tail, thus leaving him alive but in an extreme amount of pain. The manticore then swished its tail, throwing the bard like a rag doll. Then, it released the bard from its tail and violated Boltair with the tail, giving the party ample time to enter the cave."

Trevor sighed sadly.

"That's when the argument started," he continued.

"About the tail rape?" asked Norvita in blind confusion.

"No!" said the Guild in perfect five part harmony. Karl and Norvita looked at each other bracing themselves for the explanation.

"From where I was standing the manticore tail couldn't have hit me," responded Zach.

"The manticore has a plus three in range," Trevor the Guild Master interrupted. "It could have!"

"No Trevor, it could not!" Zach retorted. "The creature books say that it has a strike of two and a range of three. That isn't the same."

"Nerds!" Norvita shouted again, sensing the thought train derailing. People got very, very quiet yet again. "Do I need to take my shirt off and bounce up and down to get you jack wagons to focus on what happened?"

"Don't push it." Karl said firmly, preventing any would be shenanigans. "Her boyfriend is a vampire. You see as much as a side boob, he'll rip out your throats."

Trevor the Guild Master heaved a sigh of dejection at being denied even the slim chance to see a topless girl in his living room.

"In an effort to settle this dispute," Trevor said, "We called forth the manticore from the Void. When it arrived, it freaked out and ran off."

"You summoned a merciless killing machine from the Void to settle a dispute on graph paper and then lost it," Karl summarized. I guess you didn't need to read those last few pages. I hope you did though. I worked very hard on them.

"Did you even have a plan for containment this time?"

"We had a plan." Sam said hotly.

Karl looked over his glasses at him. He folded his arms across his chest. Sam fidgeted as the sheer intimidation emanating from Karl overtook him.

"Timmy was supposed to put the binding collar on it. Instead, he wet his jorts."

"I got scared!" Timmy yelled quickly in his own defense. This wasn't the first time that Timmy had lost a creature and probably wouldn't be the last time either. With that kind of track record, you would think by now they would be more cautious on who they let do the binding. "I was like 'OMG! A MANTICORE! WTF!' and I panicked."

"And that led to the manticore escaping?" Norvita let out a low growl. Karl, let me at them."

Karl let out an exasperated sigh. Juggling Norvita and her mood swings was one thing, but plying homeroom monitor to these idiots was taxing for the former lawman. He should let Norvita rip them apart. It would save everyone a headache. However, if he did that, they would be in violation of the pre-emptive clause in their contracts. This was outlined in the employee handbook given to every new employee of the Department of the Arcane. The new employees acknowledge receipt of this book by signing an agreement to the terms and conditions for employment. I only mention this contract because the signing of this contract is in blood and has led to the strict enforcement of the code of conduct. So while it would be amusing and satisfying to watch Norvita reduce the Seventh Street Guild to the mental equivalent of giblet gravy, it would lead to their immediate termination from the Department of the Arcane. Literally, the earth would open up and swallow them both whole. Karl decided that he didn't want to spend eternity frozen in the Abyss.

He'd rather deal with the slings and arrows of the job than have the deep crows eating his liver.

"Norvita," Karl slowly said, "Go follow that ethereal trail so we can do something about the manticore."

"But." Norvita protested.

"I'll deal with the Guild," he assured her.

Norvita's lower lip quivered as she tried to pull her face into a cute pout. Karl didn't flinch. Nortiva might have been a psychic, but Karl was the father of two. Tantrums and manipulation didn't work on him. Not even a little bit. When Novita realized she wasn't going to win, she stomped up the decimated steps. Karl sighed again as he carefully removed his glasses. He set them on the table amongst the pencils and twenty-sided dice. He rolled his fingers in small circles that pinched the bridge of his nose.

"Guys," Karl began, "I'm getting real sick of coming out here every week because you guys have an argument over a spell or a creature or whatever. It wastes our time and makes you look stupid. Here's what I'm going to do; I'm going to be seizing your grimoire and role play books."

The Guild let out a collective groan. Karl suspected that they were more upset about their role plays books being confiscated than the grimoire.

"And I will be calling your moms. Timmy, yours especially. You can get them back after you report to the Department of the Arcane's office and take the Responsible Use of Magic Seminar. It'll take an afternoon." Karl instructed.

He shook his head disappointedly. "And while I'm thinking about it; guys, you're forty-years-old. You guys are successful businessmen. Timmy, you're the CEO of a fortune 500 company. Darren and Zach, you guys are the chief researchers for Du Pont. Sam, you own two thirds of a major software company. Trevor, I don't know what you do for a living."

"I'm the Editor in Chief of Alternative Realities Publishing," Trevor the Guild Master said. Alternative Realities Publishing was the producer of a series of role play books including and not limited to <u>Mages and Monsters.</u>

"Beyond that," Karl continued. "You guys are a powerful order of mages. Yet, you still live with your parents. Every week, instead of working out or going to a bar, you're here in a basement, playing a fantasy game. You're mages who can do half the things in these books without thinking about it. Boys, during this time, do me a favor and get a life. Find a girl. See a movie. I don't care. Do something that isn't this. Please don't let this," Karl held up the Guild Master's Guide, using it as a metaphor for all things he highlighted in his talk, "stand in your way to enjoying a normal life. Any questions?"

Trevor the Guild Master raised his hand.

"Yes?" asked Karl.

"Do you think that Norvita would go out with me?"

"No," is all Karl said.

After speaking with the Guild Master's mother and collecting every piece of gaming paraphernalia, Karl carried a banker's box to his Crown Victoria. He tossed the contraband into the back of the car. Norvita's fingers flew rapidly over the QWERTY keyboard of her trendy cell phone. She propped her shoeless feet on the pale coffee stained dashboard. When she acted like the immature girl she was, it reminded him of his Annabell. Largely, because his eight-year-old daughter was better behaved than Norvita. Karl tapped on the passenger side window before lowering his bulky frame into the driver's seat.

"You should have let me deal with them," she said, not even

looking up.

"And leave them with the brain power of tapioca pudding?" Karl asked rhetorically. "No, I think not. So did you find out anything on the manticore or have you been updating Facebook this whole time?"

"No," Norvita said defensively. She rolled her pretty brown eyes. "I was able to track it to the end of the block before I lost it. We're really far too late to get to it in this part of town. I was texting Weston to see if Gaiman PD had any reports of a wild animal attack."

"You need to leave that boy alone." Karl said sternly, "You'll drive Detective Lewis nuts."

Norvita stuck her tongue out at Karl's words in agitation. Weston Lewis had been Karl's partner when he was walking a beat for Gaiman PD. Weston Lewis had also found Karl after the Incident. He knew a little more than the average flat foot about what really happened in the dark corners in the back alleys of the city. When things got weird, Weston Lewis would pass it on to the Department of the Arcane. It also meant that he fed information to Karl and Norvita, especially Norvita. Weston Lewis had been in love with Norvita from the moment he laid eyes on her. Norvita knew that and exploited his feelings every chance she got. Karl found it rather disgusting. He pushed a hand through his graying hair.

"Did he see anything come across the blotter about an animal attack or any odd activity in the Primrose neighborhood?"

"No, our fell beastie hasn't eaten yet," she paused, "What do manticores eat?"

"Anything," Karl said. He furrowed his brow as he accessed the information locked away in his mind. "They prefer man flesh and they love a fighting meal. That doesn't explain why the Guild wasn't eaten."

"That's easy," Norvita said lowly, "The Guild aren't real men."

"Norvita, they summoned a beast from the Void," Karl growled. "It's going to be scared and hungry. The only thing I can think is that there was a more powerful being that the manticore would prefer."

Karl chewed his lower lip in deep penetrating thought. "Do we have a list of registered mages and witches within the Primrose neighborhood?"

Norvita held up her phone and shook it at Karl sarcastically. "What do you think I do all day?" she asked. "We can start here and work up."

"Norvita, sometimes you can be an ignorant slut," Karl pointed out, "and sometimes you're a genius. It's like playing Russian Roulette."

"Well," she said brightly, "at least I keep you on your toes."

"Let's go clean up after the Guild," Karl sighed as he turned on the ignition, "Why do they do this? The world is already too weird to escape into a fantasy world."

"Karl," Norvita said softly, "Why do you read murder mysteries?"

"I like the books," Karl answered in deep thought, "They're a bit of an escape."

"And the heroes do things that you can't," she said, "It's the same idea. The game represents things that they can't do in our society. They can wield magic and fight vicious monsters without their Order or even us busting it up. It's a release. You didn't grow up in the life. I don't expect you to understand."

"Norvita, your grandfather is Swami Patel," Karl pointed out, "You didn't grow up in the life either."

"Karl! Not the point!" Norvita reached her agitated staccato, "The game takes them back to a more lawless time for mages!"

"I don't think mages ever had a lawless time."

"Karl!"

"Fine," he sighed, "Where are we heading first?"

IV. *Insert a Fugazi Reference Here*

He turned sharply from the window to watch her as she stormed into triage unit one. Out of all the domineering and neurotic women in his life, she wasn't the one he'd expected to be mad at him. She was the calmest person he knew. She was also the one who had the most patience for him. Obsessive and neurotic, yes but always with a sense of calm and superiority. It's why he called her first instead of Natalie. She tossed her trendy bag onto the stool next to the door while she marched up to him. He gave her his patent-pending smile in a hope to avoid a second fight. That just infuriated her more. She brought a powerful slap down across his bruised cheek. He recoiled from her assault as the gash on his lip reopened. He pressed his middle finger to the cut dabbing at the warm liquid as he narrowed his eyes at her.

"You spoiled little brat!" he yelled abruptly, "What was that for?!?"

"You're making me miss my Spanish finals because of your stoner antics," she said through clenched teeth. She pushed a long strand of platinum blonde bang out of her cupie doll face. "I will murder you in public if I flunk because of you."

Asher looked over her face as it morphed into a horrifying mask of wrath. Carin, as the middle child, had always been the intense one of the two younger children. She seemed determined to be noticed by overachieving. A less than difficult task when she was wedged between a junkie and a dry piece of toast. Asher secretly, and not so secretly, felt guilty about Carin's ambitious nature. Any outside observer would think that Carin was becoming more intense over the last two years. This might have been due to the transition into collegiate life. Asher knew better. Carin had begun getting more intense when he got on the H-train and started living in a dumpster. He'd always felt guilt about the hell he'd put his siblings through. Their mother could be a little bit hyper at best, and overbearing at worst. Asher could just imagine that with her oldest son strung out on junk, she'd become a drill sergeant to the other two. Step out of line with Tracy Stone Mitchell and gods help you. He searched his sister's unrelated features for a crack in her mask of rage. It's funny, he thought, Carin and Jordan looked like their mother. Asher, on the other hand, had been told that he looked like his father. This statement had been a source of irritation for both Asher and Brady.

Brady believed that Asher got away with a whole host of things because of his resemblance to his late father. No matter how long Tracy was married to Brady, she always seemed to feel desperately for the loss of her first husband. This belief became solidified by Tracy's laissez faire attitude when it came to Asher's addiction. This wasn't Tracy being lazy or not caring about Asher. Asher had always made it a point to not be around during his times of trial. They would have done something crazy like an intervention. Also for some time, Asher hid from the world. He hid because he was unable to cope with the stress of being a disappointment. In fact, until he'd sobered up he hadn't spoken to his family in five years. Tracy had never worried too much about where her son was at any time. This wasn't in fact due to his father, but something far deeper. I'd go into more detail but that's getting off topic. Plus, spoilers.

Asher had always been annoyed by his resemblance to his father. He was three when Stephen Stone had died. Any memory of the man was a vague dream that hung just outside the border of his waking mind. His father's features, his voice, even his mannerisms were just outside his reach and that infuriated him. To make it worse, he'd never even seen a picture of the man apart from then one his grandmother had and that was sadly of his childhood. It was as if the only record of his father's existence was Asher. That was a lot of pressure for one guy.

"First of all, you flunking anything is one of the signs of the end of days. Two, I'm painfully sober," he leaned in and stressed the word painfully to illustrate his point, "and finally, I didn't do it."

Carin placed her hand on his face and carefully inspected the long gashes and purple black skin marking his Frankish features. Their mother was still in Mexico, but with Carin there, studying his injuries like there was going to be a test on them, it was almost like having Tracy with him. Carin, at times, was so much like their mother it was spooky. They even had similar mannerisms down to the involuntary upturn of the eye fold when they thought hard. And as he peered into her slate grey eyes, she gave him the same sad smile that their mother gave him when he was sick. Her eyes sparkled suddenly like they were glazed over with glitter. Asher pulled his head back with an involuntary jerk, feeling oddly uncomfortable. She retracted her hands to her chest. Carin's cheeks burned a bright pink.

"S-s-sorry," she was flustered, "I got … distracted by your eyes. They are so pretty."

"We have the same colored eyes," he pointed out to her. That was the only thing he had in common with his siblings. They all had steely gray eyes.

"Oh, Ash," -- he'd always hated the nickname "Ash". It was the slightly effeminate nature of the nickname. It was because it made him feel like Bruce Campbell. He didn't want to be the comedic hero of a cult horror movie franchise. He didn't want to be a hero at all. Little did he know that he was the hero of our story. This is a prime example of dramatic irony. Keep on the lookout for it in the future. It's my favorite literary device.

-- "They are so not." she whispered, "Yours are way prettier. They look like moving storm clouds…" She stared into his eyes as her voice trailed off.

"Hey! Incest Puppy!" Asher snapped his fingers against her ears. Carin shook her head as she ran face first into reality. She shoved her hands into her pockets. "You are SO weird sometimes."

"So says the human jigsaw puzzle," Carin retorted, being twice as bitey out of her own embarrassment. "So, who tried to kill you? Was it one of your junkie friends that beat you up or did Natalie finally snap?"

"Neither," he'd never quite understood why his family thought he ran with a hard crowd while on the junk. Had they seen a documentary on gangs and their treatment of junkies? He was pretty sure that his experience was probably atypical though. When he was on drugs, he only hung out with two people. First of them was Iggy. While Iggy was the hook up in Gaiman Heights, he was about as intimidating as a brain damaged labradoodle. More importantly, he hadn't seen Iggy since he'd gotten clean.

Then there was Amy. Amy was Asher's ex-girlfriend. Despite this fact, she bore him no ill will. In fact, she was his ride to Narcotics Anonymous on Tuesdays and Thursdays.

"Ash," Carin said. "if someone…"

"It wasn't anyone," he interrupted her. "A mountain lion or something broke into the house. I was watching the Dukes of Hazard. You know the one where they jump the General Lee over the gorge and the lion came through the wall where the HD TV is on….or was. Man, Mom and Brady are going to be pissed. I think it ate one of mom's poms."

"Miaka or Yoshi?" she asked as if the fate of the world

hinged on the answer to that question.

"Miaka, I think," he scratched a spot on his neck that itched when he thought very hard. I couldn't find Yoshi. Mom's going to be mad."

"I somehow doubt it," Carin said thoughtfully. Altars were still intact. The familiar was still alive. Asher hadn't been killed. Their mother would deal. "How did you get away from it?"

"I killed it," he felt a laugh choke out of his throat and mix with his words. Every time he told this story, and by now this was the third time he'd told this story, it made him smile. "I used that katana that Brady has hanging on the wall of the kitchen."

Carin studied the blood tarnished katana at his side. Her eyes slowly traveled up the shining blade towards the hilt. He pushed his hair back. Her eyes then came to lie on his wrist and forearm. Her Japanese wasn't great, but you didn't have to go to cram school to recognize that the white hot kanji imprinted on the Okinawa blade matched the wood blocked tattoo that blazed violet on his forearm.

"Oh, I don't think that it belongs to dad," Carin drew out her words carefully. She slowly made eye contact. "I think that it belongs to mom."

"Why would our mother own a katana?" he asked. The words simply didn't make sense to him.

"Why would dad?" Carin already knew that the answer to that question. The reality of the matter was that the katana was more likely their mother's. Their, well her, father wasn't that cool. Asher shrugged and immediately regretted it. Pain shot through his side as he suppressed a grimace.

"You know," he said finally, "it's been a weird day; the lion attack and all, but the really weird thing about the attack was the attack. Seriously, it wasn't the lion coming through the wall. It

46

wasn't the lion coming through the wall. It was the katana. I've never held a sword in my life, but when I held it, it was like I always knew. Like I'd spent my life learning swordplay. Weird, right?"

"No," Carin said finally, "It's not that weird."

"Why are you and mom always so understanding about the weird stuff?" As previously stated, Asher's twenty-seven years on this planet had been marked by some of the weirdest events in human history. He was constantly surprised on how accepting his mother and sister were of that sort of thing. "If I said something like that to Jordan or Brady, they'd say I was lying for attention or on drugs or something like that. Why are you two so cool about weird things?"

Carin thought about it for a long time. Part of her wanted to tell Asher that what happened to him was normal for her. She wanted to tell him what she and their mother did with their free time on Friday night. Weird things happened to Asher. He should know why. But, she also knew what the Crone had taught her. She couldn't reveal the true world to a veiled person. It would break the sacred tenets that bound her to their Crone. Betraying that trust meant she'd have to leave the circle. She would be shunned by her sisters and be a huge disappointment to the high priestess. And disappointing Tracy Stone Mitchell was not an option.

"Daddy and Jordie just lack imagination," she said carefully.

"I wouldn't hold that against them. Brady is a good guy."

Asher stretched his long torso. "Did you bring the clothes I asked for?"

Carin nodded as she dug through her trendy and capacious bag. After producing three notebooks, six pens, a bag of hairclips and a bottle of lotion, she pulled out a pair of brown corduroy pants, a bleached white undershirt, a blue and white striped short-sleeved work shirt and a pair of weather beaten brown shoes. She sat the assembled clothes in a neat pile on the exam bed.

"You know, Asher," Carin remarked, "There are other places to shop for clothes than the thrift store."

"It's hip," he answered defensively. "The vintage look is in, right?"

"Yea, back when "hip" was a cool word to use." She shook her head in amusement. She hoped she never got that old. "I'm going to step out so you can get changed."

No more than four seconds after Carin had stepped out of the room, Natalie Campbell turned sharply around the corner with a loud squeak of her athletic shoes. There were very few things that were scary about Our Lady of the Angels Hospital. It was important to keep it that way so they could compete with Gaiman General which was a community hospital. Our Lady was a clean, updated facility that sat on the cutting edge of modern medicine. This had been largely due to the leadership of Conrad Matthews.

Doctor Conrad Matthews was a brilliant doctor when he still practiced medicine. As he'd gotten older, he'd moved into the administration side of the hospital. Dr. Matthews was the second-oldest member of the Order of Truth and Light, the oldest and most powerful order of mages in Gaiman Heights and the third highest-ranked member of the Order. He made it a point to have a warm and welcoming environment for his patients and staff. It made it easier for the white healing light to flow through the hospital and be useful. This feeling of calm and wellbeing was easily shattered by the scariest thing in this hospital. That nightmare came in the form a statuesque blonde in dark blue scrubs on the warpath.

Natalie wasn't mad because he'd taken the bus to the hospital. He didn't have much of a choice, she could rationalize. It wasn't that he'd called his little sister to bring him clothes, although, that was a tender subject. She was at work and Carin wasn't. It was the fact that he'd tried to sneak into the ER without her knowing he was there like she was an idiot. Honestly, she was more upset with herself than angry at him. This pattern had been Asher's M.O. in his wilder days. When she and Asher had first gotten together, he used to prowl ERs and urgent care units with an outrageous story or something to that effect looking for painkillers. For Asher, this wasn't merely a form of drug-seeking behavior. I cannot stress enough the concept that Asher's life was being run by the utter insanity of weird things that happened to him on a daily basis. This kind of madness followed him like a lovesick puppy. Asher naturally assumed that perhaps people could always see things. The answer is no. Natalie's reaction and views of things that Asher said happened were more common than Asher's experiences. It was normal for the average and therefore veiled resident of Gaiman Heights to view any fantastic story as a clear and blatant lie. Often this was a friend or a loved one who had recently become unveiled trying to describe the world as they saw it now to people. Twillingast Asylum was filled with people who had become unveiled and were labeled insane. I only mention this because people need to be reminded of things and sometimes need a connection to something I said in Chapter One.

Where was I? Oh yes, now I remember…

When Natalie found out that Asher had snuck into the ER while she was at lunch, it felt like history was repeating itself. Then the story she heard behind giggles of nurses whispering to each other made her snap. In her blind fury, she decided that if he was going to fall off the wagon, she was going to make it hurt. Carin saw her and felt the pending storm blowing down the hallway. Carin did what anyone would do facing gale force winds. She tried to make herself very, very small.

"Lion attack?" Natalie said flatly, mostly to herself. "You've got to be kidding me."

"Yea, that's what I thought too," said a scared Carin, "But he's really banged up."

Natalie gave Carin a cold and sinister look as darkness flittered behind her pretty eyes. Natalie had done her rotation in the E.R. She still did a shift every other Saturday in the free clinic. At this point in her young career, she didn't believe the majority of what anyone told her. People who typically wheel themselves to the E.R. instead of taking an ambulance, in her opinion, tend to exaggerate when they finally get to see a doctor. It was the nature of the beast. When you wait for several hours to see a doctor and you get either a bitter physician's assistant or some young doctor just out of medical school, you'd probably lie too.

I mean, I have.

More importantly, it had been Asher's mother --and more recently, sister -- who had supported Asher's wild stories. It was Asher's lies (or what she had thought were lies) and the attitude that, she believed, had enabled Asher to live the life leading him to his chemical dependence. Natalie was much like Brady and Jordan. She wasn't aware of the world beyond the veil. In fact, Natalie was a rare breed of Gaiman native that not only actively ignored the supernatural world but had to otherwise face a complete break. On this side of the wall, this mindset created a level of irritation that came only when exposed the supernatural. This came out when she spoke with Asher's family. It didn't take an empath to feel the animosity towards his mother and sister that lived in Natalie. Yet, Tracy made it a point to support their relationship. In her neurotic wisdom, his mother realized that Natalie's paranoid domination was keeping Asher sober. It had always been, as Mim had pointed out, a strong woman that kept the Stone men in line. That, as Tracy explained to Carin, was the best protection she could give to Asher. She was going to approve of Natalie.

As Natalie threw the examination door open, Carin retreated like one of her mother's Pomeranians, Yoshi and Miaka, during a thunderstorm. She'd retire to the hospital commissary for a breather. She knew better than to be around during an Asher/Natalie fight.

Besides, she had a phone call to make.

Natalie had prepared her verbal arsenal prior to entering the room. She had made an outline of things that she held over Asher's head since they'd started dating. Every mild irritation and minor misstep was combined into a neat ball of rage that powered her almost Barbie like frame. If she wasn't prepared for a fight, then he'd talk her out of her perturbed mood, something she didn't want at that moment, and he'd talk her into something more warming. Asher was the smoothest talker she'd ever known. His words and attention could talk her into anything. This wasn't anything supernatural. Natalie just hadn't dated anyone who wasn't sexually or socially anemic.

He turned towards the door, his mangled faced screwed up and ready. He took a deep breath, squaring his bruised body in preparation for the torrent of a long hard fight. She inspected his lanky frame. His legs wobbled in a non-existent breeze trying to maintain his posture. Her eyes fell on the pink tinted gauze that stood out in a field of black, blue and red ink that scarred his thin torso. She then, inspected the rest of him with a clinical eye. Her eyes finally traveled up to his gash and road mapped face. The anger she felt for him suddenly rolled down her spine and fell into her shoe.

"Oh, God, Asher!" she exclaimed in horror. Quickly, she

rushed to his side, placing her hand on his face. "What happened to you? Who did this to you?'

"You know," He said quietly. He was getting tired of explaining himself. "I don't owe people from my junkie days."

"I didn't say…"

He shot her a venomous glance. She didn't say it, but she thought it loudly enough, *"Please tell me it isn't Iggy."*

"I was attacked by a wild animal," he said almost stupidly. "Like something that runs around on all fours and eats raw meat. Not some coked-out junkie."

"So, it was really a lion?" she said slowly. She wasn't going to accept the weirdness.

"Yea," he said as his fingers trailed through his greased hair again. "It must have escaped from the zoo."

"What zoo?" she asked, still perplexed by the whole event. "Arkham is two hours away and they shipped all the animals to Washington, DC after that kid fell into the octopus tank. He was eaten by that giant squid six months ago."

"Then from the circus?" That, somehow, made less sense. Why did it feel like the weirdness parade was about to get longer?

"Are you okay?' she asked, focusing on small bursts of flames as oppose to the whole fire. She was trying to calm down. "Any itchy skin? Any fever?"

"No, itchy skin or fever." Asher said. "I'm fine."

"Did you get a tetanus shot?" she asked more quickly. Really, between her and Carin, he didn't need his mother.

"Yes," he said flatly.

"Rabies?"

"Natalie, please," he said tiredly. He appreciated her concern but this, frankly, was too much.

"I just want to make sure that you covered everything." she said weakly. Asher wondered, in these moments, what kind of mother Natalie would be and what kind of neuroses their child would have. "A lot of people forget about getting a tetanus shot after an animal attack."

"Natalie," he reminded her. "I used to be homeless. I might know a thing or two about animal attacks."

She smiled thinly at him. "What did they give you for pain?" she finally asked.

"Yea, about that?" he said. "I was told that, despite the fact that I have a torn shoulder tendon, a transverse gash on my side and three broken ribs, I couldn't get a painkiller stronger than an aspirin. Apparently, there is a note in my file that says I'm a drug-seeker which is weird. I know I was pretty strung out for a pretty long time but I don't remember coming to our Lady for anything. Now either, I'm being profiled which is just wrong or illegal or a very pretty blonde lady doctor has created a fake medical file for me which is also, I believe illegal."

"Asher," Natalie said a little too brightly, (that' meant she was about to lie to him), "It's not that I..."

"When the cat falls off the bed and breaks his hips he gets kitty lortabs." he cut her off viciously. Today wasn't the day for this. "When I get mauled by a lion, I get Tylenol. That doesn't seem fair. Then, I find out you've falsified medical records to inform people about my drug problem. Not cool."

"Bag of Bones doesn't have a seven year drug habit." she pointed out.

Bag of Bones was an old black cat that Natalie had found hanging by its neck from her Christmas tree last December. He had one yellow eye and patches of its coarse black hair were missing. Even so, Bag of Bones was very healthy for a cat of his age. When Natalie took the cat to the vet, the vet assured her of that Bag of Bones was a healthy forty year old cat.

"You mean in cat years?" she'd asked the vet.

"Nope," the vet had replied, "in people years."

That was a fun diversion. Now, back to the story.

"That may be the case," Asher said, pulling the white tank top over his head and down his body. "But a little trust? That would be great. Nat, I know I have a habit but I also know that I don't want to be that person again. Natalie, trust me to exercise restraint. I don't talk to the person I hung out with when I did drugs. I hold down a steady job. I go to meetings. I do everything I can to be sober. Now, let me be the person I want to be."

Without a response to his impassioned speech, she lifted his neatly pressed tank top. He flinched as her light fingers pulled the surgical tape from his skin. Natalie leaned close as her eyes roamed over the stitched skin. Her gentle fingers pressed on the swollen flesh. Asher let out a low groan of pain. She cast her pretty eyes up at him.

"Well, Eldon did an awesome job stitching you up." She smiled at him. "For a junkie you heal up pretty good. No hemorrhaging or signs of infection."

Her hands brushed over the ridge of his belt line. His stomach muscles contracted under her soft caress. He ignored the strain as his stitches pulled. Instead he drove his fingers into her wheat-colored hair. When he had first met Natalie, she was wearing a pleather nurse's uniform. He remembered it specifically because there were red crosses on either breast just over each erect nipple

54

that stood out in the October night. No matter how sexy that outfit was -- and that was a very sexy outfit -- she would always be sexier-looking natural and feeling warm and caring like she was at that moment. There was nothing sexier than her in a pair of scrubs with her hair up in a messy ponytail. The ensemble was complete with serene look on her face. He loved that calm, compassionate look she got when she was tending to one of her strays. Well, that and in the right light you could see her underwear through her scrubs.

Today was Thursday. That meant she was wearing the black lace thong with matching bra. Life was good.

Her fingers trailed up a line of Latin, heading towards his chest. Then, the palm of her hand rested at the curve of his sculpted pectoral muscle. She pulled him towards her roughly as a pained grunt passed through his lips. She tugged his tank top back up over his bruised head. His cut lips homed in on her warm pink neck, peppering her skin with kisses. His bandaged hands squeezed her hips against his waist. Her breasts heaved in a lustful groan.

"Asher, honey," she said breathlessly, "We shouldn't...hmm..oh...not here."

"Well," he whispered into her neck. His hands traveled to her firm behind with a tight possessive squeeze. "I won't tell anyone if you don't."

"You have three broken ribs and a hole in your side. It isn't safe, Asher," she said half heartedly as their paired bodies inched towards the medical exam bed.

"Doctor," he said coolly. "I think you'd know what positions are the safest for us to lie in. It would be irresponsible if you didn't."

She pushed herself up onto the exam bed. Her lips searched for his hungrily. He tugged off her authoritarian scrub top. Privately, he smiled as pulled at the silken strap of her bra. Black lace, he thought, how comforting. Most men would be concerned at the fact that their woman still wore underwear like it was the first date. Asher found it reassuring. Natalie could be, at times, rather intense and a little cold. This is a fact that had been brought up on her performance review at least twice. She wasn't always closed off and frigid. She reserved her sexiness and compassion only for special people. It made him feel important that he saw that side of her. The day she stopped wearing sexy underwear was the day she stopped loving him. Right now, she trusted him enough to lower her defenses and show him that side of her and that made up for everything else.

The fact that she showed only him that bra made him feel alive.

"Asher Stone," she purred, pulling his weight onto her aching frame. "you are such a bad influence."

He gave Natalie his patent pending, heart-melting smile. She gripped his wild hair, guiding his lips back to the nape of her neck. He let out a primal growl as he sank his teeth into her wanting flesh. Her frame quivered in heightened anticipation.

The door opened with a loud bang. Natalie forcefully shoved Asher off of her. He screamed in pain at the sudden motion, holding his side. His hurt rolled down his cheek in fiery tears. Natalie hurriedly pulled on her scrub top. He placed his hands on the examination table, gasping violently though the sudden jolt of pain. He might have healed normally, but he felt pain like an addict. Carin rolled her eyes at the half-dressed couple as she grabbed her bag from the stool. This was pretty tame compared to the things she saw at McKean State University. She was a sophomore in college. This was Disney.

"You have five minutes," she said flatly. "I'm leaving with or without you."

Carin let the door slam shut with a vibrating thunk. Natalie found her body being consumed with an embarrassed blush. Her eyes stayed trained on a crack in the tiled floor as she handed him his work shirt. Her cheeks turned a bright red as he took his shirt. Asher leaned over and kissed her cheek before sliding on the garment.

Yea, he thought, bring on the weirdness parade.

V. Dealing With the Supernatural

Hello and welcome to a new chapter that was added to this edition. Originally this chapter was lost under a pile of Rolling Stone magazines and better crafted fantasy novels. The creators of this work who lost it again during a move then found it. It was recovered and then rewritten. The author of this piece rejected the chapter. She then went on a small bender and forgot completely about it. However, after several months of hard negations with a large wooden mallet, the Department of the Arcane has persuaded the writer to include this chapter in this version of the novel. Enjoy!

The human mind is a delicate piece of machinery from a physical standpoint. The brain itself, is a gray collection of cells the size of a cantaloupe and holds billions of neurons. Even with a cushion of spinal fluid and incased in bone, it is easily damaged. While delicate in design, the makeup doesn't seem that complex however, what lies inside that gooey piece of machinery is something truly amazing. The random firing of neurons creates a person's language, thoughts, personality and dreams. It's what makes a human, well, human. The ramifications have baffled psychiatrists, theologians and philosophers for generations. One of the most interesting things about this very important organ is how this machine handles stress.

In high stress and traumatic events, the brain shuts down to protect an individual. If one didn't protect oneself then it would be impossible to function afterwards. For example, a car accident victim will not remember the accident due to the adrenaline pumping during a fight or flight scenario. The brain will block what is unnecessary to survive.

It isn't just times of physical stress coming from a traumatic event that shuts down the brain. The brain will also block out psychologically disturbing events as well. Case in point, infants who are put into foster care and are reared into early childhood will not remember their babyhood, but start retaining memories around the ages of five or six. With the protection that the brain affords, it is not surprising that people forget about their brushes with the supernatural world. The human brain simply cannot cope with that world.

The average human will see five different supernatural things in one day. Generally, when someone sees something odd they ignore it. Humans make a practice of avoiding involvement in odd things. For example, do you see the odd neighbor who is dancing right now in his backyard dressed like little Bo Peep with his dogs? The answer is no. Why? Because you want no part of that. This is commonly the case with supernatural interactions with the mundane world. Most people want nothing to do with weirdness. They will often rationalize or just ignore what they've seen. It is the truly off that causes people to take notice of the goings on around them. An occasional glance at a ghost or flashing lights in the sky is not enough to unhinge a normal person. This is generally written off as the unexplained and people move on.

There is occasionally a believer who sees something that confirms their beliefs. Of course, if you go looking for something you'll eventually find it, so it's simply cause and effect that this occurs. These are the ones the most likely to be unveiled. They are also the most likely to be dismissed as insane. That is not to say that all those who are unveiled are believers. In fact, any human can be unveiled. Despite the conceived success of paranormal research, there isn't any easier way to become unveiled. Simply hunting for the supernatural ones will not cause one to become unveiled, however it does make it easier -- like licking a plague beast will increase your chances of contracting the plague. Once that happens, your metaphorical lymph nodes swell with the supernatural.

How does one become unveiled? There are a variety of ways one becomes aware of the other world. The most common is a severe haunting. Most mundane people can perceive ghosts. People will notice cold spots or furniture moving and so on. An aggressive and violent haunt will open the eyes of a mundane person to the spectral world. This is a great annoyance to anyone who can perceive ghosts. If a psychic tells you that they can feel the spirit of a loved one who isn't whining about being dead, then the psychic is a goddamn liar. Ghosts will tell you all about how much they hate being dead.

While aggressive haunts will open the eyes of the mundane there is a specific type of person ghosts will prefer to haunt. Those people who have died and then come back see the most ghosts. It's generally because ghosts believe that those who have had a near death experience understand their plight better than those who haven't. People who have this alleged gift, feel it's their job to help ghosts move on. This is a great misconception. Ghosts aren't exactly looking for help to move on. They want to hold on to what made them happy. That was being alive. So, they are jealous of the ones who transverse the funerary curtain. Generally, ghosts like to punish the living by complaining about being dead. However, just seeing ghosts doesn't unveil a mundane human. Ghosts are or, more correctly, were humans. Even though it's fantastic, it's still falls into the world of the mundane.

The second most common way one becomes unveiled is through demonic possession. Demons, as well as their angelic counterparts, view the mundane world differently than those who were allegedly created a little lower than them. They have a more expanded view of who or what is in the mundane world. Due to the nature of possession, demons will share this gift with their host. The host won't be aware of this gift after the demon is removed. Being possessed is like being under water and less aware of what is happening. This is one of the many attributes left from the possession that remains with the host. This is not a major problem for the recovering possessed. It doesn't even rank in the top ten problems for the formerly possessed. The most pressing issues for the post-possessed overshadow the culture shock of being unveiled violently.

The third most common way a person becomes unveiled is the most disturbing. This way is by magical assault. More often than not, when someone is hit by magic they become aware of the magical realm. The typical way this happens is through direct assault using supernatural means. Accidents do happen, but those aren't as common as they used to be. This is largely due to the intervention of the Department of the Arcane and the rules that have been put in place to protect the mundane. This, of course, doesn't account for illegal use of magic which is responsible for the eighty-five percent of magic assault. Despite this number, assaults are less common than you think. Before a more civilized and structured time, the use of sinister magic on the mundane was very common. After all, protection of secrets has always been a top priority and overkill was not exactly a word in a mage's vocabulary. When the world got smaller, those who worked magic learned to conceal their craft. The good became respectful of their common neighbors. That left those who practiced the darker arts to rain terror on the mundane. Their acts are marked along the pages of human history. Sadly, policing the perpetrators of bad magic has fallen to the noble orders of mages and the holy witch covens. Not only do they protect the mundane but strive to repair the damage caused.

How does one deal with the unveiled? This depends on how the person reacts to being unveiled.

There are two ways an unveiled person deals with being exposed to the supernatural world. The first way is to go insane. Let it be noted that with proper treatment an unveiled person can live a normal life. However if one does go untreated it can lead to insanity. Picture, if you will, being exposed to life-altering information in the most traumatic way possible. It would tear your brain into a thousand tiny pieces. In addition to that, the first thing you want to do is tell your friends and family everything. Telling someone that you see ghosts and monsters around every corner does make one sound crazy, doubly so if no one else can see them. Many of these newly unveiled can be very vocal about this madness. Slowly, after a long period of time, one can believe that you are going insane. There are several asylums filled with the mad unveiled.

The authors of this piece want to state that not all individuals with mental illness are unveiled. In fact, the majority of mental health patients are not. These people truly need to be taken care of fully. With that being said, the populations of mental health facilities of Gaiman Heights are filled with poor souls who have gazed upon the shadowy corners of the waking world.

The other thing that occurs is aggressive behavior. When someone angrily avoiding the supernatural is hit by the paranormal, it ends violently for all parties involved. Not only are they ripped from their comfortable normalcy, but they want vengeance. If this reaction isn't curbed immediately, the aggressive unveiled run the risk of becoming one of the most hated supernatural residents. This group is called the hunters. Hunters are beings that will track down anything that has a supernatural scent and then slaughter them without remorse. There are various groups of hunters or clans throughout the world. While they have different cultural and religious ideology, they have one thing in common: they believe all supernatural things are evil and must be destroyed. Hunters were a larger problem before the standards of acceptable behavior for the supernatural was codified. Between better interventions for the unveiled and more codified rules, the clans of hunters have been slowed down. Because of this hard work, the clans of hunters have almost been driven from America.

Almost.

I suspect after being hit with this info dump you are asking yourself a few questions --namely, where the hell is the story? We'll get back to that and you'll not regret buying this crap. I mean you've invested this much time into the story; surely you'll stick it out. These questions are less important, however, than the one you should be asking which is why the average resident of Gaiman Heights is not banana sandwich crazy. It's simple really.

First of all, it's because there are better and more unified rules on intersecting with the mundane world. Humans and the supernatural have lived side by side for quite some time. To do so, the supernatural are tied to the bounds of the veil. What that entails is any practitioners of magic who live within the confines of the mundane society must never intentionally expose their mundane neighbor to magic. No one wants to deal with an unveiled human.

However, in integrated societies, accidents do happen. That brings me to the second point, protective measures for the mundane world. The binding words have been set up to help enforce the veil. Placed on the four cardinal directions around a natural resource, the binding words protect against accidental exposure from small acts of magic. Simply put, when the mundane person sees something odd, they will simply forget they saw anything. Most people in the range of binding words will not be affected unless the magic becomes too much. I'm not really sure what happens in that case. I haven't thought that far ahead.

VI. The Game is a Torso

By the time that Karl and Norvita arrived at the split level on Maple Street, the Gaiman PD had a squad car parked in the well-manicured driveway. Karl's face contorted with frustration. Dealing with the mundane and, more specifically, the police was difficult for Karl and Norvita. Half of the force knew Karl from his days walking a beat. They all knew about the Incident or what they thought had happened during the Incident. Karl had become cautionary tale for every rookie cop when talking about having to shoot a suspect. They were wrong about Karl's breakdown. It had very little to do with the shooting of the suspect but that is neither here nor there.

Then, the Department of the Arcane paired him with Norvita, who was a hot mess in her own right. This made them look and sound stupid when they said they represented a government agency in the field. Would you believe an insane ex-cop and a teenager?

I would, but I wrote the book.

The Department was fully aware of this handicap and it had planned for the obvious problem. For this reason, Karl and Norvita were assigned to the Department's domestic unit. They patrolled in the neighborhoods that police refused to go into or would never get called out to like the Primrose neighborhood where the mages and alchemists raised their children. They also patrolled the areas that no cop would dare to go, like the vampire infested South Gaiman.

Norvita's fingers flicked over the screen of her smart phone, searching for an emergency number. After all, if the cops were here then they wouldn't be able to conduct their investigation. They needed to consult with the home office. Karl slowed down the

Crown Vic to park and then reached for her hands. He gently pushed her phone down into her lap. Norvita opened her mouth to protest like a Padgett Sound Machine gun. No one had the right to tell her not to panic. Then, she saw the languishing figure leaning against the sleek patrol car. She smiled impishly, looking back at Karl.

Weston Lewis was barely out of junior college when he had been partnered with Karl. He was a fresh-faced ex-football player of twenty-three with dandy blonde hair back then. He had Hollywood implanted romantic notions of being a rookie cop paired with a well-respected veteran. All of those notions were shattered by the Incident in the West Hills. Weston Lewis had been deeply scarred by the Incident for reasons unshared with the rest of the world. It had merely been a matter of chance that he was spared Karl's fate. If Karl hadn't led the charge down the alley, then it would have been him. He'd be in a busted Crown Vic with Norvita.

That wouldn't have been all bad.

In the three years since the Incident, Weston Lewis had been promoted to lead detective in charge of the Interdepartmental relations for the Gaiman Heights Police Department. That meant that he had a cushy job with his own office. It also meant that when something weird -- i.e. werewolf attacks, vampire sighting, or fairy rape -- got called into 911, it was sent to him. He'd then pass it on to one of the agents at the Department of the Arcane. Of course he had his preference.

He preferred to give those cases to Karl and Norvita. In his mind, those two deserved first dibs for two reasons. One reason dealt with his loyalty to Karl. Karl was a good man who got dealt a bad hand by the fates. From one incident, Karl lost his family, lost his job, and nearly lost himself. That incident wouldn't have happened if Karl hadn't been doing his job. He was protecting and serving like he swore he'd do. What did Karl get from the people he swore to protect and serve? He was made a joke on the force. If they could just see Karl when he slid into Batman mode, not only would Karl be back on the force, but he'd have a shiny gold badge as well. Part of Weston Lewis hoped that his friend would return to the job. That he would be the Karl Spangler that he once knew. Of course if that happened, then Weston Lewis wouldn't have an excuse to see Norvita anymore.

Weston Lewis had been in love with Norvita from the moment he laid eyes on her. There were so few attractive women in Gaiman Heights. From a combination of the harsh New England weather and the odd occurrences of the city, women aged ten years faster than the rest of the world. If they weren't old looking then they were marked by some kind of weirdness. Norvita was the prettiest, most normal-looking girl in this city. Weston Lewis tucked a wad of Copenhagen between his gum and cheek as he poured out the remains of a Pepsi bottle. Norvita made a disgusted face.

"Behave," Karl hissed in her ear as they got out of the Crown Vic.

"Sam," Weston Lewis said between spits into the soda bottle, "Dean."

"I don't want to be Sam!" Norvita exclaimed in a high-pitched squeal. "His hair is ugly!"

"Fine, you can be Dean."

"His eyes are too far apart," she protested.

"Focus, Norvita, we're here for a job," Karl reminded her as he gave Weston Lewis a nod. "What do you have for us, Weston?"

Weston Lewis walked the pair up to the split level. Norvita let out an excited squeal as she ran wildly ahead of the other two towards the home. She practically dove into the gaping hole in the side of the house. Norvita's hands went up in delight over something she saw before disappearing into the rubble. Weston Lewis gave Karl a sideways glance. Karl opened his mouth and then stopped. Something things were better not explained. Not every situation needed his well thought out commentary.

"Oh, holy Moses!" or Norvita could do it for him, "Something exploded in here. It was powerful and I want to lick it!"

Karl squeezed the bridge of his nose and groaned in embarrassment.

"Barlow and Valens were patrolling the Primrose Neighborhood by accident when they found this," Weston Lewis explained to an exasperated Karl. "A concerned citizen called it into the station, which got them out here to investigate the wreckage. They radioed it into the station as a homicide. I think that had to be on what they found inside the house."

Weston Lewis spat into the bottle.

"I figured that since they were in the Primrose Neighborhood, I should call the Department before Fink and Carlos tramped through someone's sanctuary. Y'all got some insight on this?"

"Did you see the body?" Karl asked clinically.

"Yes, I did." Weston Lewis spat into the bottle again. "I wasn't too sure if I needed to call you and Norvita or if I needed to call animal control. It's, well, different."

"Show it to me," Karl said.

Weston Lewis led Karl through the suburban war zone to the dining room. Lying in the middle of the remains of an Ethan Allen dining room table was a mangled primal body. Its great paws curled in towards its thick fur and scale covered body. Its spiked scorpion tail was tucked between its powerful hind legs. Karl squatted next to the corpse tugging a pair of latex gloves over his tired hands. He leaned forward as his fingers sifted through the scales lining its back. He used the back of his thumb to push his glasses back to the bridge of his nose. He brought his glance up to Weston Lewis in an inquisitive gaze.

"Where's the head?" Karl asked plainly.

Weston Lewis led Karl from the dining room to the trashed living room. Buried in the fluff of what used to be a couch, laid the rest of the dead beast. Karl gently picked up the beast's head and turned it over in his hands, inspecting the creature's skull with intense criticism. It certainly looked human. Its sandy blonde beard was tinted pink-red with blood. Its violent eyes were frozen open at the time of death. Karl brought its head to eye level for a closer inspection. He peered into its pale yellow-green eyes. The pupils were thin slits across the iris. Karl pulled the mouth open wide revealing a line of teeth and then a second and finally a third row of sharpest of sharp teeth. Weston Lewis choked on the tobacco spit in surprise. He took an extra breath to compose himself as he spat what was left into a bottle. Karl stood up slowly with a sigh. This day had suddenly got more interesting.

"Yea," Karl said weakly, "It's one of ours. Weston, we'll take it from here. I'd tell you what's going on but you don't want to know."

"Yea, what you do scares the holy crap out of me. The less I know the better." Weston Lewis managed between spits. "Call me if you need anything."

Weston Lewis leaned back towards the other end of the house. Karl knew this part of the dance and said nothing. There wasn't anything that stopped this.

"And Norvita... if you aren't busy later..."

"I am!" Norvita shouted quickly from a far off corner.

Weston Lewis gave a sad nod as a piece of him died inside. He quickly departed from the house in defeat. Karl made a note to speak to Norvita about her behavior. He couldn't keep watching the poor man go through this. He stood up, dusting off his washer worn khaki pants. He stepped over the body in a long stride. His eyes darted around the ground level of the house as a realization sank in. Karl started walking carefully, his eyes looking over each piece of the remains. This is an odd suburban house, he thought, even for Primrose. The rug under what used to be the table in the dining room had a Hopi Medicine Wheel woven into the fabric. Each west facing wall throughout the house was emblazed with a Hand of Fatima. Karl walked down a hall, his finger running over aged books as he inspected a jade Fu Dragon and a soapstone bust of Bastet that sat on the shelf with the toms. Karl suspected that if he kept looking, he'd find more protective totems. So, he thought, for someone who doesn't show up on the registry, there are an awful lot of protective totems. Where were they hiding? Karl scratched the corner of his eye.

"Norvita," Karl called, "did you find anything?"

"PUPPY!" she squealed in reply.

Karl turned abruptly towards her outburst. He was immediately greeted by the smell of kibble breath. The light red muzzle of an excited animal nuzzled into Karl's conflict smashed nose. He petted the puppy on its silken head. Norvita pulled the tiny dog into a fierce cuddle with a radiant smile.

"Can I keep it?" she asked, batting her long lashes at him. Karl shook his head at her. "What?!? I found it."

"One," Karl started, "That dog is smaller than Mischief. He'll eat it."

Mischief was Norvita's gray house cat. He wasn't an aged cat like Bag of Bones. Mischief had a habit of killing things that were smaller than himself. The cat was about eighteen inches long and most of that was his fluffy squirrel-like tail. The majority of Mischief's game had been mice or even small pixies. You could tell when it was a pixie. His fur would turn a bright blue and he'd float around Norvita's apartment.

"Two, it has a collar. And three," Karl scratched behind the dog's large ears being greeted with a wag of its tail, "Who's a good puppy? Who's a good protector?"

He held the tiny dog's head in his hand as it panted excitedly. Karl looked at it in the eyes.

"Who's a good familiar?" Karl commanded sternly.

"I am!" the dog answered confidently. Norvita blinked quietly as the familiar resumed wagging its fluffy tail. She did live in Gaiman Heights, after all.

"The crescent moon pattern on his muzzle is a dead giveaway," Karl responded before she even asked. "But with the totems and protection spells, it was a safe bet."

Norvita spun the familiar around in her arms to looking for the magic switch on the puppy. The two exchanged glances as she looked over the familiar. The dog lapped at Norvita's cheek. Its tail wagged excitedly at its new friend.

"How did you even do that?" Norvita finally asked with a perplexed look.

"Familiars talk when you ask them a direct question or to give sage advice," Karl explained. "Other than that, they act like normal animals."

"And he's a good dog because he's a familiar?" Even for a lifelong resident of Gaiman Heights, familiars were complex.

"No, I told him he was good dog because he's a good dog." Karl scratched behind the familiar's ear. It yapped excited at Karl. "I wouldn't have said it if it weren't true. This house doesn't show up on the registry, does it?"

"This house belongs to a Doctor and Mrs. Brady Mitchell." Norvita set the familiar down to read the file she had pulled up on the phone. "The only name that shows up on the registry is Carin Mitchell. She was registered last year upon entering her circle of sisters. It looks like she's starting the maidenhood with the Daughters of the Moon."

"Yea," Karl said, his face twisting in complex thought. "Not powerful enough for an intelligent familiar."

"How do you know it's an intelligent familiar?" Norvita asked.

"Familiar," Karl said. "Give Norvita some sage advice."

"Well, certainly," answered the familiar. "Quit screwing around with the cop."

Norvita blinked as she considered his advice. While it was good advice, it did prove that Karl was right about her and her cruel intentions towards Weston Lewis. She didn't want to believe that about herself, so she was going to ignore the familiar's advice. She shrugged her shoulders.

"And our young witch can't be smart enough to be a totem collector," Karl continued. "What is Dr. Mitchell a doctor of?"

"Archeology," muttered a subdued Norvita.

"Relic hunter," Karl shook his head sadly.

"Norvita, we may have an unlicensed magic user on our hands."

"What about the junior witch?" Norvita asked.

"Considering that there is a familiar and it's intelligent?" The familiar barked from an unseen corner of the wreckage. "The one we're looking for is a long-term magic user. She's got a record somewhere, especially if the girl is in the Daughters. They just don't let anyone enter their circle. We'll get Dira and Aguirre to round up the girl."

Norvita struck her tongue out. Agents Dira and Aguirre were stuffy and unfunny slabs of human flesh. One of them was wooden and the other was a golem. Needless to say, they weren't pleasant to be around. Karl shook his head as the wheels clicked awkwardly.

"That doesn't make sense, though. If the manticore was looking for a more powerful meal, why here? Our real power broker is one witch or mage and can't be as powerful as the Seventh Street Guild, not with those guys as a collective. Someone more powerful was here."

Karl glanced around with a critical eye, trying to make sense of everything.

"Karl," Norvita asked. "Where's the manticore?"

Karl motioned towards the dining room and the fractured pieces of the manticore carcass. Norvita blinked her pretty eyes as she tried to imprint the wreckage as energies and feelings. She then glanced back at Karl. She'd expected him to be happier about the case resolving so quickly. There was nothing alive and clearly it was self-defense. Instead Karl had the look on his face that he got when he was trying to remember his PIN number at the ATM. He was annoyed but that wouldn't last. He was still working carefully.

"Well, this one wrapped itself up pretty quickly," Norvita said, attempting to change the subject. "Can we get cheeseburgers?"

"I thought you didn't eat meat," Karl said with a humorless tone that was as dry as the Atacoma Desert.

"Karl! That's racist!" Norvita yelled. "Just because I am of Hindu descent you assume I don't eat meat! That's a stereotype and I'm offended."

Norvita shook her head as her lower lip quivered.

"I thought better of you."

Karl let out a tired sigh in response to Norvita's outrage. Her accusations would have been taken more seriously if she hadn't overacted like this before in the past. It wasn't even the first time today that she had reacted in the extreme about racism. Karl was getting tired of her childish behavior.

"First off, it's not a stereotype. Hindus practice vegetarianism. You know that whole "each life is sacred and the resting place of the Brahma" thing," Karl said, adopting a Gregory Peck like quality to his voice. "And last week you pitched a fit when we went to the Fatted Calf because they didn't have a vegan alternative."

"Karl, that was last *week*."

Karl should have known better. Norvita only went fully vegan when she and Carson were fighting. When they made up, she went back to an iron rich diet. "Besides, we should get lunch and charge it to the expense account. They don't know we found it."

"Good try but we have to wait until Ivo shows up to dispose of the body," Karl said sternly. They did have protocol and Ivo always appreciated fresh meat. Karl felt a little concerned. Did he really come off as a pushover? Annabell, his eight-year-old, tried to do the same things that Norvita did. The only difference being that Anna was more successful than Norvita. "There is something not right in all of this."

"What?" Norvita asked, perplexed. "What's off?"

"For starters?" Karl began rhetorically. He had a list. "The dead manticore."

"I wouldn't call it dead." Norvita interjected. "In chunked pieces for a manticore stew? Yes. Do they do that when they die?"

"That's the thing, there isn't a recorded death of a manticore." Karl explained. "You can't kill a manticore or -- at least I as I understand it -- let alone decapitate it."

"Couldn't a witch kill it?" Norvita pointed out correctly.

"Only black magic could destroy a living being. A manticore is a ruthless killer, but it's a living creature," Karl lectured. Norvita leaned back. This was going to take a while. "Judging by the talismans that I've seen, it's white magic that is practiced by the witches in this house, but not our slayer. White magic is protection. What happened here wasn't defensive magic."

"So we aren't looking for a corrupted witch, but a rogue mage?" Norvita summarized. She did this a lot with Karl's lectures. It helped her get the right points. "A rogue mage that is super powerful, but uncorrupted by his power? I don't feel anything evil. Karl, that makes less sense than a young witch killing a manticore."

"Why?" Karl asked, "What are you getting?"

Norvita looked around for a moment as a soft gasp rocked through her body. She closed her eyes and extended her long elegant hands out forming a "T" with her body. She rose up on the balls of her feet in an orgasmic rush. If Karl could have perceived auras, he would have seen the light purple sparks dancing on her warm brown skin and off her fingers. He couldn't perceive auras. I'm just saying that if he could, that's what he'd see. She rolled her neck as her back arched. Her head shook out her long black hair. Finally, her eyes fluttered opened as she let out a lustful moan. Her complexion turned hot and flushed with joy. She pushed her hair out of her face.

"Oh, God, Karl," she said breathlessly. "It's like sugar-coated wonderful and red bull in a pink feather package. Forget the cheeseburgers; I want that!"

"What is it?" Karl said as he paced quietly.

"I don't know, but it's like a rainbow." She stopped. "It doesn't know either. How sad. It doesn't know how beautiful it is."

Karl rubbed the back of his neck as the puzzle pieces fell into place. Norvita watched him, her eyes sparkling with laughter as something caught his attention. She loved it when he pretended to be a detective. There was something cute about envisioning him as some man in a deerstalker with a pipe. Karl looked around the house with a confused glance. He hated that something felt off about this case. How could you be a very powerful being and not know what you are? The mage and witch community always informed their children about their abilities when they first manifested around puberty. It was the responsible thing to do. Apart from the very few incidents, like the Guild, there weren't any real problems. Their children were all well behaved, they had to be. Failing to be good stewards of their traditions could lead to shame and dishonor to the circle, order, or family, and great consequences for the family. It also led to the loss of privileges to practice magic within city limits. This wasn't the case here. This was a powerful being that wasn't aware it was a powerful being. Either it was an inanimate object or completely stupid about what it was. How was that ever possible in a house with two practicing witches? Karl's eyes drifted down the hallways. His detective's eyes settled on an empty saya that clung to the wall. He leaned over, picking the saya out of its home. His learned gaze crept over the embroidered kanji on aged shogunate leather. He looked at Norvita while chewing his lip in thought.

Then, he saw the photograph next to the saya.

The frame may have been cracked but the aged photograph

remained intact. The photograph depicted three young children arranged by age. The youngest, or the youngest looking in Karl's opinion, was a curly-haired girl in a red velour dress that looked like a red velvet cake. Beside the girl were two boys. Despite the difference in ages of the boys, they were dressed in identical sweaters and khaki pants. Karl couldn't help but laugh. Before the Incident, Monica, the ex-wife, had done the same kind of photo shoot with his girls. She, much like the mother of the children of these kids, had paraded Annabelle and Lenore out in front of a large Douglas Fir tree adorned with lights and ornaments in a December long ago.

Karl knew this was a sign of an over-involved mother.

He stared at the picture. The oldest boy stuck out in this scene like a sore thumb. For one, he was older by at least six years from the middle child. He was also a good foot taller than the middle child. Second marriage, thought Karl, it's the only way to explain why the oldest had burned red hair and looked less Irish. Karl adjusted his glasses as he plucked the picture from the wall. He inspected the picture with an appraising look. That's when he spotted it. Peeking out from under the oldest boy's shirt sleeve was a twisting line of black and gray line of ink circling his wrist. Karl's blood ran cold as he leaned in.

Karl didn't need his encyclopedic knowledge of the occult to recognize that kind of work. Karl had the words "Non Vi, Sed verbo. Non tiempo mala." twisted around his left wrist. It was his lasting souvenir from the incident in the West Hills. He knew better than he wanted to about what ink meant. He felt his body get cold and tight as a sickness worked through his body. Who would do something that awful to a child? Even the demons would have been more careful. Karl squinted as he tried to cross reference the ward in his brain. That wasn't the run of the mill ward. This was far too powerful for just a normal ward. Wards kept destructive things out but conserving the strength he wondered what had been inside the child. Suddenly, something clicked in Karl's head as the puzzle came together in a sick way. The only thing he could think is that something that powerful would have ripped the child apart unless it was still inside the boy.

Karl's stomach turned in cold knots as his realization ceased his forethoughts. Norvita paused and turned towards him, trying to ease the tension. Karl looked back at her in anger. She recoiled like a threatened deer. She didn't need to read his mind. Karl was obviously upset about this case. He wasn't just upset, he was falling into rage. This is something Norvita had feared. Part of her worried that one day Karl would fall into rage and that would be enough to burn away what was left of his human soul. Norvita squinted at him, reading his aura. It wasn't happening, not yet anyway. Karl was still rational and still human. She had to think fast.

"We should go check with the Department Archives," she said gently. Norvita knew that if she could get Karl to focus on the procedure of the case he would leave the darkness. "Maybe someone is registered under another name. You love doing research."

Karl nodded as head swam in a blazing rage. If it wasn't enough they were now hunting a rogue mage, but evidently a mage was using children to do what he suspected was a ritual possession. No, they didn't need to go back to the office. Karl didn't know everything about ward weaving. He knew someone who did. They'd be heading somewhere after this. Man, Karl thought, I better get a bonus this year.

VII. The Ballad of Patrick and Ruby

Their story is the haunting melody that sings on the summer wind haunting your dreams. It's the kind of old story that you hear whispered quietly by young lovers in the back seats of cars when spring turns into summer. With ever telling and retelling of this somber play, their story swells and ripens like a tomato on the vine. That tomato is ready to fall off the vine and fall into legend.

Tommy Hurley had loved Ruby Johnson since before he knew what the word "love" meant. She moved into the house next door to his mother's house when he was five years old and stopped him dead in his tracks. The second Tommy laid eyes on Ruby; he dropped his G.I. Joes and stared in awe. Ruby was a pretty girl. In fact she was the prettiest girl in all of Gaiman Heights. Her translucent skin flushed pink and white against her coal black hair. Her lips were naturally a warm red that hid her best feature like a velour curtain; her smile. She had a smile that sparkled like diamonds on a midnight backdrop. There wasn't anyone who didn't like Ruby. She was the shining light in any room that was graced with her presence. Tommy definitely thought she was special. Tommy asked Ruby out in eighth grade and hadn't let go of her since.

It was late spring when the road to ruin started for the young couple. Tommy proposed to Ruby at their Senior Prom during one of the slowest songs ever written. She accepted his proposal with a squeal so loud that it shook the foundations of the buildings at McKean State University. They were set to marry in the fall of that year. Tommy wanted to get married before he went into the Army that November. Ruby decided that she wanted to stay in town. She didn't want to leave her parents behind. This was just exactly fine by her mother. Ruby was maturing into a pretty and smart young woman. She had to be protected from the big bad world. Her mother was very, very concerned that the magical light that glowed from inside Ruby would be tarnished by the secular world. It was what made her special. That's why people loved her so much. Well that's not why Tommy stayed in love with Ruby. Tommy stayed enthralled with Ruby because she had a perfect smile.

The love wasn't a one sided unrequited passion on the part of Tommy. Ruby loved Tommy as much as Tommy loved her. She loved him because he had a good soul. She could see it when he looked at her lovingly. The white light that surrounded him sparkled more when he smiled and that made her smile more.

There were never two people who were more perfectly matched for each other. It's why Ruby's parents were thrilled to death that they were engaged. It was Ruby's mother that had insisted that they get married sooner rather than later. Luckily for her, the young couple agreed with her. There was nothing that could spoil the young lovers' early days. Then a dark cloud appeared over their lives.

That dark cloud was named Patrick Strahan.

Patrick wasn't born in the city. He blew into town during the last tornado that ripped through the Gaiman Valley. He had landed in the old farm house across from the Johnson's home purely by accident. He just crashed into a perfect place for his nest. Patrick was an impossibly thin youth who had inserted himself into Gaiman Heights as if he had always been there. Oddly enough, no one knew much about the lean young man with dark brown hair and soulless eyes. There wasn't anything to know about him. It wasn't that Patrick kept to himself; he hadn't existed prior to the whirlwind.

However, there was one thing for certain. Now that Patrick existed, he was going to hunt for what he was craving.

Patrick was looking for a mate. It was time to breed.

Ruby fell in love with Patrick one summer day. In her bedroom, Ruby had a large bay window that overlooked the street. Twice a day, Ruby would sit in the window and brush out her long black Irish hair. On the day that she fell in love with Patrick, she was brushing her hair like a fairy princess. She even hummed a soft melody between strokes. She idly glanced across the street trying to think about what to think about. That's when she saw Patrick staring right through her. Ruby gasped in surprise at the voyeurism from her neighbors, but she wasn't afraid. She should have been. Anyone would have been terrified. Ruby wasn't, however. Despite having everything, Ruby was the nicest person you'd ever meet. So when she saw Patrick, she wasn't scared; she smiled and waved at him. Patrick was taken aback by her boldness. He turned paler as he sheepishly waved back. Despite the fact that he radiated an uneasy feeling that she could feel across the street and was encased in a blood red aura, there was something innocent about him. It made Ruby feel like, maybe you couldn't judge a book by its cover. Maybe bad people could be redeemed from their evil. Also, her favorite color was red.

That was how Patrick and Ruby spent their courtship. Poor Tommy wasn't any the wiser about the budding romance until the Fourth of July. The town of Gaiman Heights held a carnival during that holiday weekend. Tommy took Ruby to the young people's dance on Saturday night. Tommy didn't drink often, not back then as much, except on Special Occasions. This counted as a special occasion. That Fourth of July was going to be Tommy's last as a single man. It was going to count as a party night. He left Ruby by herself in the light of the community barn. She sat on a bale of hay as her light blue gingham dress fell over her knees like a curtain of modesty. She brushed her long dark hair out of her heart shaped face. She felt so alone.

So did Patrick.

He deftly approached, placing a hand on her shoulder hesitantly. She turned to him with a startled glance and as she calmed herself down, Ruby smiled brightly at him. Patrick smiled back nervously.

"Well, hi there, stranger," she said brightly at him as she sat up prettier.

"Stranger?" Patrick choked out a ragged laugh. "We've lived across the street from each other for three years. I'm hardly a stranger."

"And in three years, this is the first time we've spoken." She extended her hand to him, her smile still bright. "I'm Ruby Johnson. It's nice to finally meet you."

Patrick took Ruby's hand gently. In the very second that skin touched skin; they both felt sparks flying between them. Ruby's pretty eyes went wide as a soft gasp passed her lips. From the bottom of her hips a wave of power pushed through her body. Her body rocked as she rode the sensation that she could only described as pure joy. She might have fallen into a sudden childish crush with Patrick as she exchanged longing glances with him but now she was completely in love with him. He, on the other hand, knew for a fact he'd found his life mate.

He resolved, in that moment, that he would make Ruby his bride.

"Patrick," he said in a voice that was smooth like painted glass tiles. "And the pleasure is all mine."

"You gonna hold my hand all night?" she asked in an amused

tone, "I think my fiancé wouldn't appreciate that."

"Oh," Patrick said, slightly crestfallen. He'd forgotten about Tommy. "I just, I mean."

"Do you want to dance?" she asked, eyes sparkling.

Patrick nodded weakly. She stood up and took Patrick's hand as she floated to the dance floor. Patrick nervously shifted his feet as Ruby placed her soft lily white hands on his shoulders. He moved stiffly as her skirt waved casually around his feet. Ruby looked up at him with her clear blue eyes.

"Is something wrong?" Ruby asked, searching his forgettable features in concern. "You act like you've never danced before."

"I have," Patrick lied. "Just not with an angel like you before."

It was Ruby's turn to be shy and awkward. Her pale features burned red with embarrassed blood swimming in her cheeks. It was a cheesy line but it buried deep in her bones and made itself comfortable. Tommy didn't make her feel like this. Patrick made her feel whole.

"Can I tell you something?" Ruby asked abruptly. Patrick jerked in surprise looking down at her. He nodded quietly. "You know, people think I'm crazy when I say this but I can see things. Like things that other people can't see, like right now? I can see the prettiest red circling around your body." Ruby smiled sheepishly.

"You can run away now," she added with a giggle.

"No, I won't. I know now that I don't have to hide." Patrick said as he leaned against her pointed ear. "I can see your wings."

Ruby took a step back as shock drained her color from her face. Her eyes danced in utter confusion from his unfamiliar words playing in her ears. No one had ever made a comment about her wings. After a silence for all these years on the subject, she assumed no one could see her gossamer wings. She used to talk about her wings, but as the years went on she'd stopped. In fact she'd almost forgotten that they existed until Patrick mentioned something. She felt them twitch as she looked away.

"How can you…." She whispered as she gasped in air.

Patrick placed his fingers delicately on her chin. She let out a pleasured breath as he tilted her head back. Her angelic blue eyes flickered like cold candles as she looked into the depths of his soulless black eyes. She sighed wistfully at his touch.

"You and I, Ruby, aren't that different," he said, and as his words worked into her marrow, Ruby shuddered at his verbal touch. She leaned up to him with her lips brushing against his. Patrick had no choice. He kissed her red lips passionately. The ground shook and pulsed lightly under their feet.

"What are you doing?" exclaimed a cracking, shocked voice.

There is not sound in the universe sadder than a heart breaking. As Ruby broke off the kiss, that sad sound greeted her by smacking her in the face as she rocked back on her feet and heard his words. Tommy had sobered up pretty quickly at the vision of his Ruby kissing another man. Tommy's distraught body shook its head. Ruby's healthy complexion turned a ghastly white as her nose burned with the onslaught of tears. She fearfully backed away from Patrick, watching Tommy's spirit getting crushed under heartache. Her lips quivered, trying to force out her stammering voice from static embarrassment. Patrick remained quiet through this drama. Quietly, he turned his head to the side.

"T-T-T-Tommy," Ruby finally stuttered out of the silence. "It isn't what you think."

Tommy wanted to be angry with them. He wanted to grab

Patrick by the collar and punch the other man in the jaw. He wanted to call Ruby a whore and leave her there. He wanted to muster all the rage he should feel for them but when he tried, he felt a stabbing hurt rock his soul. Tommy shook his head sadly before leaving as quickly as possible. Ruby gave Patrick a regretful look as she followed Tommy on a quick step. Patrick watched her leave ruefully. A smile slowly crept across his pale lips. She may have left with Tommy but Patrick knew one thing. Ruby Johnson would be his bride.

Ruby found Tommy sitting by the creek under a wind-scarred birch tree. Her eyes danced as he threw a smooth river stone into the high creek water that hugged the carved shores. She fell into a hypnotic trance watching the ripples flare out from the kerplunk of the water. No matter how quiet she was, Tommy could smell her. He turned his gaze upon her with the contempt one has for betrayal written on his face. Ruby carefully sat beside him. Tommy looked back at the water and sighed.

"Why?" he asked coldly.

"It was only a dance," she said, putting a hand on his shoulder. "I love you, Tommy. I can dance with other people and still love you."

"It wasn't because you two were dancing," Tommy said guiltily. "It was how you two looked at each other."

"Thomas Joseph Hensley," Ruby exclaimed. "What do I have to do to prove to you that I'm faithful?"

"Marry me," Tommy said abruptly. "Let's go right now. We can drive to Stockridge tonight. I have my daddy's truck. Please, Ruby let me have this one thing. Your momma wants us to get married as soon as possible. Let's do it now."

Ruby blinked, considering an abrupt ceremony. Something told her that if she didn't bind herself to Tommy, she'd lose him forever. Despite the squeamish pull towards Patrick, she did love Tommy. Once her choice was made, she took his hand as she stood up, taking him with her. She pulled him into a passionate kiss. Tommy looked at her with a broad smile. He squeezed her hand as they ran off into the night.

Somewhere in the distance, Patrick let out an ethereal scream.

Tommy and Ruby were married on the Seventh of July in a courthouse in Stockbridge. At the time of the "I dos", a hole was ripped in the side of Tommy's parents' house. This compounded their irritation with their son's sudden nuptials. Tommy decided that it was best to not make their home with them. Ruby's parents on the other hand, were ecstatic. They welcomed the new Mister and Missus Thomas Joseph Hensley into their home. They gave the couple a small reception to celebrate their union when they arrived.

After the party, the couple retired to their makeshift honeymoon suite. Patrick sat and watched through the bay window. He seethed as Tommy pulled Ruby's clothing off her body. He growled and his black blood boiled in his veins as he watched their intimate ballet of consummation. Patrick hung off the roof as his skin turned black. Some mundane human was touching his bride and that was unacceptable. This common person had no right to touch his goddess.

The Hensleys lived a quiet married life at first. Tommy took a job at the local Woolworth's as a stock boy until he went off to basic. Ruby went to typing school in an effort to find a job. She had gotten a part time job at Dr. Robertson's office by August. If they kept up with their work, they could have their own place by September. Life was going well for the young couple until the night Patrick claimed his bride.

Ruby suffered from bouts of insomnia. She would say it was because the voices kept her awake and never elaborated. To quiet the voices, she'd wander the halls of the house for hours. Many mornings she was found asleep in the attic. Her wanderings led her past the large window at the top of the stairs. She stopped as her skin suddenly crawled. Her eyes were compelled to glance outside. She gasped in surprise.

Patrick was standing on the stale summer air just outside the window. He was surrounded by a bloody otherworldly hue that burned brighter than creation's dark. He placed a bony hand on the glass of the window. Ruby jumped back in surprise before her eyes locked with his. She suddenly heaved her breasts in a gasp of pure ecstasy. The light that shone from their exchange pulled in a blood black light, releasing tendrils that curled around her body. As her body let go of its long held breath the window ripped itself from the frame. A great wash of power overtook her, ripping the mortal flesh from her body. Her mouth opened as she let out a loud moan. She took a step backwards into the hallway just as Tommy walked out of the bedroom. He froze at the sight of his young bride glowing like a collapsing star. Ruby's wings unfurled like a white linen sheet in a locus wind, lighting her cool blue body like a rainy street at midnight. Tommy blinked slowly as his mouth hung open.

"Ruby?" he asked in a whisper.

Ruby looked over her shoulder at her mortal husband with an unblinking eye. Tommy was dumbstruck by the inhuman beauty of his wife. Her skin glowed a bright blue green with a cold light. Her tireless eyes blinked as her love for Tommy pulled her back to a mortal plain. She extended her bioluminescent hand to him. Tommy graciously let his fingers brush hers. He felt the weight of the world slide off his shoulders as he was filled with a general sense of wellbeing. She smiled at him as she sank back into a mortal form and fell into a kiss.

Then a violent gust of wind rattled the summer air as it blew into the house. Ruby snapped her perfectly rounded head back towards the farm house, breaking her salvation's kiss. Darkness came over Ruby and her body let out a primal scream from the bottom of her angelic soul. Her face burned now with blood red eyes. She shoved Tommy away from her. In a horror movie jerk, her possessed body staggered towards the hole blown out from the gust. Her wings spread wide and took flight towards the horizon. The whirlwind appeared and instantly consumed her form. Tommy ran after Ruby after fruitlessly. As she disappeared, he cursed the wind. A second great gust blew Tommy forcefully into the wall. Tommy slid down the wall defeated by the forces beyond his control. He stared in that spot until the sun broke through the clouds and dark.

It was Ruby's mother who found the shaken and disturbed Tommy there.

"Oh, dear," she said. "She flew off with the Morning Star. Come on downstairs. I'll get you a cup of coffee."

They sat in the kitchen as the morning changed into afternoon. Tommy stared at the creamy swirling patterns in his Folgers. Ruby's mother sat down across from him with a wavering sigh. He watched her with a bleary sleep deprived eye. Tommy wasn't upset. He was too confused by what he'd seen to be upset. It's not every day that you see your wife transform into a supernatural beast and then disappear into a whirlwind.

"I'd always hoped that we'd be able to stop her from being taken from us," Ruby's mother said quietly. "The priests said that could happen. You see, Tommy, Ruby wasn't born. Me and Jimmy had a hard time having a baby, so I prayed on the first star. Then, I saw a star fall from the sky. The next day there was a beautiful baby girl on our doorstep. I asked the priest about her. He said that she was a gift from God. That she was special. I was always afraid that she'd be taken from us. Tommy, she wasn't meant for evil. Maybe if you loved her harder or had gotten a blessing from the priest this wouldn't have happened. She would have chosen to be human."

"This is my fault?" Tommy asked, dumbfounded. His initial shock gave way to hurt. You're really blaming me for this."

"Yes," she said.

"It can't be," he replied.

"No," she said. "This is your fault."

Tommy had expected her to say "No, these things happen," but she didn't. Instead, she said the exact things that pushed him down the spiral.

He didn't fare too well after that day. The guilt of not saving Ruby consumed every part of his being. A happy young man became a great silhouette of himself. It was then that Tommy started seeing things. He saw horns on the gas station attendant. He heard whispers of unsung songs. When Tommy started to see ghosts, he began to self-medicate. He took up drinking. When that didn't help, Tommy went looking for something stronger. If you make the right friend, you can get the good stuff. Tommy made the right friend who made things better. There was only one problem.

Tommy's monstrous visions were getting worse.

Worse isn't the correct word. He was never scared of anything he saw. Things had become more vivid. Tommy's eyes had been opened to a world which had caused madness for some. Tommy would have gone mad himself if it hadn't been for the steady stream of narcotics being fed to him. He felt nothing in his narcotic haze. He'd lost his commission, his home and, more importantly, his wife.

Truthfully, Tommy was waiting to die.

It was late September when Father McBride at the Church of St. George intervened in Tommy's life. He'd caught Tommy one too many times sleeping in the fellowship hall. The Priest felt compelled by God or, at least, by older parishioners o have a word with the boy. The two men sat down in the rectory and discussed Tommy's residence at the church. It was then that Tommy recounted the story you just read in full truth. I won't be repeating it seeing as that would be foolish and unnecessary. We have spent enough time on this chapter and we have the other part of this story to get to. Father McBride leaned back and scratched his head.

"First of all," Father McBride said, "you're a goddamn fool to buy anything from Iggy Smith. That boy is crazier than a bag of ferrets; but Tommy, nothing that happened to you and Ruby was your fault."

"Really?" Tommy said, feeling a modicum of guilt leave him.

"Shit, son," the priest said, "This is Gaiman Heights. Everyone loses their first girlfriend to a demon."

VIII. God Grant Me Serenity

Thursday afternoons in Gaiman Heights saw the meeting of Narcotic Anonymous at Trinity Episcopal Church. The assembled tired faces that massed in the aging building's fellowship hall were attempting to cope with the outrageous strain of living everyday life in Gaiman Heights. Asher had started attending the weekly meetings when he woke up from his seven year opiate binge. He realized then that sober life was weird. Asher had decided that despite the weirdness he liked being sober. Of course staying sober meant more than just hanging out with new people. Sobriety meant he needed support. He wanted to be with people who were going through something very similar. He found that in the meetings.

Not everyone was like Asher in the sense that Asher had turned to drugs to deal with the weirdness. While most people do need some form of release to cope with the stress of experiencing the other side, not every breakdown resulted from the assault of seeing the unseen world. Some people were like Dr. Bob. Dr. Bob was a pediatric oncologist. If he wasn't addicted to something, then that would be a problem. Or they were people like Megan. Megan was the mother of two and from what Asher could gather, a professional victim of circumstance.

Asher and the girl beside him (and her story is just as interesting as Asher's, but we won't be sharing it today. I'm sorry. I haven't really written it yet.), listened to Megan's latest crisis which might have involved her husband not giving her enough money or attention or both. Asher wasn't exactly sure. He faded in and out of that conversation. The girl beside Asher batted her long lashes as Megan squealed in a sudden vibrato about her children who never listen and her husband who didn't understand. The girl blinked empathetically at Megan's sobs.

Asher was bored. Megan seemed to dominate the group almost every week. He wasn't sure if it was because no one else wanted to share their lives, but she did this every week. It wouldn't be as bad if it weren't the same story every week. It was always the same story of her less than interested family. He looked off as his mind wandered through the coldness of the afternoon. His eyes settled finally on Tom. Tom was the head junkie of the group that met on Thursday. He'd been there the longest in the program. He found himself being pulled into the hypnotic trance of Tom's nodding at every single word validating the sobbing words from Megan. Tom always listened and never shared. Tom would share one day when it was appropriate. Until then, no one would be fully aware of his story. You should, of course, know Tom's story. I just spent a chapter telling it. This is another case of dramatic irony. There will be a test on this later. I do hope you're taking notes.

Asher then turned his lazy attention to the girl with green eyes who was sitting beside him. Part of Asher would always be in love with the girl. Amy was his first love. Everything about her was amazing. She was beautiful, with skin the color of buttermilk and hair as red as a wild fire. Amy wasn't just pretty. Amy Nilsson was also working on a PhD in Physics at McKean State University. She was so smart that she knew things about Asher that his mother didn't know. How could he not love her? He loved her and respected her too much to hate her for dumping him. He knew that after these meetings, she'd go off to teach her Freshman Astronomy course. She'd then go for a run. Lastly, she'd get a shower and then get ready for her night job.

Amy Nilsson went on at ten at the center stage of the Firebird lounge in Old Gaiman. She called herself Anne Pheteme.

Asher leaned closer to Amy. He hesitated and quietly shuddered in restrained delight as he inhaled her cool scent of lavender and glitter. Desperately, he wanted to put his mouth on her. In an effort to restrain from nipping at her neck, he bit the inside of his mouth. Amy quirked a brow suspiciously at him. He shook his head as he tried to gain some level of self-control. He lifted his lips to her ears.

"Do you think that Megan got addicted to oxy just to add a little drama to her less than episodic life," he whispered into Amy's left ear.

Amy giggled suddenly as a smirk danced on her lips. She sat up gracefully in her chair, still giggling. Quickly, her eyes locked on to Tom's disapproving look. She lef her face fall in shame. Asher looked over at her smirking in enjoyment of his own joke. Or he was until her bony elbow jabbed into his recently mauled side.

"God damn you, you junkie whore!" he swore violently at the top of his lungs. Bitter, salty tears trailed down his cheeks burning his open face wounds.

All the noise within the church and in a two mile radius had ceased abruptly. Slowly, Asher looked around the fellowship hall quietly. Each pair of tired eyes shot him an accusatory glance. Asher inspected each of the gray faces as he tried to muster a sheepish grin. He glanced at Tom. Tom blinked cooly, analyzing the situation. Today, Asher learned there is no place quieter than a church fellowship hall after a blasphemous swear. He was learning ever so much today.

"Do you have something to add, Asher?" Tom said with the reproachful dignity of a high school teacher.

"No, I," Asher stuttered. He cleared his throat. "I wasn't calling Megan a junkie whore. I was calling Amy a junkie whore.

See, I said something that she didn't think was funny so she…"

He laughed nervously. Somehow, the room had gotten quieter, if that was even possible.

"Um," He scratched the back of his head. "Can I go to the bathroom?"

"I think that would be the best for everyone," Tom said.

Asher sequestered himself in the small bathroom. He breathed in the scent of aged copper and peeling lead paint. A cringe twisted across his lips as he slumped against the porous cement wall, trying to catch his labored breath. Asher squinted at his reflection in the mirror as the bald light bulb swung lazily, spilling a sickly yellow light into the tiny room. With an intense stare, he leaned forward while gripping the old sink as he tried to inspect his face through the soap scum. The edges of his opened wounds that marred his elegant face had started to flake with scabbed dead skin. With great care, he slid onto the closed toilet seat as his body ached in exhausted pain. He let out a contorted breath as he opened his work shirt. As the last button came undone, he felt a cold pain. Asher had become terrified that his stitches had ripped and, now, he was bleeding out. How could he explain this to Natalie when he went back to the E.R.? She would flip out if she found out he was with Amy. Natalie lived in paranoid fear of Asher going back to his old ways which included returning to Amy. Amy was a part of that old life. He couldn't do that to Natalie. He loved Natalie.

He furrowed his brow as he pulled down the pink tinted gauze. Asher let out a sigh of relief as he inspected his war-torn side. Amy had thrown her jagged elbow at him but his stitching remained intact. He wiped the tears from his eyes. A pained laugh echoed through his bruised side. In spite of everything that happened, he was gleefully still in one piece.

Suddenly, there was a gentle rapping at the bathroom door. He leaned back against the cold porcelain with a pained grunt.

"Go away," he called out. "I'm shooting up drugs in here."

The door grating along the linoleum as it was forced out of its swelling frame filled the room with a reverberating thrum. He jumped as he saw a fiery red head peer carefully around the door. His questionably stable back hit the toilet as Amy pushed her body into the bathroom. She folded her long delicate arms across her dancer's chest. He eased back as she looked him over. Her foot tapped out an impatient rhythm. The only thing that he could do to ease this situation was to flash that patent-pending smile. In an instant, her body eased. She loved his smile. Everyone who saw it fell in love with that smile. She brushed a strand of hair out of her plain face as her own warm smile crept over her lips.

"Cute," she said lightly. "How are you holding up?"

"Considering that you have razor sharp elbows?" he said, "I'm fine."

Amy shook her head as she leaned over his sitting frame. Her soft hands trailed down his side which made him jerk in pain; more so when her slow fingers lifted his undershirt to assess the covered damage. Her large jade-colored eyes were transfixed on his handsomely bruised face. Gently, she swept down to his torso watching the designs on his skin dance with each breath. A pleasured moan escaped her lips as she pressed her fingers against his inked torso. Asher shifted in his seat drawing her closer to his body. His fingers lazily searched her loose curls ultimately gripping her skull seductively. Her lips searched the skin between his neck and nipple. He let out a low wanting growl as he wet his lips. Amy's eyes went wide when she became aware what she was doing. She stood up pushing Asher away as her face went pink.

"Asher Stone," she breathed out. "You're a bad influence."

"Me?" he said. "I'm not the stripper who cheated on her boyfriend and got him addicted to junk."

"No," she said defensively, "you're just the loser geek who made friends with Gaiman Height's only drug dealer."

She paused, looking his body over again.

"Did you get new ink?" She reached forward, pressing her fingers to a fresh line of black running down his neck.

"Yea," he said, looking down his frame with a weak smile. "My birthday was last month."

He placed his hand on the freshest ink on his body.

"It was the last one my dad paid for, according to Evil Edward," he continued. "Weirdest thing for a parent to give a baby boy."

"It's kind of cool," Amy said thoughtfully. "It makes me wonder if your dad was some kind of circus freak or in a motorcycle gang or something like that."

"I wouldn't know," he grumbled.

The details about the life of Stephen Stone were a mystery to Asher. Not only were there no pictures of the man, but no one spoke of or about him in Asher's presence. If it hadn't been for the existence of his grandmother, he would have thought that he'd been made in a lab through magic.

That's silly, he thought, people were born not made.

Amy returned to her warmer state and crept back to Asher's side. Her hands lay flat on the top of his pectoral muscles. She sat back down on his lap as his body relaxed and he leaned back, watching her. Her eyes locked into his gaze. The storm behind his gray eyes moved violently like a hurricane making landfall.

Suddenly, he felt a great warm light enter his body and fill his bones. He could feel white hot energy saturate his marrow and mix with his white blood cells. He let out a soft grunt as he felt his ribs shifting back into place. His hand went to rest on the curve of her hip pulling her against his body. One of her hands brushed up his neck to his neat pompadour. His mouth watered as her lips brushed against his lips again. Something about all of this confused Asher.

"A-A-Amy," he said in a low voice, "what are you doing?"

"What you want," Amy said with a lustful groan as her pelvis grinded against his lap.

"I respect Natalie for what she's done for you. I mean, she got you clean, but she can't give you everything you need. I can."

Asher contemplated the prospect of snogging with Amy. She was a very attractive woman who, in his wilder days, he did things with her (and once with Iggy) that would have made the most hardened porn star blush. So, with those memories fresh on his mind, his body quivered feeling the heat rise from her aroused frame. He chased after her with wet kisses eagerly planted along her cheeks --it was inappropriate, but he would have her right then and there.

What stopped him wasn't the idea of defiling a church bathroom with his genetic material, but an image that walked into his head. It was the image of Natalie sitting on their secondhand couch looking up at him. Then, her head would sink into her hands with a long sob. He knew that look. After she'd yell at him and scream in full angry passion, she'd be hurt, the kind of hurt that only comes with betrayal. He could cheat on Natalie easily, but could he live with hurting her? He adored Natalie and vice versa. Even with her psychotic fits, Natalie had given him everything and devoted everything to this relationship. To throw it all away for one moment of Amy's warm and eager body, it would be too much.

He knew that, in that moment, he could never hurt Natalie, not intentionally. If he broke Natalie's heart in his moment of weakness, he knew that he couldn't live with himself. Asher's body stiffened with resolve as he placed his hands on Amy's collar bone. He pushed her away trying to get her off his lap. Amy looked down to him with half lidded eyes.

"Get off me," he said in a descending whisper that hit her ears like the threatening rumble of thunder. Amy sat back with her lower lip quivering.

"What?" she replied in barely audible whisper.

"Witch," his low tone gave way to a power streaked and terrifying growl. His palms pushed hard into her skin and bones. Her eyes grew wide as her body became stiffened under the grip of powerful magic. Light blue sparks flew off his fingertips and wrapped around her. "I said get off of me."

Amy didn't stand, so much as levitate off Asher's lap, much to both of their surprise. Her hurt face remained transfixed on his shining countenance as she flew into concrete wall. How could he invoke a ward against her? She loved him and she was a good witch. Didn't he know that she belonged to the same coven as his mother and sister? No, he couldn't know, but that's more dramatic irony again. In fact, Asher literally had no inclination about his own magic or how to banish anything. He banished Amy from his lap by accidentally mispronouncing the first word that came to mind. If Amy was confused by this, Asher was two steps away from insanity. His hands shook as his jaw fell agape. His own misunderstanding of the events that were unfolding ran across his face like a news crawl. Asher should have said he was sorry, or eased the ward, or both. He should have at least stopped and helped her. Of course, he didn't.

Asher was piloted by panic.

By the time Amy regained the ability to speak, Asher had sprinted down the hall and into the street. This morning had started weird and something told him that things were about to get weirder. He had to find a way a to cope.

IX. Little Sisters are the Worst

There was nothing like sneaking into your parent's house to make whatever you're doing feel ten times naughtier. If she was getting laid or drunk, this would be way more exciting. She wasn't. Carin held on to the fantasy of being as irresponsible as the other girls her age. It was only fair. Asher got be like that. He gave up on being responsible and did something frivolous as a lifestyle.

She had tried to be irresponsible once. It had been during the annual football game between McKean State Otters and the UMASS-Salem's Wicked Somethings. Carin tried to tailgate with the brothers of Beta Phi Mu. Carin's partying lasted exactly fifty minutes before she went into a panic attack. She then spent the rest of the day in the library trying to get caught up on her course work. Carin would never be "the" irresponsible one, but her actions this afternoon made her feel like she was. This, however, was in fact the greatest act of responsibility she could do. She had told her mother what had happened. Her mother had taken it very well. Then again, there wasn't much that did surprise Tracy Stone Mitchell anymore.

"That's fine," Tracy had said via satellite phone, "As long as you and Asher are okay, I don't care. Just when you get a chance, make sure that the altars are intact."

She had a break before Algebra. She had a chance to do her honor-bound duty to her matron. However, when she drove by the remains of the house, there was already a patrol car in front of the suburban split home, so Carin drove past her house and parked a block away to commence Operation Pretend I'm A Rebel. She snuck through the Robinson's back yard and then climbed the tree that housed an old tree house (she may have been humming the Mission

Impossible theme). She sat against the opening, watching carefully. She cringed as she watched Patrolmen stomping through her blessed home. She wasn't sure how much she could take of this tension. It's why she breathed a sigh when a red Volkswagen arrived on the scene. Clearly, the Department sent someone to protect the world from the stupidity of the mundane. That meant things were wrapping up with the investigation and she could go ahead and go on in. Carin's relief was short lived as she watched in irritation as the ex-footballer stepped out of the Volkswagen and joined the scene. Out of all the back up one could request, why did it have to be Weston Lewis?

Weston Lewis might have looked and acted like a simple cop. It might have been coincidence that he was partnered with the one who'd gotten possessed however, everyone in the supernatural community knew about the Lewis Clan. They were hunters -- even if they were trained dogs, they were still hunters. The Lewis clan was a rare breed even by hunter standards. For starters, it was very rare for a clan of hunters to be a blood family. Hunters see a familial bond as a weakness and therefore a liability. Much like religious orders, when a hunter is initiated into a clan, he forsakes his family to fight with his new brothers. So to involve wives, children and/or siblings is something unheard of by most hunters. The Lewis clan was a family first and hunters second. They believed this made them stronger as hunters.

Two, most hunters rarely hunt for just one type of creature or have the same something they will end up slaying. Generally, hunters track all manner of other worldly creatures for the safety of the mundane humans. The ideas of secrecy in the supernatural world causes the hunters believe that most supernatural creatures are evil. The Lewis Clan however, for generations have hunted vampires and only vampires leaving other creatures to be dealt with on a case by case business. Vampire hunters or -- as they are called by the vampires gangs -- Van Helsings, are not uncommon or unique to Gaiman Heights. Typically, there is an increase of vampire hunters with every vampire book, film or TV released on the subject. The Lewis clan is unique in the regard that they are the only clan of hunters sanctioned by the Vampiric House of Burgess of New England. According to the gossip (and vampires have the best gossip), back in 1825, the newly elected Princess of Gaiman Heights Prudence Goodchild hired Milan Lewis to police her increasing and violent population. Milan brought to Gaiman Heights his wife, two brothers, and three sons. Ever since then, the Lewis clan has been policing the wayward in the vampiric community. Sometimes, it's better to have your dirty work done outside the broods.

Weston Lewis wasn't a vampire hunter. He chose to use his talents to serve and protect in a different way. That didn't mean he was above paranoid suspicion of the supernatural community. He was hunter kin. That meant that, one day, Weston Lewis could snap and turn on the secrets he kept.

Carin's thoughts of her task being easy were dashed finally when she saw a busted up old Crown Victoria pull up in her driveway. She knew what that meant. The Department of the Arcane had really become involved, which was to be expected. She had half hoped that with all the cops hanging around that it maybe was a simple animal attack. Carin knew, of course, knew that if the Department of the Arcane was involved, then it was important. She had a deep well-taught respect for the Department of the Arcane. Despite learning the tenet that sisters help sisters, her mother would remind her frequently of their role in their society. Carin didn't care. She never got in trouble, so her and the Department of the Arcane stayed away from each other. However, she almost spat when she saw the occupants stepping out of the Crown Victoria. She groaned at the sight of Karl and Norvita.

There are few groups in the supernatural community that were as hated as the Marked. They were viewed with a squeamish cringe by most of the community. Most magic users are born into a legacy of magic. Having one forced into such an existence through subversive means makes one very uncomfortable, more so when it's a demonic possession that resulted in the abilities. This is because of the misconceptions by others in the supernatural community that center around demons. Saying that all demons are evil is generally stupid. While that's a subject for discussion later in this book, I will say this: demons and the possessed have a bad reputation based on a few bad apples like many other groups. Carin scrunched her nose as she watched the Marked man leave the car to speak to Weston Lewis. She couldn't complain about Karl too much. He had kept her from being stripped of her powers last Midrunitch when she put the leader of the Seventh Street Guild through a wall after he'd tried to grope her breast. It was the last time she would ever go on a blind date. Karl wasn't bad. If anything made the pair terrible it was Norvita.

You didn't' have to be in the supernatural community to know Norvita Patel. Everyone knew Norvita. You couldn't go through McKean State University without knowing Norvita. Norvita had a reputation that followed her. She was a loud and abrasive brat. She flirted mercilessly and spent a great deal of time partying. Carin had tried to become friends with Norvita after the Delta Mu party when Norvita drank half of Theta Kappa Tau fraternity under the table. After their initial meeting, Carin and Norvita's friendship had cooled considerably. Carin started to see the side of Norivta that everyone saw and was disappointed. She had hoped that there was more to Norvita than what she presented, but there wasn't. Norvita Patel was everything that she seemed to be. Carin had expected the daughter of the Patel dynasty to act more like an adult. Instead, Norvita acted like the rest of the immature children in the sophomore class at McKean State and Carin hated her. Well, Carin didn't really hate her. More likely, Carin was jealous. She didn't feel like she could ever be that reckless, no matter how many mad dreams she may have entertained. She was the only person in her family who performed magic outside of her mother. That meant that she was responsible for the legacy for her family. It wouldn't be Jordan. If Jordan had ever done anything exciting then that would really be a sign of the end times. He was just there. Of course Asher could have some natural talent. It would explain why all the weird things happened to him. Carin sneered again for a moment as she thought about Asher. He got away with everything. It just wouldn't be fair that on top of this that he was magical. Although, if Asher was a witch, and pulled the crap he did, then Carin could perhaps get away with a little irresponsibly.

Carin sighed as she watched the pair enter the ruins of her parent's home. She wearily set her head down on the floor. Waiting for people to leave your parents' home was boring. She let out a tired yawn as she shut her eyes. Quietly, she curled into a ball and fell into a light sleep.

It was the sound of barking that shook her from slumber. She snorted as she rolled back to her stomach. She looked back at the house and wiped drool from her face. In a window from the back of the house, there was a small red-brown dog yapping excitedly at her. She let out a sigh of relief at the sight of the dog. At least Yoshi was all right. She could report that the familiar was safe. Carin leaned forward surveying the driveway. The Crown Vic was still parked there. Her jaw hung open as she started to plan. Clearly, they didn't see or know that there was a familiar in the house. She licked her lips in deep thought. She had to come up with a diversion. She wondered if she knew enough to be able to do that. Furthermore would it be considered personal gain and a violation of her vows to do so? Of course not, she resolved, this was taking care of family business. She was doing this for her mother, which wasn't personal gain at all. That made her a good child. She smiled brightly before stopping herself. Feeling superior meant that it was personal gain. She cringed beating her options around until:

"Karl," Norvita yelled shrilly, "Wait!"

Carin looked up in enough time to watch the Crown Vic speed off. She couldn't have asked for a better diversion. Within five minutes, she climbed down quietly from her perch. She snuck down into the house through the empty garage. When she walked into the kitchen, she was greeted by the small jumping dog. Carin smiled as she knelt down. She petted the dog on his auburn head.

"Hey, Yoshi," she said quietly, stroking the dog's ear. "Keeping the house safe?"

Yoshi yapped excitedly with a bouncing tail wag. Carin smiled.

"Good," she said. "Take me to the altar."

Yoshi barked once as he trotted towards a back room. Carin followed behind the dog. She listened quietly as the sounds of suburbia filtered in through the open wounds of the house. The street was oddly quiet today. It was as if part of the house exploding had released a calming white magic throughout the neighborhood. The house didn't look terrible though. She knew that it would have been worse if it hadn't been for the wards her mother expertly crafted in the wood of the house unseen by mundane eyes. Carin blinked as her face curled into a scowl. She was learning to do her mother's work. She wasn't that good at it and it bothered her.

Carin looked down as her feet tripped over something heavy

and soft. Her voice choked off in her throat leaving her mouth dry. She'd never seen anything as big as the corpse lying at her feet. Her body shook in terror at the lifeless matter. Her hands reached out as the ground came rushing towards her. Carin found herself crawling towards a wall. She convulsed trying to expel the fear and her lunch from her body. All she could muster was a sour dry heave. Carin finally let out a sob. Asher, she thought, got off lightly. If she was in his Vans, she wouldn't have been able to cope.

Yoshi yapped at her to follow. Carin wiped her mouth before finding her feet. She staggered behind the dog into an east facing bedroom. She pushed the door open and walked into the room with queasy steps. She let out the third or fourth sigh of relief. The other thing her mother was good at was constructing altars that didn't look like altars. Karin knew it was an altar. She could feel the power from the altar. It had remained intact. She had nothing to fear, not from her mother anyway.

From the other creatures in the house though, that was a different story.

Behind her came the sound of heavy feet crushing her calm as flat as the carpet under the remains of the manticore. Her eyes darted in the afternoon darkness as she backed into the bedroom. She closed the door noiselessly. Her breath stopped as she uttered a small prayer. Things were going so well for her in her hiding place until she heard Yoshi yapping excitedly at something. Carin's eyes went wide at the noise. The familiar was now unprotected. Carin knew that she would be in a world of hurt if she didn't do anything to save him. She forgot about her safety and ran from the bedroom. She went roughly three feet before she was greeted by the intruder. Carin came eye to chest with a hulking creature. She suppressed a shudder as the large beast flexed its green skinned muscles with snarling breaths. She froze as big hands grabbed her shirt and pulled her up to eye level. Its snout buried into her neck and snorted into her scent. Troll, she thought, their vision is bad but their sense of smell was amazing.

The troll let out a growl.

"Veetchling," said the troll in a deep Slavic voice, "Vat are you doing here?"

"I-I-I came to get my mother's familiar," Carin blubbered almost incoherently. Tears ran down her cheeks as she started to sob. "I live here. Please don't hurt me."

"Vy are you crying, veetchling?" asked the Troll. "Do you tink I would hurt you, foolish girl?"

"Yes," she whined.

"Veetchling," the troll said as gently as a troll could, "O vould hope better from you. You say racist tings. Ivo doesn't harm veetchling or magi. They are Ivo's best customers."

Carin flushed with embarrassment. Ivo Warmace ran the most exclusive restaurant in Gaiman Heights which she'd gotten reservations in once. The Warmaces were the only civilized family of trolls in Gaiman Heights. In fact they were polite and as nonviolent as a group of trolls could be. In an instant, Carin knew she was indeed being racist.

"I'm sorry," Carin said hurtfully. "I wasn't thinking."

"I will forbive this," Ivo replied. "You, veetchling, have given Ivo a manticore. Very rare. We will make much money. You will help send Ivo's daughter to Sarah Laurence."

"That's great," Carin said lightly perplexed. "I didn't kill the manticore."

"Oh," Ivo said in surprise. "Who did, veetchling?"

Carin shrugged as best she could.

"I don't know," she said, "I guess Asher did, but it doesn't seem fair to be a loser with super powers."

"Asher of Stone?" Ivo asked in astonishment.

"Yea, why?"

Ivo thought for a moment about her words. He then thought about Asher. He knew who Asher Stone was. It was hard to find anyone in this city who didn't know who Asher Stone was. Ivo, however, had been present at Asher's first birthday party which had been at his restaurant. He and his wife, Neela, had brought the cake to the small child. It had been the last time he'd seen Stephen. Six months later, Stephen threw himself into a crack in the void to seal it off from the mundane world. No one had forgotten what Stephen did for the world. As honor bound creed, people owed it to Stephen to protect Asher. It seemed that Ivo couldn't leave Carin there undefended, so he made a choice.

"Vell, Veetchling," Ivo said abruptly, "time to go."

"You didn't answer my question," Carin said.

Ivo wasn't going to answer her. He knew that there were things that were beyond his pay grade. This was definitely beyond his pay grade. The standing order was that questions about the family Stone were to be diverted to the director of the Department. That was where he was going to direct Carin. He did this by throwing her over his shoulder. She screamed in protest as he walked casually through the house. Yoshi followed behind them in a trot. Carin wondered if her day could get any worse. The answer was yes.

X. Inked Information

Norvita was curled into a tightly wound ball as the Crown Vic spun over the cobblestone streets heading towards Old Gaiman. Karl's driving, though erratic, hadn't scared her (though his Steve McQueen impersonation was enough to have scared any sane person). No, what frightened the young psychic was the foul mood radiating like a mushroom cloud off of Karl since they'd left the crime scene and the manticore to Ivo. Karl was quiet, but she still knew he was mad. It wasn't hard to tell. One, his upper lip tightly sneered along his darkening completion. His eyes narrowed as he thought. She could have chalked that up to Karl being irritated with Old Gaiman. It could have been except for the rhythm being drummed in a pattern of a war song pattern by his fingers. Karl's eyes became darkened with vengeance. He was livid and she needed to know why. She had an idea that hadn't been discussed really. Norvita had made it a policy to never read Karl's thoughts on purpose. She liked Karl, despite putting him through a world of shit; she liked Karl and nothing makes you dislike a person more than knowing what's going on inside someone's head. Also, she found that spying on your partner's most private thoughts led to extreme mistrust. However, after he all but growled at her when she touched the car radio, she felt that she was entitled to know why.

Subtly, she crept into the back of Karl's mind. She moved through the joyous experience that was the birth of Karl's second daughter. She then fell into the blackness of the year that he couldn't remember. What a weird path, she mused to herself. Then, as two and two were put together, Karl's conclusion dawned on her.

Karl, as you may know, was one of the unfortunate souls

called the Marked. The Marked were a group of people who had, at one time or another, been possessed by a demonic force. The term comes from the tattooed wards that wound around their left wrists. Norvita knew Karl's ward by heart. His said, to recap, "Non vi, Sed verbo. No teimpo mala." Or, "through words, not actions. I will fear nothing evil." It was an ordeal. She knew his concern. The experience of a demonic possession is a rather painful one for both the demon and the host. Anyone who has gone through that kind of hell can and will tell you that hell is to live with another person inside your brain. Norvita's face softened instantly.

"Oh Karl," she whispered mostly to herself, "children get possessed too."

Karl gave Norvita a cold and venomous look that stopped her heart from beating for a minute. Norvita recoiled into the passenger seat as her body shook on pure instinct, struggling to get away from that feeling that was burning her soul. She'd never been scared of Karl before this moment. After all, Karl was a clam and austere man and was slow to anger. The only time Karl threatened to lose his temper was when a child was involved, which in three years had only happened twice. That's when Karl closed down his human self and his consciences got quiet. She knew that's when the other voices came to stay with Karl. She got scared when that happened.

One of the benefits of possession was the leftover demonic powers. Some were innate or required little effort to use, like Karl's encyclopedic knowledge of the supernatural. Others had to be tapped into, like inhuman strength or a psychic attack like the Demon's Wake. To use those talents, a Marked would have to give up a piece of their humanity. Even the use of the innate abilities corrupted the human soul over time. Anger came quicker the longer Karl lived with Anger came the temptation to use other gifts. Norvita knew that Karl was progressively becoming less human. The day that Karl became a full demon, she feared, it would be because someone hurt a child.

"And a demon of any size would rip a child apart," he said finally. "It's why the Hordes prefer adult hosts for hostile invasions. Harder to burn through. In a pinch, they'll possess a child but they prefer female children. This isn't a possession. That ward wasn't keeping anything out. The ink was light blue. The Hordes can only read dark red or black. The wording was all wrong. There isn't a command to keep something away. It's more of a nice ask to stay. That kid isn't a Marked."

"Then, Karl," Norvita asked, "what is he?"

Karl leaned back in the driver's seat, his brow smoothing as he relaxed into a lecture. His vengeful grip eased off steering wheel. His natural calm finally caught up with them at the stop light. He smoothed out wild hairs as his lips pursed in thought. *Always,* she thought to herself, *whenever he gets like this, ask him a question about something. He loves being smarter than everyone else.*

"That kind of work is a binding ward," Karl explained finally. "Someone is using that kid as a vessel."

Nortiva blinked her rich dark eyes. Her light blue glittery eye shadow sparkled in the red light of a well-timed stop. Her thoughts extended their court into contemplation as the light changed to a passive green. Karl sped into the hard left with the determination of a stock car driver. Norvita's brightly highlighted hair fell into her face, breaking her train of considered thought. She leaned against the window, watching the ancient cobble-stoned world of West Hills melt into the abandoned world of Old Gaiman in a wordless haze. That's when her thoughts returned to her.

"A vessel," she asked finally, watching the antiquated store fronts pass. "But for what, Karl?"

Karl shook his head. Nothing felt right about this case and he couldn't quite put his finger on what felt wrong. He couldn't find anything for what this vessel would be in his reserve. It was as if someone had taken that information and deleted it from history. Even his treasure trove of knowledge was empty. That bothered Karl deeply.

"I don't know, Norvita." Karl admitted in a great amount shame. "For it to be housed in a living vessel though, it has to be something very powerful."

"So we don't know what it is and we're going to...."

"To talk to Evil Edward," he cut her off.

The constant issue for someone in Gaiman Heights was the financial stability of the witch and mage populations. Due to the diversity of cultures, the former allegedly holy ones had to find ways to integrate with in the mundane society. Many of these people converted their ancient skills into modern society. The best example of this modern entrepreneur was Edward Anoi.

Edward Anoi had traveled from his island home to Gaiman Heights over fifty years ago when his people came to the mainland. Then, he was a young man with raven black hair and dark skin that would have made Gauguin's lover jealous. He was the heir to the religious rites and practices that had been in his family for more than fifteen generations. Edward Anoi channeled his archaic skills into Edward Inks. His true name was hidden behind the moniker of Evil Edward. Most of the mundane, those who ventured into Old Gaiman -- few and far between -- thought he chose an edgy name to drum up business.

This was a lie.

Evil Edward was really Edward the Dark; defeater of the black arts. It is not uncommon for mages who fight black magic to have a name like Evil Edward's. They find it confuses the enemy. Evil Edward's battle against evil forces was fought by weaving wards and incantations on human flesh to expel the grotesque from the mortal world. While the core of his business was mostly the mages, witches, and, of course, the Marked, Edward Inks was also the only tattoo shop in Gaiman Heights and meant that he also served the mundane world more often than not. Ward work paid well, but the crux of his business came from the mundane students of McKean State. He used to fight dragons. Now, he was tattooing them on drunken freshman. The irony was not lost on Evil Edward.

Evil Edward's shop smelled of antiseptic and metal. The walls of the fluorescent-lit store were covered with bright displays of tattoos that one could have gashed in ink lines on their flesh. Norvita was distracted by a butterfly tattoo whose wings extended out into a pattern that mocked Evil Edward's tribal heritage. Karl's nose wrinkled tempestuously at the store air. He had a strong dislike when it came to Old Gaiman. People in that part of town didn't regard the rules of the city like their brothers spread out in other parts. It was like they thought it was their own city without the mundane.

They *were* here first. The mundane world was just going to have to deal. This irritated Karl had who never had a choice of being unveiled.

The proprietor of Edward Inks was stretched out at the receptionist's desk. His body tensed hearing purposeful feet on his tiled floor. He looked up from his copy of Guns and Ammo. It wasn't really Guns and Ammo. He used a light incantation on his copy of Vanity Fair to keep up appearances for his customers. He liked Vanity Fair though. It was a well written magazine that had things he cared about. He wasn't too crazy about their political leanings but everyone's got a fault.

"Karl, Norvita." said the aging Samoan Shaman happily. "What brings you to this side of town?

"Business," Karl said coldly. Norvita's voice choked on the animosity from Karl. She gave Edward a regretful smile. "Edward Anoi, also known as Edward the Dark and Evil Edward. We need to see your license."

"On the wall, brother," he said, leaning back further in his chair and putting his cowboy boots on the shiny desk.

"Your other license?" Karl's voice increased in volume lightly.

"On the wall brother," Evil Edward repeated. "I don't practice my craft outside the shop."

Karl's steely gaze rose just above Evil Edward's head to the wall above him and in the center of a loose cluster of state issued operator's license and approved health inspection stickers was the more important license. On a piece of stately blue patterned paper and embossed in gold, the Department of the Arcane declared that Edward Anoi was a registered and licensed mage. He was oath and honored bound to uphold the laws and codes put forth by the Department or be stripped of his powers and bound from the craft.

"Huh," Karl said in disbelief. "You display that in public like that?"

"Most of my clients are either marked, mages, or witches," Evil Edward shrugged.

"They expect to see it. The mundies never look at the walls. If they do, they think it's a joke. What's up?"

Karl tightened the muscles that connected his jaw to the rest of his tired face as he looked down at Evil Edward. Things had gotten friendlier than Karl had hoped for. If you have a ward done, you had it done by Evil Edward and there was no two ways about that. However, this was business and Karl couldn't forget that's why they were here. He had a mission to solve a mystery. Karl had to remain focused. Magic had been performed on a child in a slanderous way. That was an act that Karl could not abide. He peered over the frame of his glasses. Norvita knew what that meant. It brought to mind a sleek samurai noiselessly unsheathing his deadly katana. Her pupils retracted as she watched his interrogative fencing arm swing back.

Karl was going in for the kill.

"What do you know about Tracy and Brady Mitchell?" Karl said smoothly as a katana swing.

"They sound like a couple from a soap opera," Evil Edward said flatly, bracing against the verbal slash. "Unless you're talking about Tracy Stone Mitchell."

"Tracy Stone Mitchell?" Karl's pitch had changed drastically. Norvita had never heard what Karl sounded like while on the verge of panic before that moment. This is what it had to be. It was as if Karl had screwed something up profoundly. "She's not kin to Stephen Stone, is she?"

"Steve's widow," Evil Edward confirmed. "He was a good man. Something happen to Tracy?"

"That's what we're trying to figure out," Karl said, almost dropping the rage that drove them to this point. "A manticore destroyed their house. Norvita and I are trying to figure out why them. In the course of our investigation we noticed that one of the kids is pretty inked up. You do any work on the Mitchell kids?"

Evil Edward pursed his lips as he contemplated the question before him. The back of his trunk like body pressed against the chair as thoughts worked through his mind. He'd never technically been a member of an order of mages. As a shaman, he served his tribe now and then. That was some time ago. He had no set tribe now in the city. Without a set tribe, Evil Edward served his community. He was among the people he protected. Cloistering himself off in a stone library like other mages seemed counterproductive to his mission. The magi are diverse with many different beliefs, however, Gaiman Heights magi had a few things they agreed on such as Coltrane was better before he got clean. They also believed that meat tasted better cooked on an open flame. The one thing they definitely agreed on was certain pieces of history were not to be discussed within the earshot of the mundane. He rose solemnly.

"Perhaps, we should take this conversation to my office," is all he said.

To be invited into the inner sanctum of a magic user is a rare honor. Being invited into the room, often a room facing east, where a witch places an altar is a sign of intimacy. To be invited into a warlock's lair means he either finds you delicious or you don't mind the smell of burnt bald eagle. A fae won't invite you into their sacred space pretty much ever, but that's a story for another time. For a mage to invite a non-mage into one's study, where a mage keeps his tomes, is a sign of great respect. Evil Edward's study was kept in the back office of his store. Norvita went flush as she walked into the shaman's study. Her hands shook excitedly as she felt a surge of power.

"Oh, Karl," she squealed, "I can…"

"Sssh," Karl hissed.

Evil Edward settled in a high backed chair as Karl and Norvita sat down on the cushioned chairs that were close to the ground. The shaman stretched out before letting his hawk like eyes rest on the pair.

"I've not done any work on a mage named Mitchell," Evil

Edward said finally. "But if it were anyone else but you, I wouldn't share this. The Crone scares the hell out of me and I fear her wrath, but you and Norvita have light souls. You're the good guys. You have the right to know."

"Don't lie to me, Ed," Karl spat. "I saw the pictures in the Mitchell house. Their oldest son had more ink on him than the Library of Congress."

"The girl's a witch who just matured into maidenhood," Evil Edward retorted.

"Tracy brought her in for the rites and binding covenants. Most witches don't do that in house anymore. She provided the materials and the blessing. I did the hard part. The youngest isn't anything to write home about, so I doubt I'll see him."

"At this point," Norvita interrupted, "I'd say you're getting off topic, but I feel like all this exposition is building to a point of significance."

"Nah, I was running on a tangent," Evil Edward admitted. "But thanks. I almost forgot you were there."

"How?" both Karl and Norvita asked in unison.

"She was being uncharacteristically quiet while waiting for a punchline," Evil Edward explained. "And yes, I worked on the oldest kid. Some of my best spells are on that kid, but he's a Mitchell about as much as Norvita is a virgin."

"Hey!" Norvita yelled.

"Asher is Stephen Stone's son. I'm honored to say I worked on Asher."

"Why?" Karl finally managed to ask. "Why do that to a child, Ed? You know the rules."

"Because when Merlin Duke and the Crone tell you to craft

wards on a child, you don't ask questions." said the shaman. "I would have done it anyway. Stephen was a good man. He saved me from the Abyssal swarm back in '85. When hell rises, it comes after my kind first."

"Dr. Duke and the Crone asked you to place wards on a child?" Karl said stupidly. No part of that statement made sense in his head. It was strictly forbidden to perform serious magic on a child unless it was an emergency and to have the two most powerful beings in all of creation instructing someone to do that was an odd juxtaposition.

There was also the idea of the Crone working with anyone. The Crone, according to legend, lived on Warrior's Peak by herself and had for the last five centuries. It was generally believed that she was seldom seen. This was greatly inaccurate. On Saturday, the Crone would go shopping with her friend Beverly. Beverly was legally blind; however, the Crone had never learned to drive. On Market Day, the Crone would act as Beverly's eyes while Beverly drove.

Still, the Crone speaking directly to someone in Old Gaiman was hard to fathom.

"Wait," Norvita said, "don't Doctor Duke and the Crone hate each other? You know like epically? Like their worlds would collide hate?"

"Baby girl," Evil Edward began, "hate doesn't describe the feeling between those two. Besides, when something that'll change history happens, you get the strangest allies."

"Then what happened?" Karl asked. "What brought those two together? What makes Asher Stone so special?"

The shaman gave Karl a stone cold look. This had never been his fight and he wasn't about to be a part of it now. Evil Edward knew this wasn't his business.

"Information like that, my brother," Evil Edward said quietly, "is well beyond what I'm allowed to say. You want the whole story, you should talk to Dr. Duke. I will tell you this; this kid is the most important person in this city."

Later....

Norvita and Karl sat in the Crown Vic without movement for a long time after that. The air of confusion passed between them as did recycled air from the heating system. Norvita couldn't figure out the pieces or how they fit together. What was worse was Karl couldn't figure it out himself. This was a new problem for them.

"He's powerful and doesn't know?" Karl said in disbelief, recounting the story so far. I do hope you're paying attention. I'm not kidding about that test. "And Duke and the Crone are involved. Norvita, none of this is adding up. How are you raised by a witch and are the son of Stephen Stone and remain veiled? Or, for that matter, how can you be strong enough to kill a manticore and not know that you can?"

"Karl, who's Stephen Stone?" Norvita asked with a soft blink.

"He was number two in the Order of Truth and Light." Karl explained. "One of the most powerful magi to ever live. If you believe the stories, he was descended from the Crone, if that's even possible."

"Then if he's so powerful," Norvita asked, "why is he dead? I thought the more powerful a mage is, the harder it is to kill them."

"Because in 1986 the Void opened up and the Abyssal

Hordes had their Spring Break. Hence why we have spandex, New Wave, cocaine, and Reganomics. In order to close the rift, Stephen threw the most powerful thing he had – himself -- into the gap to shut it." Karl said sagely. "Now I know there is a chance he could be alive, but god help him if he did survive. Abyssal are some of the worse demons out there."

Norvita didn't question Karl after that. When he knew something, he was always right. Secretly, she never wanted to know the full sum of Karl's personal experiences. The ones she knew about, the ones he'd shared, terrified her. She turned her attention back to the dreary spring day."

"So," she said finally, "no cheeseburgers?"

"Nope," Karl said, searching in his pockets for a piece of candy. "Sorry?"

"It's okay," she said. "Carson'll understand."

XI. Magic in the Park

There were a few things that made Asher feel like a human being. One of these things was going to work. Before he'd fallen into the brutal spiral of addiction, Asher had been the department manager for the Stop and Save in Gaiman. Needless to say, he didn't have that job any longer. However, Asher had been lucky enough to procure a job with Torg Olensen. Torg was an older gentleman with sky blue eyes and Nordic blond hair. His large powerful arms held the fossils of thickened muscles. A casual viewer would say that Torg was a former linebacker. This isn't true. Torg used to swing a hammer and the sky would rumble and the earth would shake. Now he and his brother Ollie ran Thunder Strikes. Thunder Strikes was the only bowling alley in Gaiman Heights. They had opened the alley back in '75. The Olensens were fixtures of the community even if no one could remember them arriving to the city. It felt like they'd always been there. Asher looked around awkwardly at the polished brass as Torg inspected Asher carefully. Asher gave Torg his patent pending smile.

"No," Torg said in a gruff voice, "it's league night and I can't have you hurt and on the floor."

"But Mr. Olensen," Asher pleaded, "you don't understand. Today has been weird. I need to strike a balance."

"Asher, listen, I like you, kid," Torg said. "I really do; but we've had this talk before. Normal sober people have days off. Especially after a dog attack."

"Lion attack," Asher corrected him.

"Stone, go home," Torg ordered. "Get some rest."

There was no earthly way he was going home. In the span of a day, he'd been attacked by a lion, killed said lion, been hit on by his sister and Amy, and wielded a katana like a refugee from a Kurisawa film. Things were far too weird to just go home. Asher looked down at his twitching fingers as his brain processed his personal confusion. He was waiting to see the sparks again. He'd never seen sparks fly off his fingers, not like that before. His life had started to feel overwhelmingly weird. That meant that the voice inside his head was saying it was about to get weirder. There had to be a way to get through this day without a mental breakdown. He had to find a way to cope.

Suddenly an image popped into his head. He focused on a black eyed sprite with a head full of pink hair. He could hear the claxon of the sprite's voice haranguing in his ears. Asher couldn't resist the temptation anymore. He had to go see Iggy.

Therein lay the inherent issue with that desire. Iggy was almost impossible to find. He was possibly the last living gypsy in North America. Iggy had no home. He didn't own a phone. As far as Asher knew, Iggy never received mail or paid taxes, which begged the question of where or how did Iggy live. The only way Iggy gained shelter, as far as Asher knew, was by gifting his way into homes of single mothers and staying until they kicked him out. He'd meet these ladies while doing his first great cover, street magic. Iggy was Gaiman Heights' only drug dealer, but he only sold drugs to finance his street magic which still made less sense than anything else that Iggy did. Iggy had been doing the same tricks for the last twenty years; he didn't need money to update the tricks. Maybe, he needed the money for all his legal fees.

If Asher was right, he knew where to find Iggy.

In the 1970s, as a part of urban renewal, the town council of Gaiman Heights embroiled itself in a bitter land dispute with many different gangs to create several different public parks. The bloodiest battle came to a head during the fight against the Hare Krishnas for the land beside the McCaffery River. At the end of this mini-Gettysburg, the town manager and the mayor had been slain and several town council members were maimed. At the end of the war, the Krishnas were banished from Gaiman Heights. This created Martin River Park, named for the mayor who valiantly gave his life for its founding.

In the center of Martin River Park was a statue of said fallen mayor that had been given to the city by the Gaiman Heights' chapter of the United Daughters of the Confederacy. Hanging from the statue was the figure of the enigmatic Isaac "Iggy" Reed. He looked around at the captive audience with maddening delight dancing in his onyx colored eyes. Iggy never got high off his own supply because he never needed drugs for a buzz. A crowd's admiration was better than speed -- but only small crowds. Asher asked Iggy once why he never went professional.

Iggy had shrugged. "I was kicked out of one home," he'd say. "Why would I want to leave this one?"

Asher couldn't argue with that.

He looked just how Asher remembered him looking. He wore an oversized black cadet's jacket with silver buttons that shone as brightly as they did on the day he stole that coat. Under the jacket were a faded Adam Ant T-shirt and a pair of beaten dark blue jeans that with holes around the cuffs that were ripped into existence by the heels of his cowboy boots. The only thing that was neat about Iggy was his hair. Iggy had a perfectly sculpted faux-hawk. Granted it was bright pink, but it was always perfectly neat and clean.

Iggy spread his gangly arms out dramatically. The sleeves of his jacket swayed like a war banner in the Spring breeze. His crowd of wives and toddlers stared up at him, transfixed by his glory. He owned the crowd in that moment. If he told them to riot, they would be ripping this city apart. He flashed his jaded grin at them wildly. If I didn't know better, thought Asher, I'd say he was high. Again, he wasn't. Despite being the seller of drugs, Iggy was a total straight edge. He didn't drink alcohol or do drugs, much to the surprise of everyone.

Iggy held his hand flat. He rolled his sleeve up and then snapped his fingers. A bright red flame appeared in the middle of his hand. Iggy's free hand waved dramatically around the flame. The flame danced as it changed to a vibrant black purple then to a sacred white. His enthralled audience ooh and ahhed on his cue. Iggy brought the dancing flame to his lips and blew. As the flame went out, bright gold flakes peppered the crowed in a light flurry. A deafening wave of applause rung out over the crowd like Christmas Day over Whoville and attacked Asher's overly sensitive ears. Iggy bowed garishly at the applause.

"Thank you, thank you. Now for my next trick I..." Iggy suddenly got quiet. His ink spot eyes searched the crowd of generic faces excitedly. His eyes grew wider as an all too familiar smell hit his nose. His smile grew more manic as recognition set in.

"Show's over. Go home. Asher! Asher! Asher! Asher!"

There was a blur of pink and punk. Then, there was a fleshy thud. The next thing Asher knew, he found himself on the hard asphalt. His eyes stared up at the cold spring sky. Asher let out a grunt as he suppressed a pain riddled grimace. Iggy laid on top of Asher as he clung to Asher's fractured frame. Asher sighed as Iggy buried his face into Asher's chest. He purred happily.

"I missed you!" Iggy squealed happily. "I knew that you'd come back to me."

"Hey, Iggy," Asher said with strained breathlessness, "Mind getting off my chest?"

Iggy looked down as his face fell, following his eyes. Begrudgingly, he pulled himself off Asher as he stood up. After several minutes of struggle, Asher weakly got to his feet. He cringed as his weight settled in his shoes. Things inside him didn't feel right. He wondered if it could be possible that Iggy had broken a fourth rib. Iggy looked at him brightly. Mischief danced in his eyes as he inspected him.

"Man, Asher," Iggy said, "you look like you've been mauled by a manticore."

"What?" Asher felt a burning sensation in the center of his left temple. He'd felt this scarring pain before this moment. It was a side effect knowing Iggy. Iggy's weird tangents made Asher's head hurt.

"It's something my grandmother used to say to me," Iggy explained. "She'd say, 'Shit, son. You look like you've been mauled by a manticore'."

"Your grandmother said a lot of weird things," Asher said.

"Well, she did take a lot of drugs," Iggy conceded. He smiled excitedly at Asher again. He threw his arms around Asher's neck, pulling him into a tight hug. "I've never been so happy. Asher, I love you!"

Asher coughed nervously at Iggy's words. People walked past them in painful slow motion. It was true. In his own way, Iggy had always loved Asher. He also had no qualms of showing it in the most physical way possible, regardless of the setting. In spite of being used to this, Asher was still very uncomfortable with the public display. A feeling that grew as he felt judgmental eyes penetrating their embrace. Asher patted Iggy's back with a complicated sigh.

"I-I-I know," Asher stammered. "Iggy, I need to talk to you. I've had a pretty weird day. I was hoping that you were holding."

Iggy pulled out of the hug, keeping Asher at arm's length. His eyes danced with tightly wound circles of delight as his grin manically covered most of his face. Iggy gripped Asher's shoulders tightly. Asher knew what the feeling of apprehension that was building into a black ball of hate hanging under his ribs meant. This was a bad idea.

"For you Asher," Iggy said. "I will always be holding."

No sooner than his tension built, Asher's apprehension passed into memory. Iggy took Asher's hand and merrily skipped down the trail that led out of the park. Asher stumbled as his feet struggled to keep up with Iggy's gallop. The judgmental eyes that had taken an interest in the pair now actively ignored them. Martin River Park was bathed in shadows as the mid-afternoon sun moved behind a curtain of cloud.

Iggy dragged Asher to the western mouth of the park and into cold reality. The western exit was Iggy's favorite because it was close to his second office; the corporate Park and Ride. Asher hated the exposed forest of dormant cars. Gaiman PD was notorious for patrolling the park and rides. Asher knew that if they got caught, Iggy would run, leaving Asher holding the bag.

Asher couldn't afford to go to prison. Even with the tattoos, he was far too pretty.

Iggy came to a sudden halt at a pink Cadillac that was old enough to have voted for Kennedy. Asher stared at the Grateful Dead sticker on the left side of the back bumper.

"You bought a car?" Asher said in disbelief. Iggy dug into his pockets for something. "You own property?"

"Nope," Iggy replied as he produced a large key ring that was the same color as the car. He hummed as he walked around the car, in one of the many obsessions of Iggy's that Asher never quite understood, thrice. "Stole it."

He should have expected as much from Iggy. Why pay for something when you could take it? It wasn't stealing if you needed it. Asher's first memory of Iggy was him being chased out of Asher's childhood home with a fireplace poker. Asher's mother had caught Iggy trying to take her keys. She caught the man just as Iggy was leading a very small Asher out the garage door. As he watched Iggy struggle to open the trunk, Asher wondered what single mother didn't have a ride to work today.

Iggy popped the trunk with great triumph. Asher shoved his head into the pristine trunk to welcome his narcotic bounty. As his eyes inspected the clean purple-pink interior of the trunk, his heart sank to his diaphragm. The biggest dealer in Gaiman Heights and not a granule of opiate could be seen in his trunk. This clearly was a joke…right?

"Where's the junk?" Asher asked as irritation and panic scratched in his veins begging to be saved by a sweet mix. If this was a joke, it wasn't very funny.

"Oh," Iggy replied casually, "I have it on me."

"What is it?" Asher asked hastily. "Heroin? Morphine? Oxy?"

"Chloroform," Iggy announced loudly.

Asher's face twisted in confusion. He opened his mouth to question Iggy as a chemically damped cloth dropped down over his lips and nose. Asher let out a muffled scream as he went into panicked shock. His body spasmed as he tried to avoid breathing in the sickly sweet fumes. Iggy's deceptively strong frame pressed against Asher's convulsing body. He held our hero rigid and shoved the rag harder into his mouth with his hand firmly planted over the cloth. In what felt like the longest thirty seconds on record, Asher fell into drowsiness. His head lolled back against Iggy's shoulder reluctantly surrendering to the effects of the drug. Iggy leaned against Asher's ear.

"You left me once," he whispered. "You won't leave me again."

The last thing Asher could remember was his heavy frame nestling uncomfortably in the trunk of the old Caddy. Iggy leaned down and kissed the top of Asher's head before shutting the trunk. He clicked his heels before dancing to the music in his head to the driver's seat. He settled comfortably behind the wheel. This was a red letter day. Asher came back to him. He and Puck were going to eat good tonight.

Don't act surprised; you knew they'd be back.

Iggy spun out of the Park and Ride like a Meatloaf song and turned the radio up so loud that the base registered on the Richter scale. He sped towards the widening streets of Old Gaiman and, specifically, Goodfellows Comics. He sang victoriously with the radio. He couldn't have planned this turn of events better. If he was any more pleased with himself he'd have to be a Kanye West song.

That was, of course, before the abrupt appearance of flashing blue lights filling his rearview mirror. Iggy's face came tumbling down into a frown as he saw the form of a black and white patrol car. He slowed his hasty retreat and pulled over to the side of the back street. Iggy was completely and utterly insane. Anyone who knew Iggy for more than five minutes could confirm this fact, however, he wasn't stupid. He knew that the worst thing a person could do while making mischief was to do something stupid and impulsive. For example, running from the police would be incredibly stupid and impulsive. He glanced up, watching the silhouette of a uniformed officer approaching the pink caddy. It would have been fine. He could lie to a uniformed cop. That wasn't hard. What was hard was the fact that a plain clothes detective joined the uniformed officer. Iggy grimaced. He knew then that this wasn't a normal traffic stop. No one with a detective would make a normal stop. The patrolman tapped gently on the window. Iggy steeled his face with a manic grin as he rolled down the window gingerly.

"Well, hiya officer," Iggy said as friendly as a slow summer breeze. "What can I do for you today, my good sir?"

"License and registration," said the patrolman.

Iggy had never owned a license nor wanted one. Like most government functions, he didn't see the point in participating. It wasn't a major problem for the pink haired fairy. As he leaned forward towards the glove box he muttered a small rhyme under his breath. Iggy snapped his fingers three times and, out of nothing, he had the forms of identification that every officer asks for. He leaned back as he handed the work to the patrolman who started back to the car. Before the patrolman had a chance to run the information, the detective stopped him. Iggy watched as his confident grin turned into a primal sneer as the detective walked towards where the patrolman once was. Like a bad penny, Weston Lewis was on the scene. Iggy watched with disgust as he ambled calmly towards the driver's side, his cool gaze cocked and locked on Iggy.

"Iggy," Weston Lewis said with all the authority given to him hanging off the vowels of his words. "What do you think you're doing?"

"Going to see my grandmother," Iggy said matter-of-factly. He couldn't talk his way out of trouble with Weston Lewis. That didn't mean he wasn't going to try.

"Step out of the car," Weston Lewis said flatly.

Iggy sighed but complied with the request and reluctantly stepped out of the Caddy. Weston Lewis eyed Iggy with utter disappointment and then spat into a plastic bottle contemplatively. Iggy leaned forward towards Weston Lewis and bated his eyelashes at the detective trying to suppress his manic grin. Weston Lewis wasn't amused by his charm. He simply shook his head at the fairy.

"Iggy," Weston Lewis said, "cut the crap. You can't drive. You don't own a car and I know for a fact you don't have a grandmother. What are you doing?"

"Returning my grandmother's car to her. She's very, very sick." Iggy replied.

"Officer MacArthur will be searching your stolen car," Weston Lewis said as his irritation grew. Dealing with Iggy Smith put everyone in a bad mood.

Iggy took this moment to assess the state of his current situation. He could ride out this traffic stop easy. Iggy had been in tighter spots with meaner people than this. The problem here was Weston Lewis. Weston Lewis was more than aware of what Iggy was and that meant it wouldn't take the detective long to figure out how special Asher was and where he was. This was a problem for Iggy because that was a surefire way to lose Asher forever. Iggy could not permit that to happen again. He had to run, knowing that Asher would be found again. He was hungry for the things that only Iggy could give him. So while Officer McArthur tried to open the Caddy's trunk, Iggy stared at Weston Lewis. A devious thought played across his face culminating in his dark eyes dancing in delight.

"Retreat like the night," he whispered. "Let me travel on the light."

In a puff of logic, Iggy vanished. Weston Lewis took a step back, swallowing a bit of his tobacco. Goddamn fae, he thought, they get me every time. He'd have to ask Karl how to deal with them later. He'd also have to figure out an explanation to give to Officer MacArthur on how an unarmed suspect got away from him. He cough-spat into the bottle mulling over these problems.

"Detective Lewis," Officer MacArthur called, shattering Weston Lewis's concentration.

"We've got a problem, sir."

Weston Lewis walked towards Officer MacArthur who was frozen in horror as he stared down into the open trunk. He let his lazy gaze walk down towards the mass that had gotten the uniformed policeman's attention. There lay a bleeding crumpled mass of human being in the trunk of this car. Weston Lewis uttered a small prayer when he saw the mass breathe calmly. This was a new twist of sick, thought Weston Lewis. This wasn't their case, it couldn't be. Fairies rarely were so sloppy about kidnapping a human being. This was something more than they were comfortable with Iggy. This was a matter for the Department of the Arcane.

"Radio for a bus for this kid and find me Spangler and Patel," Weston Lewis ordered.

"They'll want to talk to this one."

Weston Lewis popped another wad of chewing tobacco in his mouth. Iggy was getting very, very dangerous.

XII. The Crone

The gray clouds relinquished a fine mist of wet over the city as a black SUV left Old Gaiman from the large garage behind the castle and headed to the small community of Wildwood Grove. Wildwood Grove was originally a lone grove of oak trees and a large house that sat at the top of Warrior's Peak. Then the paradigm shift from agrarian to industrial hit and those who could flee out of the city did. The grove that stood was cleared to make way for a shifting tide of progress. In its place, identical houses sprung out of the ground to join the house on the hill. Time and the economy changed in the Grove. The average age of the residents increased as young couples became parents and then grandparents. The only thing that remained the same was the house on the top of the hill. It was an impressive Victorian, before people knew what Victorians were, that stayed in perfect condition despite the length that it had been there. That was where the SUV was headed on this Thursday. It was more interested in the occupant of the Victorian than the Victorian itself though.

The owner of the house was far more interesting than anything in the house anyway.

There were many standard fixtures that seemed to linger in Gaiman Heights. Most of these fixtures were rocks or buildings that aged and got cold as the years passed. The other thing that remained was Miriam Stone. No one would remember when she moved into the Victorian (except for two very proper Native Americans -- they had kept the receipt) however, there has always been someone matching Miriam Stone's description in the house and that would always be the case. Miriam Stone would tell you that she moved into

Wildwood Grove in the spring after marrying Dennis Stone who was a local barber. They had met in Boston one day at the Constitution and he brought her back home. Oh, she was so beautiful back then with fiery red hair and smooth ivory skin. He was so handsome with his elegant features and dark eyes. They made their home in the Victorian which Mim had picked out personally. It was where she raised her only son Stephen. He'd even been born in that home with the help of one very confused midwife. She'd tell you all these things before she started to lament the death of her husband in the early days of the Vietnam War. The only thing he loved more than her was his country and he did what he thought was right -- to go off to die in some foreign land. She'd look at you after that, offer you some tea and move on as if nothing had happened.

The only problem with this is Miriam Stone would be only telling you half the truth.

She had settled in Gaiman Heights ages before meeting Dennis. Back when the New World was green and still wild to European eyes, she made her home on that lonesome hill. She hadn't mentioned that to Dennis at any time in their marriage. That would have ruined the illusion of their relationship. She had met Dennis when she'd gone off to Boston to check on the remaining witches of the old city. It had been at the end of her long off-again on-again relationship with her long term partner. She'd never told him that either. There were things she'd never told Dennis because she loved him far too much to tell him. It wasn't a part of her plan tell him about her other life. Of course she never planned to fall in love with Dennis Stone either. She never planned to fall in love with anyone. If she had then she certainly wouldn't have gotten married five times. Despite her incredible age and immense power, Miriam Stone was a hopeless romantic. Sadly, Mim, as her mother had called her, had become sick of love. Her heartbreak hadn't been healed since Dennis stepped on a helicopter and flew out of the mortal plain. Just when she thought she could accept something like that again, Stephen fed himself to the Void. After that, she withdrew from society and rarely interacted with other people. She did come down to the town on Saturday for groceries. In the twilight years of her life, she did find some comfort in interacting with her only grandson. He called her every Sunday without fail. It made her feel needed.

A happy Crone was good for everyone.

The black SUV parked with a halting growl just outside a chain link fence that protected the yard. The two squarely-built men simultaneously slid out of the vehicle. They looked at each other before walking in perfect step towards the gate. The one on the left opened the wire made door. The two looked at each other again before they walked towards the porch.

The agents were perfectly identical in not just their step. Physically, they both had mud brown hair and were built sturdy like 19th century bedroom furniture. They wore identical black suits with stretched white shirts and black sunglasses. They even had matching "emet" tattoos on the back of their necks. They wore those tattoos as a lasting tribute to the legacy of the Cabbalist mage Rabbi Ben Rothstein. He had created Agent Dira. He was a student of the teachings of Rabbi Judah Lowen Bin Bezalel and had learned to craft golems using a few other tricks up his sleeve in addition to the old lessons. He'd crafted Dira out of clay and grave dirt. Agent Dira served at the side of Rabbi Rothstein until he shuffled off the mortal coil as old men are wont to do. Once that happened, Agent Dira found himself coupled with George Aguirre. Agent Aguirre had been taken with the golem to the point of cultivating the identical image. Agent Dira was flattered by the attention. Part of him liked feeling human, it gave him a sense of value. The other part thought it was an unusual waste.

The two men stepped up onto the shaded porch quietly. Agent Aguirre's eyes went wide behind his sunglasses as something awful gripped his body. A cold chill worked though his body as dread gripped his very soul. It was the kind of cold chill that reminded someone that they were mortal. Agent Aguirre felt himself look over his right shoulder as a shadow crept over the porch. The wind stood still and the rain held off. Agent Aguirre bit the inside of his mouth, suppressing a terrified scream. The shadow belonged to a cloaked specter that stood before them silently. His fleshless hand gripped a scythe that glistened with threat in the fading afternoon daylight. The wraith glided silently towards the agents. Agent Aguirre suppressed tears as he stood quivering in the presence of the wraith. He wanted to run in terror and yet he remained. Agent Dira was not scared; he just stared. He reached quietly towards his partner to steady himself. Agent Dira turned to watch the events unfolding behind him.

"Death," Agent Dira said dispassionately.

"Arthur." A death rattle hissed through the porch. Agent Aguirre blinked away tears as he held his jaw.

"You will not be taking Agent Aguirre," Agent Dira said aggressively. "I will fight for him."

"I'm not here for your…pet," Death replied. "I am here to collect the Crone."

The specter of Death had been stalking the Crone since the 1850s. Bagging the oldest creature on the planet would be a big win for him. Proof he could take back to the bar to say, I Am Fantastic. He could get that stunning redhead to finally pay attention to him. Death had started to stalk the old woman more frequently since the loss of her son and her almost pathological departure from the human world. He thought having nothing left would make it easier for her to come with him. It hadn't. In fact it just made things harder. Death pushed the agents out of his way. He stood before the heavy door with his hands balled into firsts. He steeled himself, preparing to knock. Death paused just as his hand balled. His lack of weight shifted from foot to foot nervously. He turned back towards the agents.

"Um," Death said. "Did, did you have business with the Crone? Because I can wait."

"We do," Agent Dira answered.

"Okay," Death said. "Mind if I tag along?"

"We will be speaking to the Crone before you collect her," Agent Dira said firmly. "Our business is most pressing."

The agents looked at each other before stepping around Death. Both of the agents raised their right hands and knocked authoritatively on the door. They let their intimidating knock resound through the wood four times. After several minutes, there was the sound of chains and a dead bolt being unlocked. The door opened slowly. Behind it, stood a small elderly woman who carefully looked between the agents and Death. She barely stood at five feet tall with pure white hair that fell in loose curls. Her sharp dark brown eyes peered over her thick glasses. Death teetered nervously as she gave the wraith a severe look.

"Welp," Death said. "Look at the time. I should be going. Y'all have a good one."

Death whistled nonchalantly as he glided awkwardly off the porch. He passed through the gate before dissipating into a black cloud. Mim watched Death leave before turning her gaze back to the agents. They glanced back at her unflinching. They were unfased by the old woman. Being the same meant that they could hide their fear behind a mask of solidarity. The Crone wasn't an easy person to face regardless of your moral status. The best thing to do was to pretend you weren't afraid.

"Huh," she scoffed. "Mormons are getting more aggressive. Can I help you boys?"

"Greetings and blessings to you, most holy and sacred Crone," said the agents in perfect unison. "We have been sent by Merlin Du…"

"He still has you greeting people like you're trapped in a Shakespearian play?" Mim cut them off. She rolled her eyes in boredom, already so bored with this conversation. "Tell him no. Whatever he wants, if he can't ask me in person, then no."

"Dr. Duke offers his sincerest apology," they said. "A recently unveiled mage killed a manticore. The mage is quite injured. Dr. Duke is overseeing his healing personally. He requests your presence immediately, wise Crone."

"And it has been a very long time since I've been at the beck and call of Merlin Duke. I am not inclined to be so again."

"Even if the mage is your grandson?"

Mim's stony exterior weakened as she became concerned. This wasn't the first time Asher had used his powers. She hated those days. Mim had no desire to see Asher share the fate of her only son Stephen. If he was unveiled then that dreaded fate was just all that much closer. She knew what she had to do. She had to circle the wagons. Mim narrowed her eyes at the agents.

"Well," she said with a sigh, "let me grab my Book of Shadows and a sweater. It looks like it could be cold. You boys really can't do anything without me, can you?"

XIII. On Demons and the Possessed

The following is an excerpt from the New Agent Training Manual from the Department of the Arcane:

Chapter 7-77: Demons and the Possessed.

Anyone who has seen <u>The Exorcist</u> or any of the flashy Hollywood films on the subject of possession knows how terrifying to the veiled eye it can appear, much like any paranormal event that borders on the unseen. The symptoms associated by the mundane world, though rarely seen, are often brought to the attention to a religious professional. The religious professional says a few words and the veiled go home happy. The demon moves on to another host. We, at the Department of the Arcane, know that this is only half the battle. Below are a few facts for the new agent while dealing with the Possessed

Some Facts About Demons and Possession

Not all demons are evil. Make no mistake, the most powerful of the hordes are the Fallen which are, indeed, evil. At this point in our training we don't need to go into detail about the classes of angels and demons. If you'd like more information, there are several books on the subject in your local libraries. While the Fallen are bound and determined to create as much chaos as possible, not all demons are on the same path. For example, the demon known as Pitch left the pit after experiencing the rare joy of cable television and the TV program <u>Angel.</u> Pitch was taken with the character of Lorne. Pitch started to model himself after the fictional bartender and club owner. With his first chance, Pitch escaped from the Pit. He first approached repeat possessee and failing restaurateur, John Rose, with a Faustian deal (named for Bill Faust, demonic CPA). He would help Rose run a successful bar as long as he could invite whoever he chose to drink in the bar. This deal stayed serviceable, as did Pitch's Pub and Grill for more than fifty years. This has gone on record as the most successful deal and possession to date.

Make no mistake, Pitch is a rarity. Demonic possession can range from dangerous to cataclysmic. The less intelligent or more feral the demon is the more dangerous they became when they possess the host. A demon with a lack of purpose in the human realm will be more confused and destructive. The more intelligent demons, while dangerous, are often better because they have a goal during a possession. These goals often depend on the personality of the demon

How Does One Get Possessed?

Most possessions are complete accidents. If you ask a demon, the corruption of humanity is not the chief priority of hordes. It actually ranks at about five on their list. The first priority of the demonic hordes is keeping their counterparts from gaining an upper hand. The celestial Cold War has been going on for a millennium because neither side wants the items that'll start Doomsday but neither side speaks to the other. This stalemate and maintaining it is priority one.

The second most common reason is acquiring the delicacies of the human world. Demons are huge fans of reality television and game shows. This entertainment was not created by the Hordes but they are constantly amused by the depths of human shallowness. If also proves to them that they have to do very little to destroy humanity. The other prized delicacy that the hordes want is sugar. Sugar is impossible to acquire in the Abyss, but is incredibly delicious to the demonic tongue. These two reasons are the cause of

95% of all possessions in the last thirty years.

The scenario that most often occurs is that demons transcend to the human realm to purchase a slurpee and a Cow Tail. The demon expels a great deal of personal energy to do this. On his way to the 7-11, the demon gets distracted by Survivor and burns up quickly. In an effort to maintain existence on this plane, they will find the closest human host that is strong enough to support their being.

How a Demon Chooses Their Host

Demons will prefer to possess whoever they think is strong enough to support them. This'll often be a reflection of the demon's personality. The demon, however, doesn't realize this until the time of possession.

Demons prefer adult humans or large animals for possession over younger children or house cats. It takes a fully developed body and a great amount of energy for a demonic entity to be supported in a corporal form. The average demon, based on that information, will kill a child during a possession. This is counterproductive to the purpose of possession, so it doesn't occur often. In a pinch, they will possess a teenager, typically female. Demonic creatures prefer females due to the romantic notions from demonic fairy tales.

The demonic hordes pay no attention to the religion of their hosts. Anyone from any religion of the world can be possessed. Think of it like this: demonic possession is like trying to find a free restroom in an emergency. You are less concerned with the location than you are with finding a toilet.

Effects of Possession on the Possessor

Possession is psychologically painful for the demon. Often demons will question how they made a mistake. They live in terror of going through the possession and exorcisms process again.

Ultimately, the delights of the human world become too great a temptation and eventually they will possess a person again. This is a consistent problem for demons. However, this doesn't compare to the problems that face the Possessed. We will discuss that in better detail later.

How to Spot the Possessed

The Possessed, to the untrained eye, can be hard to spot at first. The host rarely grows horns and their heads stay quite stationary. The initial possession starts with a sneeze which is the natural human reaction to having a demon shoved into their brain. Then, there are the slow changes. The Possessed will be excitable and very sociable. Demons are generally friendly and love meeting new people. The Possessed will also run a slight fever.

Despite being social, the Possessed will become lazy, spending much of their time watching daytime TV while spooning powdered sugar into their mouths. It's six weeks after the initial possession that the demonic flu occurs. This is a chronic illness that is characterized by projectile vomiting and sudden use of abyssal tongue as well a few other different symptoms that people associate with the mainstream media

When to Call For an Exorcist

Many people call for an exorcist at the development of the possession flu, however, if you suspect someone of being possessed, for go immediate exorcism. The sooner this is done the less damage to the host will be done. **DO NOT ATTEMPT** to exorcise a demon on your own. Exorcisms are very dangerous if done on your own and can result in possession of yourself or your partner. In extreme cases, an improper exorcism can result in the soul of the host being ripped apart. The Department of the Arcane employs demonologists and mages who are trained specifically for this occasion. Alert them to the Possession. Place the Possessed into a Level One binding circle and call for immediate assistance. If the Possessed becomes fussy, offer them a piece of candy (without breaking the circle).

After Care for the Possessed and Becoming the Marked

When an individual is no longer possessed, it is the responsibility of the Department to offer immediate care for the Marked. The chance of a second possession increases by 75% since the natural defenses against the demonic are greatly lowered, much like contracting an auto immune disease. Since such is the case, the Marked One must be protected from future possession. Once a Possessed has been unbound from the demon, they MUST be examined by a Department of the Arcane registered demonologist, assuming one has not been called during or performed the exorcism.

The demonologist will formally examine the Possessed. They will then determine what kind of demon possessed the victim. It will finally be concluded whether the demon was malicious or not. Based on that information, the demonologist will craft a protective ward for the Marked. The ward should be applied to the Marked by a ward weaver. The ward will be placed on the left, or shield, hand. Wards are typically written in Latin to confuse the demon. The newly Marked then will be debriefed.

Long Term Care for the Marked

Becoming one of the Marked presents new challenges for these individuals. For many of the Marked, the difficulty comes from trying to explain to friends and family the drastic change that came from the possession. Often, veiled society won't accept the explanation of demons so the Marked will find a variety of excuses. The most common explanation is the Marked was fighting the demons of drug or alcohol abuse. Their families and friends will accept this charade as the easiest explanation. Others have alienated themselves from friends and family through their behavior so much at this point that they don't bother.

Isolation is a growing concern for the Marked. After being unbound from the demon, a piece of that demon will remain with them. The Marked will hear the voice of their former guest speaking to them. This will cause panic in the Marked, who will then isolate themselves quickly, fearing the worse. Yet isolation is one of the quickest ways for the Marked to fall to their demonic traits.

The chief problem facing the Marked is adjusting to their demonic abilities. Not only is part of the demon's consciousness left behind, but also its demonic talents. These often include being faster and stronger as the individual gifts based on the species or class of the demon that possessed them. For this reason, the Department of the Arcane offers a variety of integration services for the newly created supernatural citizen.

A Word of Warning from Doctor Merlin Duke to the Marked

You still have part of the demon that possessed you inside you. The Hordes will try to corrupt you since you are partly one of them now. Your life will be much harder now. Do not give in to wrath or greed. That will corrupt your flesh quickly.

The Department encourages you to live a normal as possible life. Be as human as possible. If you forsake these demonic gifts and let them be, then you will not corrupt. If that is not possible, use your gifts for good. You are more human than most. You will know what good feels like better than before your possession. It's the best way for you to hold on to your humanity. Seek a useful path of true believers.

Be aware that one day you will be corrupted and fall. You

will become a wicked spirit sent for the corruption of mankind. We will be there to protect the world from you. We will find you. Make no mistake, if you choose a wicked path, we will find you and we will vanquish you with no mercy.

Always walk in Truth and Light.

XIV. Welcome Back From Intermission

Carin fidgeted as she spun around in the plastic chair. Her fingers drummed on the table. She looked up again nervously at the gray walls. Shame boiled at the back of her sore and scarred throat. She'd try to throw up again to no avail. The notion of being arrested -- even by the Department of the Arcane -- was, all in all, upsetting. There wasn't exactly a good way to explain to her professors why she wasn't there to take her exam. McKean State was the second oldest public university in the state. It being located in Gaiman Heights meant that the student body was a mix of the mundane and the supernatural students of the area. That did mean that some of the staff often were privy to the supernatural world. She couldn't exactly tell her professors that she had been detained by the Department of the Arcane though. She had her vows to think about. She would not betray those words.

So, to recap, her home was destroyed. She had been arrested and now she was going to repeat her freshman year.

Carin buried her head in her hands and let her elbows rest on the acrostic metal table. She let out a muffled scream. She had a rough road and she knew who to blame; Asher. It wasn't the first time he'd ruined her life. Carin's youth had been spent being knocked down and passed over because of Asher and whatever thing he'd done to himself. Now, because of him, she was a homeless loser with a record. Her nose scrunched as she fought back tears of frustration. The world revolved around Asher and what Asher did. That wasn't fair. She'd worked just as hard as anyone to get where she was in her life. Maybe, she thought, I'll become a junkie too. Then people will like me more than Asher. Carin sighed. This day couldn't get any worse.

"Carin Eloise Mitchell," said a stern voice from her nightmares. "What in the name of Blessed Gaia is going on?"

If you find yourself saying something can't get worse, stop immediately. It can and will get worse. In fact, if you are able, have someone kick you very hard in the leg before you are able to say it couldn't get any worse. Carin's eyes went wide, unleashing swollen tears that ran down her cheeks making wet puddles on to the table. She didn't know when her mother had entered the room. It was as if the matriarch materialized out of nothing, but she had probably walked in during Carin's panic attack. Carin's attention to detail went down exponentially when she had one of her panic attacks. Carin sat up as jolt of alertness went through her. Her heart bounced off her rib cage as her mother sat down. Carin swallowed a mouthful of bile as she locked eyes with her mother.

"It was Asher's fault," Carin said quickly as if they were having the same conversation.

"It was Asher's fault that you walked into a crime scene?" her mother asked, confused by the outburst.

"No," Carin said as she shook her head, "That the house got jacked up."

Her mother sighed as she regarded her daughter.

"So, you snuck into the scene of a manticore attack that was crawling with Department agents," said her mother…

I know this seems repetitive, but chapter nine was also a while ago. I didn't want you to forget. I assume you are reading this bit by bit, as opposed to one fell swoop. You know, like how I wrote it.

"…That is either stupid or dangerous or both."

"I just wanted to do what you wanted for me to do," Carin said quickly. "And the cops were there and I didn't know what else to do and I'm really sorry."

"And while that was a dumb way to go about it, you're safe and the altar is untouched," said her mother. "I'm very proud of you. You stared into the face of temptation and didn't give in. You'll be a great witch one day."

"I didn't want you to be disappointed with me," Carin sniffled. She ignored that she wasn't a great witch yet. She knew she wasn't great at the craft yet. Some days she thought she would never even be good.

"Oh, Carin," her mother said warmly, "I'm not disappointed with any of my children."

"Including junkie Asher, because he's a total dick when he's high."

"Carin! Watch your language," her mother said sternly. "But yes, that was disappointing."

"You know, he killed a manticore," Carin said, feeling just a little bit superior. She wasn't a disappointing junkie.

"Yes, I know," her mother said softly. "It's incredible."

"I know, right!" Carin exclaimed. "He's not even one of us."

Her mother looked back at Carin as her face grew quiet. She contemplated the cracks in the linoleum finish of the table as guilt worked into her mind. She let out a pensive sigh as realization hit. There had been a long standing argument between Doctor Duke, the head of the Department of the Arcane, and the Crone on dispensing information for or about Asher. The Crone had made an order to enforce this agreement among the covens. No one was to breathe a word about what Asher was. It had made sense back then. If people knew that a power like the nexus was portable and easy to get to, he would be the target for every mage, witch, and warlock in the Gaihaim Valley. But his mother knew this was a bad idea. It was killing her Asher. If he knew about himself then, maybe, they wouldn't have watched him decline into addiction. They had discounted how smart Asher was. Now this order was harming Carin too. She was making rash decisions that could have gotten her killed and ruining a relationship with Asher. Her mother shook her head. She couldn't do this to her family anymore. This was breaking her apart to continue to keep lying to her children. She had to tell someone. She'd considered telling Brady, but first things first. She would debate telling Brady later but she had to stop lying to her children now. She took Carin's hand and smiled sadly. Carin tensed up as she looked up at her mother. Her mother didn't give her that look unless something terrible happened. Carin felt tears well up in her eyes again.

Oh, no, she thought, *Asher's here and he's dead.*

"I know we've told you that, but it isn't true," Tracy said. "Your brother is like us and quite powerful. I never told you because Asher doesn't know. It didn't seem right for you to know when he didn't."

"So, Asher's a super powerful being and no one told him," Carin summarized. "That's pretty fucked up."

"Carin! Again! Language!" her mother snapped. "Yes, that's pretty fucked up, but this ends today. I can't keep doing this to any of you."

"Cool!" Carin bounced. "So what do we do?"

"We?" snorted her mother. "Nothing. You are going back to school. I'll get Karl and Norvita to take you home."

"Mom!"

"Carin, a super powerful being is going to be unveiled. It's going to be upsetting. I don't know how he's going to react or who is going to get hurt. I think it's safer for you and Yoshi to go back to McKean State."

Carin opened her mouth in protest. This wasn't fair that Asher got to be special. In an instant, her mother shot her a cold glare. Carin shut her mouth and shamefully looked down at the table. Her fingers rolled along the bubbled surface. Her mother nodded, quietly satisfied with the end of this conversation. Carefully, she exited the room. She'd later make it up to Carin. Right now, however, she had a more pressing matter. She was going to have to have words with her former mother-in-law.

Tracy marched the down corridor, her noble gray eyes narrowed with conviction. She had been prepared to yell and scream and to drive home her point but that quickly passed as she walked in well measured steps. She had started to think about how yelling at the Crone or Duke ended. They both responded to yelling with more yelling. Nothing would get accomplished. It was a miracle that those two ever agreed to anything. She knew what that what miracle was. One of them, typically Dr. Duke, would utter Stephen's name. A sense of quiet would descend over them and they would speak calmly out of respect for a ghost that haunted both of them. She let out a shuddering sigh as her heart broke again. She had married Brady to, not as Mim suggested, to erase Stephen, but for love. He was a smart guy who was a little weird, but a good man. There was no amount of time or kindness that would make her forget she was in love with Stephen Stone. You never fell out a love with someone like him. She knew he was gone, but she could feel him walking behind her. Even now, she could hear his cool voice in her ear.

"Tracy, be still," he'd say to her. "Getting mad doesn't help. Be what I love about you. Be the assertive, kind woman I know you are. Don't let them tear you down."

She blushed as a powerful memory gripped her shoulders, causing her pace to slow. His fingers brushing through her hair as he spoke in calm hushed tones into her ear. His weight standing behind her making her feel safe. Her hand touched her collarbone as she tried to catch her breath. Stephen was too good for this world. He was always eventually going to transcend the mortal flesh like everyone else, but she could be happy for the memory of her time with him. She had pieces of him still lingering around her. She knew that it was part of the binding words that they had inscribed on their skin early in their marriage rites. She cringed as her inked wrist ached. She rubbed the "esse" in *Nunguam neese, esse alsgue,* trying to make the hot throbbing in her wrist cease. It wasn't helping. It never did. However, she had other things to focus on right now.

She had a wrong to right.

As she turned down a hallway towards the administration office, she was greeted by Karl. The Marked man straightened up with a calm nod. He realized that he looked odd without Norvita, but Norita was busy squealing with Carin. He thought it sounded like squealing. but they seemed to be to getting along rather quickly and eagerly. Karl wanted to talk to an adult now. That meant he had to adjust his perspective gently. Tracy smiled quietly at him.

"Lady Stone, good evening," Karl said earnestly. "You'll have to forgive me if I don't do a formal greeting. I'm not fully updated on the Department rankings."

"I can tell," she answered calmly. "I haven't been Lady Stone for a long time, but hello Karl. Nice to see you again. Is your boss busy?"

"Last I saw him, he was leaving the infirmary with the Crone," Karl said. "They, they were loud."

"That's typical." Tracy rolled her eyes. "When Stephen and I got married they got so bad that the buffet table was struck by lightning. What's in the infirmary?"

Karl looked back at Tracy with a gentle calm demeanor. He thought how he, as the father of two, would want to know if it were him. He'd want to be told without hesitation and not in some sort of gentle way. He would want to know first thing, as opposed to finding out by wandering through the door. He didn't want it to be the quiet lack of information. He felt his jaw sag as he looked back at her. He couldn't find the words. He sighed.

"Asher," is all he said.

"Take me to him," Tracy commanded.

She had been led down several different hallways to a large white room. She walked down a row of cots until she found the one she was looking for. A soft smile crossed her lips as she approached the cot. Asher didn't move. He didn't even react to her presence. She would have been more worried, but his chest rose and fell as his wounds mended rapidly. She leaned forward and kissed his forehead.

"Don't hurry on my account," she whispered. "I'll be here when you wake up, *mon petite*."

XV. When Worlds Collide

Asher awoke several hours later with the light panic that comes from waking suddenly. The first thing that went through Asher's head, as his eyes dreamily opened, was "*Man, this is the nicest dumpster Iggy has ever left me in.*" It had been a custom of his friend to leave Asher, after he passed out from his altered state, in a waste management receptacle. He glanced around oddly perplexed by his surroundings.

For once, he didn't smell decay and death. If one has spent any time around garbage you know what kind of pungent aroma it emits. There was a definite lack of odor. He wasn't cold and dirty either. Asher, finally, felt the warmth and comfort of a warm room. Despite being covered in a thin white sheet, he could feel a healing warmth deep within his cells. His eyes slowly focused on the walls before darting around a high ceiling. He furrowed his eyes, looking at an indescribable ethereal scene. Asher blinked in heavy confusion. I'm not wearing my own clothes, he realized. He didn't recognize the soft cotton pants and shirt that covered his body. Great, he thought, another hospital. He breathed in, waiting for the black embrace of pain.

There was no pain. The only thing Asher felt was the white warmth of healing where things should start screaming in fiery pain. He rolled to his side perplexed. He was in a hospital. He should hurt but he didn't. That meant something new. Something absolutely wonderful about this hospital. Was he high? He paused for a moment to decide whether or not. He could feel the earth spinning under his body. No, he felt tangible, which mean that he was sober. This was odd.

Then, he focused on the figure beside him.

She had made herself at home in a highly ornate chair with a bright colored knitted fabric dropped over her khaki-colored linen pants. A pair of black and green plastic reading glasses hung on the edge of her petite nose as she wove another strand of stiff yarn into her work. Her graying brown hair was pinned back in a low ponytail that brushed the collar of her purple kurta. He smiled quietly.

"Mom," he said with a dry weakness in his voice, "are we in Back to the Future Part II?"

She slowly looked up from her work with that sad smile. If Asher had any worry that he was dreaming, the look on his mother's face cemented the fact that this was real. She scooted the chair closer to his bed. Her elegant fingers brushed through his wrecked pompadour mostly for her comfort.

"No, sweetie," she said softly as her body radiated calm. "Biff Tannen isn't your stepfather. How are you feeling?"

"I feel," Asher sat up in surprise. He couldn't believe the lack of pain in his body. He poked his stomach and felt fine. "I feel pretty good. Mom, a lion attacked the house. I'm sorry about Miaka and Yoshi."

"I know, dear. It ate Miaka. Yoshi and Carin are sleeping the day off somewhere, I hope," she said quietly. Suddenly there was a raise in the volume of muffled voices. She suppressed an eye roll. Asher recognized one of the voices.

"Is that my grandmother?" he asked.

"Yes, your grandmother is here," she said through gritted teeth.

Asher's head turned down the row of identical white covered beds towards a less than ornate door. Each passing moment the voices in the hall grew louder. He watched silhouetted figures gesturing and waving their arms at each other. He glanced back at his mother.

"Who's Grandma fighting with?" he asked.

"That's Dr. Duke," she dropped the mask of calm for hard irritation. "He runs this place."

"Doctor Duke," Asher repeated. "Am I in a hospital?"

"Sort of, *mon petite*. You're in the infirmary wing of the Department of the Arcane."

"The what?"

"Don't worry about it, *mon petite*," she said quickly. "Just get some rest. They took a lot out of you. I'll tell your grandmother to keep it down."

They took a lot out of him? Asher opened his mouth to ask another question. Before he could ask, she stood up and walked down the row of beds that led to the hallway. Asher thought for a moment before he slid out of the bed. His feet hit the warm marble tiles. Things were weird again and his mother knew why. He was owed an explanation. Besides, he wanted to see the doctor who inspired that kind of anger and rage in his grandmother.

Asher stopped just beyond the door, opening it a small crack. He watched a violent tango of words. His grandmother was there before him. Mim stood at about four foot eleven. Her angelic white hair thinly covered her ancient head in large uneven curls. Her skeletal arms were covered in a cabled Irish sweater and firmly folded across her chest. Her eyes were big and wide with rage behind her thick Coke bottle glasses, which bobbed with every angry yell. She scowled at the tall man who was staring her down. Asher blinked, perplexed. He was the oddest looking man Asher had ever seen and Asher had seen plenty of odd people in his life. He was a thin wiry man with a paunch that indicated his age like rings on a tree. That wasn't the weird part. It wasn't even the bright orange Hawaiian shirt with cream colored hibiscus flowers coordinating with a pair of dark brown corduroy pants. It wasn't even the white sandals that capped off the outfit. What made the man weird was the cowboy hat. More specifically, what was hidden under the brim of the Stetson. Asher caught a glance at the old man's craggy face. Something about the old man's fear-inspiring eyes made Asher uncomfortable. The kind of discomfort one feels staring at a mysterious and ancient artifact. The man left Asher searching for meaning in his life. He waved his razor wire arms at Asher's grandmother frantically.

"You're impossible, woman!" his voice jerked and convulsed in his yell. "Do you even hear yourself sometimes?!?"

"Can it, Mage!" Mim's ancient pseudo Northern accent stabbed angrily into Asher's brain with a cold vengeance. Pain and anger pulsed through his veins like a heartbeat. "You think that your soulless book-learned traditions are the only true path. Your lot spends so much of your time locked up in your sanctum you don't see how really dangerous the real world is. Go outside for a change."

"And we will always give our people a choice!" said the man.

"He shouldn't get a choice!" Mim yelled. Asher now had a migraine. "He's not like us and he's not like them either. He's something new. Duke, we need to protect him from us and from him."

Asher's rage-filled heart pounded harder in his body as he felt a twitch of panic shoot through him like a bolt of blue. He stood frozen there listening to a conversation that he knew was about him. Asher wanted to run back to his bed and hide under the covers. He thought that would wake him up from this nightmare.

"He still should have a choice, Mim," Dr. Duke argued. "Our

people will always have a choice."

"Ha!" Mim expelled bitterly. "You give your people choices. That's a joke."

"Are we going to go through this again?!?" Dr. Duke groaned in irritation. "You damn well know that Stephen volunteered for that mission!"

Asher's eyes went wide as he heard an all too familiar name to him. His mother rarely spoke of his father. He knew that he had a father and what his name was. That was it. This stranger to him knew more about his own family than Asher did. Asher balled his fists in furious jealousy. Light blue sparks flaked off his arms. No, he told himself, this isn't real. This was a nightmare. He had to wake up. Why wouldn't he wake up?

"Tracy," Dr. Duke commented, "You've been awfully quiet about this."

"Well," Tracy said in a manner most calm, "when you two fight it's hard to get a word in edgewise. However, I've agreed with the Crone in the past. Asher had to be kept safe. The result is my son doesn't know who his father was. More importantly, Asher doesn't know who he is or what he can do. That makes him more dangerous than if he knew. I've been angry for so long at the Department, but the last time we went down this road, we lost Asher for seven years to addiction. I can't do that again. I agree with Doctor Duke. It's time to give him the choice."

Mim scoffed as the united front grew in confidence. Mim knew it couldn't last. No one ever said no to the Crone. Her scoff infuriated Asher more. They had lied to him. Everyone he trusted lied to him about who he was. What was he then? If he was so dangerous why wouldn't they tell him? That thought made his back stiffen violently as his shoulder held on to his rage. A sharp blue light enveloped his body. Asher had heard enough. Asher threw the door open with a growl as a lightning flashed in his eyes. The assembled party stared at the fuming Asher in shamed silence. His gaze turned to each of them with hurt-filled rage. If he could start his campaign with his grandmother, then things would be awesome.

"Asher," Dr. Duke said, placing his great hand on Asher's shoulder. His body eased at the old man's touch. Dr. Duke looked him over with his good eye. It wasn't that one eye was worse than the other. They were fantastic eyes. One just happened to be better than the other.

"You..."

"Don't," Asher said, cutting into Dr. Duke's words. "Don't you dare tell me that I look like my father."

Dr. Duke chuckled lightly.

"I wasn't going to say something you've heard thousands of times though the resemblance *is* striking," Dr. Duke said. "I was going to say that you look rested."

Asher blinked as confusion played across his face. He was feeling awkwardly comfortable for him, which generally made Asher feel uncomfortable. However, he also felt oddly at home in his confusion. Asher arched his brow.

"Thanks?" Asher tried.

"Asher, I'll skip the heavy explanation for now," Dr. Duke launched back into business. "You see, your grandmother, mother, and I were chatting. Since this conversation is about your future. I believe, as does your mother, that you should have a say in it."

"My future?" Asher asked like an idiot hero.

"Yes, Asher, your future. You see, Asher, what I'm about to tell you is going to sound strange to you but it is the most honest truth. Your future and ours does depend on you."

"Me?" he repeated again, still sounding stupid. "Why me?"

"Because Asher, you are different even by Department standards," Dr. Duke continued. "There is literally no one or thing like you."

"Don't give me that human snowflake crap," Asher said curtly. "I'm not six-years-old."

"And you listen as well as your grandmother does," Dr. Duke retorted as Mim narrowed her eyes venomously at the mage. "You are the single most powerful creature in existence. We have been hiding you from anything or one that could harm you, including yourself. After your run in with the manticore, we need to re-evaluate."

"Lion," Asher corrected.

"No, son," Dr. Duke said. "That was a manticore. I saw the body. Either way, our method hasn't worked. So, now we're going to try a different approach. You have a choice now. I think that you might do better if you can make that choice on your own. Asher, young mages like yourself go through something we call an Awakening. It's a process that'll grant you deep cosmic knowledge of who and what you are. You can say no and we won't be angry. You won't be a target of the Department's wrath, but I can't guarantee your safety from outside forces. You, Asher Stone, and only you can' decide your fate."

"What sort of Matrix/Keanu Reeves bullshit is this?!?" Asher yelled indignantly. "Next you're going to start offering me pills to free my mind. That is a trap. I'm sober and won't jeopardize that for you. Iggy isn't trying to feed me drugs. He's trying to kill me. I know that now after he shoved me into the trunk of his car."

"We know you're clean," Tracy said sweetly. "While I agree

with you that Dr. Duke does need to stop watching Laurence Fishburn movies, this is not a joke. Sweetie, I know it's scary but it's your choice. I want you to make the right choice. You aren't alone. I had to make that same choice. So did your father. We all made that choice on our own. Now, *mon petite*, so do you."

Asher looked between the three of them carefully. His brow furrowed as he considered the words that floated in his head. His body twitched as he considered what he had to do. He shut his eyes to clear his mind. Asher thought if he didn't know what do, the fates would show him. Something would give him an answer. During his meditation, he felt the big hands of fate push on his shoulders as an inner voice hissed at him to do the right thing. He opened his eyes. He felt his body ease as a concerned look crossed his face.

"I can't be my father," Asher said finally.

"No one except Mim is asking you to replace Stephen," Dr. Duke said. Mim was oddly quiet on this subject. "We want you to find your path."

"My life will always be weird," Asher resolved. "I want to know why."

"Good," Dr. Duke said. "Let's begin."

XVI. Meanwhile at Goodfellows

Her pale arms wrapped around his leather-tanned neck like a white chiffon scarf as his Phoenician face nuzzled into the china patterns on her skin. His skilled fingers trailed up an intricate line of Delft blue patterns on her white skin under her tunic, touching the pale skin of her white breast. He pulled her into his lap hungrily as their bodies created a wave of friction passing through them in the passion of people who hadn't seen each other in ages. Her black-purple lips brushed over the crook of his neck eagerly. He turned her face up to his as he contently looked into her bright blue eyes.

"What news have you brought to me today, λουλούδι?" he asked, breathing into her skin.

She pulled herself out of his loving grasp, trying to focus on what information she might have for Puck. His fingers followed her desperately as she sat on his desk in the back office. If he had a choice he wouldn't ever be without her being well within his grasp always. Her smell and warmth of her body was missed even in the space of inches between him and her while she sat above him. She sat up straight as her semi-sheer tunic draped over her knees in a form of modesty that she had never ever had. Not that he would have minded. Her body was perfectly carved from her very being and therefore would always reflect only the true essence of herself, which he adored. Her eyes danced in a current of happiness as she looked down him with an odd amount of pride. He leaned up to brush her dark blue-purple hair out her face lovingly as he smiled back at her charming elegant face.

Puck had adjusted to his life outside of Arcadia peacefully a long time ago with little to no real problems. His earthly masque, the image that the fae present of themselves to the mundane world, had started to reflect this comfort with a small paunch protruding from his once lean stomach. His bark-brown curly hair was adorned with freshly-grown gray hair peeking up like flurried snow. Even the coarse tufts of his goatee were speckled with white. Despite his ever aging human appearance, the one thing that remained untouched by age were his eyes. Puck's eyes remained youthful and the color of fresh growing moss and sharp as the day that they had been formed from dust.

He'd settled into a mundane job for the mundane world. Well, he'd settled into a job that was as mundane as one could find and not feel bad about it. Puck owned and ran Goodfellow's Comics on the edge of South Gaiman. It made sense to him really. Many of the fair folk who lived in what they called the paper world worked in the comic book industry. Anyone who had read things like FLCL or the reboot of the Spider-man Franchise knows this fact first hand. The fae are quite fond of being what they consider extremely funny. Puck liked being able to help his brethren succeed in what they thought was fun. It made him feel connected to his home -- a world that had shunned and cast him out a long time ago -- in a way that not many things did. However, his most potent form of connection and source of information from home was his river nymph.

Before his exile from the Dream, Puck and the Water Nymph named Amaya had been paired together by their elders almost perfectly. She had been crafted out of smooth river rocks and the midnight rain by the Goddess of the Wild River. She was the youngest of her sisters so it only seemed natural to pair her with the fourteenth son of Pan. Puck had been, at the time, the youngest satyr without a mate so he became bound to her. Binding to one's protector as a nymph meant mind, body, and soul would be linked to his nymph. In every sense of the word they were one. Even after his fall, she still followed her Puck into the human world. She may have resided in Arcadia but her home was with him.

"The moon was full for three whole days," she reported carefully. "The water lilies are in full bloom. Oh! I also got a new ring."

She flew back into Puck's lap gracefully as a duck into a still pond. She straddled his jeaned lap as she settled finally on top of him. Puck let out a half serious "oomph" as she settled onto him. He grinned at her as she pressed down along his assaulted crotch, letting her bare thighs ride him gently. Her pale hand shoved itself into Puck's face. He smiled, watching a semi-shiny plastic jelly ring as it danced gently in the office light.

"I traded two silver coins with an old man on them to a robot thing at the mall," she announced to Puck. "What do you think?"

"It's very rare to get something like that from robots," Puck said, putting his hands on her rounded hips. "You are the luckiest water nymph in all of creation."

Amaya let out a delighted giggle that sounded like a bubbling brook. She wrapped her arms around his neck again, hugging him deeply. Puck let out a contented sigh, taking in the scent of rain and nightfall. The flow of their happiness engulfed them like a thick fur blanket. The thin space filled between them with an inner peace that was hard to shatter.

What could and did shatter that inner peace was a loud crash that echoed throughout the lobby of Goodfellow's Comics. Puck and Amaya both froze in place, listening to the clamor that had invaded their space. He buried his head into her cleavage in an attempt to hide as he analyzed the ruckus that called from beyond the walls. It was a rare occasion that Puck prayed in any matter or fashion. Religion was not something that the fae worried themselves with too much. He knew most powerful god-like beings. He had never felt like praying to anyone he knew personally. However, he suddenly found himself being very spiritual. He prayed for a car crash or at least a burglar. He prayed for the commotion to be anything, anything at all, other than what he feared. He buried his face into Amaya's breasts hoping against hope for anything besides what he thought it was going to turn out be...

"Please, God," he whispered. "Not --"

"Puck! Puck!" A voice cut through the still air. "Puck! Puck! Puck!"

Iago's call cut straight to their nerves with the precision of a large piece of brick for over fifteen minutes. After which, Puck couldn't take it anymore. He scooped up Amaya easily into his arms and stood, carefully juggling her weight. She clung to his frame as he stretched quietly. Reluctantly, he walked into the main part of the shop with his nymph in tow. Iago stood hunched excitedly over an assaulted comic rack with a triumphant look. He looked up at Puck with delighted speckled eyes as he almost jumped up and down. Iago rose to a standing position, bouncing on the balls of his feet with a manic excitement that made everyone feel just a little uncomfortable. Most of Iago's emotions made everyone uncomfortable. Puck felt his right eye twitch as Iggy started to pace eagerly, his fingers inspecting his faux hawk. He stopped long enough to stare at the pair.

"Oh, Hiya, Amaya," Iago said quickly. "Puck! Puck! Puck!"

"I heard you the first time, Iago," Puck said flatly. "What do you want?"

"He came back!" Iago said as tears happily cracked through his voice. "Asher came back to me!"

Puck gave Iago a long sad look, punctuated with a soft sigh. This was a repeating theme in his relationship with Iago. For over seven years, Iago had continued to fall in and out of love with Asher. Asher would leave, get sober for a week or two, and then he'd come back and it would end exactly the same way all over again. He knew where things went from here. Puck hoisted Amaya up again onto his shoulder. He looked at her, sadly lamenting his next move.

"λουλούδι," Puck said quietly, "I need to talk to Iago. Mind giving us some space?"

"Why?" she asked with sweetness dripping from her words. "What's in it for me?"

Puck leaned over with the nymph still in his arms. He picked up a copy of a brightly colored, thickly-bound manga. Air went sharply into her lungs as he handed the book to his little water nymph. Amaya squealed in utter delight while her fingers gripped the volume tightly. She pulled herself up and over Puck's shoulder and catapulted over him towards the stock room. Puck waited for the door to shut before he turned his attention back to Iago with a serious look.

"If he came back," Puck said skeptically as he folded his arms across his chest, "then where is he?"

"I got pulled over on my way here. The cops took him," Iago grumbled. He stomped his foot in irritation. "I almost had him. Puck, I could taste him."

"Cops or The Cops, Iago," Puck said in a mild panic. "If the Department is on your tail, you need to leave. I told you that last time."

"Puck, it was Weston Lewis," Iago was getting feverishly agitated. Weston Lewis was the thorn in almost everyone's side. "The Department doesn't know, not yet anyway. Oh Puck, I still have time. Not much but I still have time. I can get him back. Puck, I need him."

"And then what, Iago?" Pucked asked tiredly. "You keep him junked up so that he can't tell that you are feeding on his energy? I'm pretty sure that the magi aren't going to let you off with a warning this time. Not like they did when you almost killed him."

"I'm sorry, Puck," Iago said sharply. "Not all of us have a water nymph to give us a spicy bowl of home."

Puck looked at his best and oldest friend. There would never be anyone he spent more time with -- including Amaya -- than Iago. Puck looked at his long-term best friend carefully. When Puck gazed into the black pools of Iago's doe eyes, he felt like it was his fault that Iago had gone insane. Puck had his water nymph. It had been that marital relationship that kept Puck anchored and sane. Iago didn't have that. His people didn't connect to marriage bonds like most of the fae. In fact, Puck believed that it was jealously of this relationship that drove Iago back to the land of Arcadia after their banishment. He wanted what Puck had -- that feeling of belonging even in the paper world. Iago hadn't been as lucky as he'd hoped. Iago had been discovered and brought before their Great King. It was then that their formal death sentence was passed. If he or Puck were found in the Dream they would be sentenced to the hundred's year tear which didn't last one hundred years (it was much longer) and only ended with a final death. To hammer the sentence home, Iago was cursed with a spreading madness that was punctuated with random moments of clarity. Iago hadn't been the old Iago in a long, long time. However, the last time Iago acted like the old Iago was when he was hanging out with Asher. Puck couldn't deny Iago the one thing that Puck himself wanted so badly.

Puck wanted to be normal again.

"As much as I find your methods terrible," Puck conceded. "I guess we all need something to maintain a sense of self. I mean it's not like we can bring home here."

Iago's eyes widened into Olympic-sized black pools of excitement as the corners of his predator's maw curled into a jagged smile. He threw his gangly arms joyously around Puck's neck as he planted a kiss squarely on Puck's lips. Puck recoiled as he pushed Iago away from him in terror. No that homosexuality was a taboo to the fae. Sexuality for them is a very fluid aspect of their life. Puck had kissed plenty of boys in his time. Part of Iago's curse was spreading his madness to other magical beings through physical contact. Puck didn't want that madness.

No one wanted that kind of madness.

"Puck!" Iago yelled excitedly. "You're a genius!"

"I know I am," Puck said confidently. "But why now?"

"We can never go home," Iago said wildly. "He'd have the feral beasts of the Abyss rip us apart. Oh, why didn't I think of this before?!? It's so easy. We need to bring home here!"

"Iago, it can't be that easy," Puck said quietly. "If it were that easy, we would have done it already or the Court soldiers would already know how to stop us."

"How? We're not stealing Arcadia. Think about it Puck," Iago said as spit flew off his lips. "The only thing that is keeping us from swimming in the seas of cotton candy and anarchy is that stupid Hedge. We get rid of the Hedge, then there will be nothing stopping us. Puck, you're a genius."

"No, I'm an amazing genius," Puck said. "Even I know that there is no amount of magic in creation to cause that kind of destruction."

"There is too!" Iago yelled as the dots connected in an unseen pattern. "We kill Asher! You know as well as I do that kid is chock full of magical energy. When he dies, he'll explode. It'll rock the foundations of both worlds!"

"Rock?" Puck snorted. "Hell, Iago, with his power level, he'll tear the Hedge into pieces. Iago, what happens when the Dream overcomes this world?"

"Who cares?!?" Iago yelled. "We get to go home. Let's go kill Asher!"

"No," Puck said finally. Puck wasn't human, but he liked them. They tried so hard to be significant, but they fell short. It was cute. He didn't want to see any of those cute people die. That's where he drew the line.

"Come on Puck!" Iago whined like a fire siren. "We only have to kill one person. He's not even a real person. He's a mage. Puck, we'll kill a mage and get to go home!"

Puck took a step forward, contemplating Iago's proposal. He looked out at the grey street with indignation. He watched the dull faces of the mundane pass through the paper world as the day hung tightly on to the remains of winter. He scowled. Murder always made Puck squeamish but to liven up this side might be worth the price of blood.

He could taste the sweet salt of the winds of the midnight shore. He felt his fingers twitch with delight. Puck shut his eyes.

"This world could use some color," he muttered to himself.

"See, Puck!" Iago exclaimed happily. "No part of this plan sucks!"

Puck gazed into Iago's joy-shined eyes. Iago's fingers curled around Puck's hooded sweatshirt gripping tightly. His lips curled into a lamenting pout. Puck was apprehensive but Iago was making sense. That disturbed him.

"What's your plan?" Puck said reluctantly.

Iago bounced on the balls of his feet with an excited squeal. His eyes danced again as he hugged a hesitant Puck.

"Simple," he said finally. "We lure him into the Hedge. I know a great spot. We say a few words and then rip his heart out. We'll be drinking Mai Tais in the Crystal Palace by midnight."

"And how do we get him into the Hedge? Even if the Department doesn't have him, it's difficult enough to get a mage into the Hedge. They don't just simply walk into the Hedge."

"Oh, I'll get him in there," Iago said with a cold precision that made Puck's ears twitch with terror. "There is no way this plan will fail."

"Iago," Puck said uneasily. Iago's zeal scared him out of his righteous feelings. "Can I think about this?"

"Puck," Iago said with a warming voice. "When have I ever forced you to do something you didn't want to do?"

"Lots of times." Puck replied. "Just give me a couple of hours?"

Iago hugged Puck, confident he'd won the battle, and then disappeared into the ether. Puck stood in swelling unease. It wouldn't have mattered if he'd said no to Iago. Iago was going over that cliff and taking Puck with him. Puck truly wished he could be on board with this plan. Part of him was, but most of him wasn't. This wasn't right. He walked back to the stock room. He plopped down on the old couch.

"Hiya, Amaya," Puck said.

Amaya sat upside down on the couch. She ripped out a page of the manga and balled it up. She grinned up at Puck.

"Hiya, Puck," Amaya said as she popped the page into her mouth. "Kiss my toes."

"Amaya," Puck said gravely. Amaya looked up at him carefully. "Iago has this plan to rip apart the Hedge. It might work out perfectly, but..."

"But it's Iago," Amaya finished for him. "Things are rarely what they seem."

"He wants to kill this powerful being." Puck shook his head. "I don't know."

"You know, I could consult the elders," Amaya offered. "They know everything. I could go ask them."

"You'd do that for me?" Puck asked.

"Only if you'll do one thing for me, first," she sang sweetly.

Puck smiled, taking her pale foot into his hands. He brought her tiny toes to his lips and kissed each one. He then took the other foot and repeated his actions. His worship of her tiny feet was met with light giggles from the water nymph. Amaya slid off the couch gently. Within seconds, a neon green door appeared. As the door closed it disappeared into a fine vapor just as quickly as it arrived. Puck sighed. This was all too much for him. He had to get out of the shop and clear his head. He needed to take a walk and so he did.

XVII. A Date with Exposition Jones

Asher's hands shook violently as Dr. Duke escorted him down the long bone-colored marble hallways twisting through the Old World castle that was the Offices for the Department of the Arcane. He hadn't been sure what he'd thought this place was as a child but an office complex wasn't it. He'd hoped it was a real castle with a princess and everything and yet here he was. His eyes darted over the torch lit doors and the carved features of the walls and ceiling that told a haunting story that Asher didn't know. It was a narrative to which the words had been forgotten years ago and what remained was the pictures and images of a valiant looking prince and trials that hadn't been easy to understand. He tried to keep up with the his guide's sporadic and rapid steps as he looked at the faces that were more engaged in their battle than with people walking down the dimly lit hallways. Dr. Duke's cowboy boots made a finite echo in the serious halls making them feel more foreboding and evil. Asher watched a shadow fly in serpentine patterns on the high gothic ceilings circling its prey. Asher felt a fear grip him as the sound of fast beating wings scurried down the hallway. He cringed lightly as his ears were filled with accusatory whispers outlining every terrible deed he had ever committed from the time he could remember. Asher stopped dead in his tracks in cold fear. He couldn't will himself forward any longer.

Suddenly, a great rush of wings swept a wind through the hallway. The Great Beast landed quietly on soft paws, approaching Asher and the mage. Its wings folded down on its great torso as its elegant head held itself up with dignity and intimidation. Her broad chest heaved out a thundering growl that could cause a harder man to tremble. Asher shook like a wet Chihuahua outside in the middle of January. Asher's eyes became wet with terrified admiration of the great creature who watched him. He was struck by the beauty of its classic looks. To Asher, she was classically beautiful, especially her ancient face. Her face was smooth like it was carved out of a single piece of alabaster and framed by a mane of curly black hair. She was so scary-beautiful that she was hard to look at for a long period of time. Asher had to avert his eyes in pain as his hands twitched like it was high noon in Tombstone. Dr. Duke stepped between Asher and the Great Beast.

"Halt!" bellowed the Great Beast. "Who doth tread these halls?"

"Tis I, Merlin Duke," Dr. Duke bellowed back. "Grand instructor and High mage of the order of Truth and Light. Director of the Department of the Arcane. I bring with me Asher of the House of Stone, son of Stephen. Vessel of the all-powerful nexus. We seek an audience with the Recantor."

The Great Beast padded on predatory steps towards Asher. Her angelic head bent down, falling mere centimeters from Asher's face. Her hot breath blew across his cheeks, forcing a spiral of intimidation down him that stuck in Asher's throat. He couldn't help but find himself trapped in her rich amber eyes like a small animal staring down the last minutes of its life. She drew in his scent with a fierce snort as her jaw unclenched violently. She raised her head with a territorial growl and turned back to Dr. Duke.

"I will grant thee passage," said the Great Beast. "If thou canst answer to me a riddle...."

"Zana, can it," Dr. Duke ordered. "The boy is off to experience his Awakening with the Recantor. We weren't going to records. Ease up."

The Great Beast roared in her defeat at Dr. Duke before flapping her wings. She pushed off the ground with no sound and flew back up towards the high ceilings. Asher watched as she disappeared into the rafters before turning his inquisitive glance back to Dr. Duke. The old mage rolled his eyes in irritation at the interaction. Some days he longed for the days when he could spend his time in a tower reading and working on his craft. Today was one of those days.

"Goddamn sphinxes," Dr. Duke muttered mostly to himself. "Great for keeping secrets. Lousy Hall Monitors."

The two of them proceeded without further conversation to the shadowy, unknown end of the hall. Well, unknown to Asher, really. Dr. Duke knew far more than he ever cared to let on. This was one of those moments. He knew exactly where they were going and what would happen there. He would have explained that to Asher, but it seemed redundant since Dr. Duke had just explained to the sphinx where they were going. He wasn't a fan of repeating himself. Who is? I am, apparently.

They stopped before a door in the hallway that stood out from its surroundings like a 7 foot tall Nigerian at the Republican National Convention. For a moment, Asher wondered if they had gotten lost in the twists and turns of the halls. This had to be a neglected part of the building with the broken floors cracked and covered with a fine layer of dust and what Asher hoped were cobwebs. It had reminded Asher of the hallway of Roosevelt High where the Janitor's closet had been. For some reason, it was the dirtiest and oldest spot in the whole building. There was a door, much like this one, that was a single piece of chipped wood that had the word "Janitor" scrawled in faded black paint. This door didn't have the word Janitor scrawled in faded black paint. It didn't have anything on it. Of course to Asher, this has to be the Janitor's closet.

No one would ever want their office to be that far away except for someone who had no desire to be seen and ridiculed. How was this supposed to help him on his new quest of the last thirty minutes? Of course janitors always seem to know the score, so maybe it would be the case here. Dr. Duke breathed in the composure of his words.

"You can be nervous, " Doctor Duke said finally. "This is a new and frightening experience for you. We all go through an Awakening at some point. I didn't, but I'm not everyone. I want to remind you, Asher. Once you walk through that door, you'll know what we've always known. You'll be aware of your abilities...all of your abilities. This is an important moment for any mage. Your father...."

"Do you want me to change my mind?" Asher said coldly. The invocation of his father had bothered him when no one else ever mentioned the man. Today, it was somehow so much worse to breathe the name to him.

"No," Dr. Duke retorted calmly, "I want you to make the right choice for you."

"Then don't mention my father like that ever again."

Asher turned the rusted door knob and carefully pushed into the room. I use a lot of doors in this story. There isn't any real symbolism there and I won't pretend there is. It's an easy device to use as a transition from one scene to another scene. I mean, if you think about it, how many times a day do we walk through a door and not really even register it? We do it a lot. I suppose me calling attention to it just makes me a bad storyteller. I'll fix it later.

As Asher entered the room, his eyes darted around the antiqued furniture. He coughed as the smell of old and must invaded his nose. Asher squinted through the brown flickering light at the figure sitting at the fossilized desk. He was a squat man in jeans and a flannel shirt that was buttoned up to his doubled chin. His work booted feet were propped up on the desk while the bill of his trucker hat was pulled down over his eyes. Asher took a step towards the desk like Dorothy approaching the Great Oz. The man looked up at Asher from under the trucker hat with a bemused smile. His toothless grin was as wide as the bill of the hat.

"Hi," Asher said hesitantly, "My name is..."

"Asher Stone," cut off the man with his thick Southern Appalachian accent. "Come on in, son, and set a spell."

Asher looked to his right where an ancient folding chair had appeared beside him. Asher stared at the chair before hesitantly sitting in it. He was surprised to find it to be the most comfortable chair he'd ever sat in. The man put his feet on the floor with an inquisitive gaze. Asher eyed the man, spuriously furrowing his brow.

"Ain't you Stephen and Tracy's boy?" asked the man. "No I ain't gonna tell ya that you look like yer daddy. I know it's right upsetting for you to hear that."

"How did you..." Asher began to ask.

"Fear not, I ain't rootin' around in yer head. I'll leave that to the mind readers," said the man. "My name is Exposition Jones. My momma wanted to call me George."

"George....Jones...." Asher said stupidly.

"I'm what you would call the bard here at the Department," Exposition Jones said. "I recount the stories of people, which ain't as difficult as it sounds. You are here for the mage rite of Awakening. When a mage embraces his path, he is given insight on his place in the universe that assists him on his path. This is a deeply personal vision that has been ready for you and only you. The First Peoples of North America would call this a vision quest. Relax, you'll be given the things you'll need to see."

"Does this involve peyote?" Asher inquired. "Because I have kind of a drug problem."

"No, no," Exposition Jones replied. "That machination is best left to the shaman. I use a different method. Now, let me tune up my guitar right here."

Exposition Jones rose from his desk like a phantom unfolding. He then walked over to a corner with a light smile. In the oddly lit corner, a National guitar appeared much like the fulfillment of a cue in a weird ritualized play. Exposition Jones walked with the guitar back to Asher. He sat on the corner of his desk and plucked a few chords. He made a few adjustments on the tightness of the strings and then played again. Exposition Jones gave a nod of a satisfaction before standing up. He walked behind Asher and swung at the back of his head. It connected with a metallic clang, pushing Asher forward into blackness.

XVIII. Follow the Yellow Brick Road

The brass and silver gates of the Elysium Library rose elegantly over the ruby poppies like the subject of a Monet painting before his eyesight went blurry. Her purple-black lips curled into a grin as she looked over the wildflowers and then towards the gate feeling ever so wonderful about her walk towards the center of all information in Arcadia; this was fun for her. Amaya loved traveling through Arcadia. It was always pretty here. It always felt like things were on the verge of breaking into song and sometimes a dance number like a brightly colored musical from the 1950s. Every day for her in Arcadia was an adventure and she wanted to relish every minute of it. Her favorite place to visit in all of Arcadia was the Elysium Library. The sky seemed to shift from deep blues and purples of night to the blistering orange of day rapidly which was pretty enough but it was nothing compared to the library itself. It was a large building sitting amidst the rolling landscape that touched the changing sky. When the sun hit the library, the light danced off the smooth green stone. Some time ago, Amaya had seen a movie starring Judy Garland. Judy Garland and her friends went to a tall green building filled with wonderment. It made Amaya smile at the cellophane vision of her home. When she got back to Puck, she'd have to ask him if she could have a puppy that sang "Africa".

She didn't have a puppy with her today or a tin man or a scarecrow. That didn't mean she was alone. When Amaya was in the Dream, she traveled with a charming companion. Amaya's companion was a doe-eyed girl with a bright red curly hair. She loved Amaya and had all of her life simply because Amaya was the only family she knew.

Amaya and Puck once had conversations about where babies came from. She wanted one and Puck had explained that they weren't candy. She then asked Puck where babies came from just to satisfy her own curiosity. Puck attempted to explain the human reproduction system to Amaya and he failed...terribly. Until she took the child that had become her best friend, she believed that humans hatched from eggs that were pooped out by the mother. In fact, she'd taken the girl to prove a point to Puck. She'd had the hatchling ever since. Taking children from the mundane world is a common occurrence when it comes to the fair folk. Fairies often get bored and occasionally very lonely, so they kidnap a child for companionship. They will, typically, leave a fetch or a fake person made of straw in the place of the stolen child. Parents raise the fetch as their own child none the wiser. As for the reason the fae take a child, that is a mystery even for the fae. It is believed by many that it is simply a reflection of how hard it is for fae to give birth to offspring. Anyone can craft offspring from any number of materials, but to give birth is difficult. Some claim to take a child as a servant or something of a pet. In Amaya's case, she'd always wanted to have a very best friend in the whole wide world. So, she had the girl to be her best friend forever and ever and that was just great for her. She'd named the girl Penny after a silly human word for copper.

Going to the Library was a special treat even for Amaya. The Library wasn't easy to port into so you had to walk, which could take forever by fairy standards. So to take the time and trouble of going to the Library meant it was a super special occasion. This day called for pageantry. She knew this well so she went all out, including her use of costumes for their trip. Amaya chose a blue and white checkered dress with knee socks and red shoes. Like I said, she was a big fan of Judy Garland and this film about Amaya's home. She skipped down a time worn path with a soft giggle.

Penny was also in a costume. She wore a black and yellow tutu with a striped toboggan and fake glasses. She skipped hand in hand with Amaya. If you think this is a random costume then you're wrong. Penny's costumes were based on the scene from The Wizard of Oz when Dorothy reunites the bee people and they danced in a field of sunflowers. It's Amaya's favorite part of the movie. Where is that scene in the movie, you ask? It's not in the movie. Amaya often gets The Wizard of Oz confused with the music video for Blind Melon's "No Rain".

The pair walked past the great gates and down the crystal hallways of the Library. Slowly, they walked into the largest room in the Great Library. The deep blues of the walls and the floors danced in the sunlight that bled into the building, making the gemmed walls sparkle like the Pacific Ocean. Before them stood twelve carefully carved white marble statues that stared down on a silvery white basin in silent prayer to an unknown deity. Amaya gracefully walked to the basin with well-choreographed movements of her delicate fingers dancing in small circles around the basin as her feet danced a small dance to music in her head. Her big blue eyes looked quizzically at the somber faces sadly. She was sad when people she knew were sad looking. Then again, the elders were always looking sad. Maybe they were sad because she didn't know their names. No one knew their names. Their names were lost to conventional memory.

At one time, the elder ones ruled both Arcadia and the mundane world as the spirits of guidance and truth. As time pressed forward, bringing progress and newer pantheons, they relinquished power to more capable hands because people get tired of ruling after a long period of time. Since their time had passed a long time ago, they transcended a corporeal form leaving their spirits behind. They didn't need those bodies anymore. Their spirits lived in the Library to dispense their wisdom because really, they rather enjoyed having people bring them presents. Everyone likes presents, even -- sometimes especially -- ancient spirits. It was why Amaya and Penny were there. They were there to offer presents and talk to the spirits about super important information.

Amaya stood beside the basin. She hummed a disjointed melody as she dug into her basket. She pulled out a bottle of cherry cola and a package of chocolate chip cookies. Amaya carefully placed the cookies around the basin as Penny poured the cola into the basin quietly. Penny looked around as Amaya cleared her throat.

"Penny," Amaya whispered to her friend, "Say the words. Please, Penny."

Penny hid her face behind a curtain of hair. She shook her head no as she hid behind Amaya.

"Come on Penny. Say it," Amaya said with an irritated plea. Penny shook her head no. Amaya rolled her eyes. "Fine, I'll do it."

Amaya cleared her throat again as she raised her hands over her head. There are two customs that the fae indulged in regularly. One is paying tribute to the other fae. Any excuse for a gift is a good one. When visiting an elder, one is expected to bring a gift or a tribute. The most acceptable gift bring to an elder fae is junk food. Human junk food is a delicacy in most ethereal realms and is highly prized. If you want to make it safely through Arcadia take a backpack full of Hostess Cakes. The other thing that the fae love is ritual. The fae, by nature, are very dramatic. They will often perform grandiose gestures. The best way to a fae's heart is pageantry and ceremony.

Amaya stood behind the basin with her arms raised above her head as she looked up at the faces above her.

"Greetings and salutations to you, Great Fathers of the

Forgotten Race and to the Sweet Mothers of Time and Space," Amaya called loudly through the hall.

A third thing that the fae love is hearing their names in grand titles. The older the fae and the more noble the house, the longer and more complex their name becomes. It is considered rude and incredibly disrespectful to not greet an elder by their full title. It is also rude to not formally introduce yourself by your full title.

"Tis I, Amaya; Daughter of Indra; Queen of the Wild River, Princess of the Midnight Rain, bound in union to Puck, the fourteenth son of the Satyr called Pan. With me is my very best friend Penny. We bring thee a great tribute. Please accept these gifts of Cherry Cola and cookies."

Suddenly, there was a great gush of wind that blew through the Great Hall. It moved over the basin, letting small ripples form on the surface of the cola. It then blew over the cookies spreading small crumbs off the plate. The wind encircled Amaya playfully and then it blew through her dark blue hair, lovingly greeting the water nymph. She giggled as the ends of her hair tickled her neck.

"We could have preferred the nectar of the bovine," whispered the wind in a descending voice that filled her ears. "It is the favored beverage when we are offered the biscuits with the crafted cacao, but this is acceptable. Why dost thou beckon us to this place, water nymph?"

"I had a question but it's not for me," Amaya said kicking her feet. "But Puck and Iago have this plan to tear down the Hedge to merge the two worlds together. Is this a super bad idea or not?"

The wind ceased abruptly. The voice broke into distinct voices as it conversed with its selves in hushed whispers that echoed through the great hall as they discussed Amaya's question. Then, there was silence. Suddenly, the wind picked up again.

"The Hedge cannot be destroyed," decreed the noble wind in a loud gust. Amaya blinked intently. "The force to destroy that kind of barrier does not exist. The nexus is safe."

"But..." Amaya said. "What *would* happen if the Hedge got broken?"

"Then," said the wind. "The worlds would be united as one."

"And...then what would happen?" Amaya asked.

"Well," said the wind. "The merging of our world with the mundane world would be catastrophic."

"Why?" Amaya's eyes grew bigger, not knowing what the word meant, but desperately hoping it meant more kittens.

"The two have been separated for far too long. Before the split, they cohabitated with each other. They needed each other to survive," explained the wind. "Since their separation, they have learned to move on without each other. Now, they have filled the empty spaces with countering energies so that they no longer bear a resemblance to the worlds that once existed as a united place. They are so different. The energy is different that pushes them forward through history. The force that once united the two will pull the two asunder violently."

"What does that mean?" she asked, confused.

"They'll implode," said the wind.

"Uh....huh....." Amaya said slowly.

"You, us, Penny, and Marshmallow Peeps won't exist anymore," said the Wind. "Nothing will."

"Oh," Amaya said. "That sounds bad."

"It would be, yes," spoke the noble wind. "Didst thou sayeth that the Prince of Lies is involved in this moronic plan?"

"Uh Huh!" Amaya said brightly. "Puck said Iago wanted to

tear down the Hedge, bringing Arcadia into the mundane world."

"Most odd," spoke the wind. "The Prince of Lies bore witness to the birth of the nexus and the creation of the Hedge. He should be more aware of the destruction its end would cause."

"But he is super old and pretty crazy," Amaya reminded them. "He could have forgotten?"

"It's quite possible," conceded the wind. "We should warn the mundane to prevent this atrocity. We must send an envoy to the mundane authorities."

Amaya's hand shot up like a bottle rocket on Canada Day.

"Oh," she said loudly. "I can do it! Pick me!"

"Amaya, Princess of the Midnight Rain, Daughter of Queen Indra," declared the wind. "Thou shalt warn the mundane world of Iago's nefarious plan. Go, speak to the mages on this matter."

"Will do." She paused. "Hey, Elders?"

"Yes, Amaya," asked the wind.

"I'm really sorry you don't have a body," she said. "Because I want to hug you."

"Well, you could always hug our Sacrificial Basin," offered the wind. "That would be like hugging us, only not really."

Amaya's eyes went wide with delight as she dropped down beside the Basin. Her tiny arms flung around the Basin in an enthusiastic hug. Quickly, Penny also flung her arms around the Basin. The two sighed contently.

"I love you, elders," Amaya said happily.

"We love you too, Amaya," said the wind gently. "Now go. Time is of the essence."

"Okie Dokie," Amaya said cheerily. She stood up. "Penny! Keep hugging the Elders. I'll be back!"

Amaya clapped her hands twice calling for her green door. Penny raised her hand to give a precision military salute. She then quickly returned to hugging the Basin. Amaya stepped through the green door and off to her mission.

XIX. Still on a Date with Exposition Jones

"Owww!" Asher screamed as he pushed out of the blackness. "You toothless slack-jawed yokel!"

Asher looked around viciously for the man before blinking in utter confusion while holding the back of his head. This wasn't the derelict office he had been sitting in just moments ago. The office had slipped into a medical white that radiated an unsettling aura around him. His nose burned with the smell of antiseptic cleaner and medical supplies. *Huh,* thought Asher, *he must have hit me harder than I thought.* Asher became irritated with his situation. Why did most of his life revolve around hospitals? It was like no matter how he'd spent every hour of his day today he somehow ended up in a hospital or an infirmary and so on. He stood up carefully from the waiting room chair and looked around again mostly to reinforce his complaints about being in a hospital. Asher stopped himself here for a moment. It was safe to say that he didn't recognize this hospital at all. Asher breathed. At least all the hospitals he'd ended up in were different from each other. This was a new one for him. His perplexed eyes fell on the forms of the medical staff as they moved like ghosts through the floor with a sense of dated clothing. To Asher, it felt like a dream. There was nothing to hold on to and everything was covered in a fine mist. Things were oddly serene in this distant place.

Then, Asher saw him enter the room.

Asher's heart leapt into his throat as he laid eyes on the tall man entering the room. He felt his back ache as a warm tension poured through his body. The man stood in the center of the room just out of Asher's reach. He had the same burnt red hair as Asher, except his fell in shaggy layers barely touching his neck. Asher was filled with familial warmth as he tried to memorize the man's related Frankish features. Asher had always wondered what his father would look like. Tracy had no pictures of her first husband and the only pictures Mim had of Stephen was a picture from his youth. It wouldn't have mattered. No one ever looked real in pictures. Real physical memories of people were so much more. This would be greater than any picture someone could have shown him. Asher was staring at his father; adult and in the flesh so to speak.

He was taller than Asher had expected. From everything he'd heard, he expected his father to be thin and smaller because of his grandmother who was diminutive. He looked so strong and almost confident standing in a sea of lab coats and scrubs like he was a superhero from the 1950s comics. Asher felt a great sense of overwhelm storm through his body and sting his eyes as he looked at a man he'd never known well enough to share a memory of to another living person. A cascade of conflicting emotions tore through him like ten thousand bullets into his major arteries. His father shoved his hands into his red McKean State hooded sweatshirt as he blinked tiredness from his bang hidden eyes. He rubbed the back of his neck. Asher couldn't help but smile as he noticed that they had the same Japanese kanji tattooed on their wrists. He approached his father with hands outstretched reaching for the man. His lower lip trembled in delight for a moment.

"D-Dad?" he asked quietly.

His father looked at Asher directly and then walked away without a word. Asher's heart sank into his lower intestines as his father ignored him. Then, a soft voice spoke to him. It said not to worry. He was standing in the middle of a memory. He wasn't a part of this scene. He was merely an observer in this farce and that he should enjoy the ride. Man, thought Asher, as Visions go, this one sucks. He sank back into the chair quietly with his head in his hands.

"So, he's here?" suddenly said a familiar jerky voice. Asher's ears twitched in recognition.

"Six minutes ago," said his father. "Asher Pennywise Stone. Sir, I'm glad you could make it."

Asher looked up quickly in blind confusion as he heard his own name. They were talking about him, but not seeing him which made things awkward. Perhaps, this was indeed something more important. The voice in the back of his head assured him that he was correct, this was indeed a memory of a time past, but it was his memory. Something that Asher had long forgotten happened to him. This was the moment of his birth. Asher looked up to watch the players in this biographical stage show. He wasn't surprised to see his grandmother. IF this was the day of his birth then she should be there. Oddly, Dr. Duke's presence didn't surprise him either. In the short time he'd known the man, he seemed to have bound himself to Asher's fate whether or not he wanted that to be the case. Somehow, every part of Asher's life had had Dr. Duke overlooking him. What surprised him was that, in nearly the three decades since his birth, neither of them had aged. He expected that his grandmother had always been old but Dr. Duke had remained unchanged by the years. The only difference between the current Dr. Duke and the Dr. Duke of the past was the choice in head gear. Dr. Duke in this memory wore a baseball cap professing his support for the Brooklyn Dodgers. Mim gave Stephen a severe look at she watched the mages greet each other. He smiled at her with a smile that was all too familiar to Asher.

How do I even remember this moment if I'm not in the room? Asher thought to himself.

Hush, you, said the voice, *it's **our** memory, not just yours.*

"Stephen," Mim started with a nagging whine. "You greeted

him first on a very cold night before your own mother? I suppose I should just be happy that you called me at all, I guess. You never call me for anything anymore Stephen. At least we're here. You know traffic was terrible and can't see well at night so I had to get a ride with Dr. Duke and that was just awful. Now it's raining frogs and the nexus is missing..."

"Mom," Stephen cut her off cheerfully, "We're both glad you're here. It means a lot to Tracy that the Crone could come and see her son."

Mim snorted ruefully at Stephen's words. Asher continued to watch as the events confused him even more. Raining frogs? That was something he was pretty sure no one ever spoke about. If that happened then that was major, why did no one ever mention it? He then wondered if it had happened in the real world.

"You should have called me when she went into labor," Mim sniffed. "I could have sent a mid wife instead of us being in a mundane hospital."

"In retrospect, yea, I should have," Stephen conceded. "But I had bigger problems. I've had Dira and Aguirre out trying to clean up after us and contain the problems. Tracy's water broke when we were eating dinner at Jose O'Flannagan's."

Stephen ran his hands through his hair again. It was then that Asher noticed the cuts on Stephen's hands and face. Those cuts looked fresh to him.

"She," Stephen continued. "Well, her insults can be cutting. I just stopped bleeding from the first round of contractions. I expected that, so, that's not the weirdest part of this. I think there is something wrong with my baby."

"How so?" Dr. Duke asked.

"When Tracy's water broke there was an earthquake. Surely,

you guys felt it. Then it started to rain purple," Stephen recounted. "And he came faster than expected. Oh and the best part of all of this? Tracy glowed bright blue when she gave birth. Then, the rain turned to frogs. There is something really wrong with the baby."

Dr. Duke pursed his lips as he turned away from the group. The tension of the mounting situation twisted in his back. The onset of the two events meant that what he feared had happened. Dr. Duke didn't want to face his fears. He shut his eyes and turned his head to the side in concern. What he feared had happened and he had to embrace it. Fears don't fix anything, or at least that's what he was going to tell himself.

"Indeed, something has happened to your son," Dr. Duke cleared his throat before he declared dramatically. "The nexus has found a new host."

"Bull," Mim said. "If it had gone from Gaiman, we'd know. Hell, I'd feel it."

"And raining frogs is a regular occurrence," Dr. Duke rejoined sarcastically. No one stole his dramatic pronouncements without getting slightly snubbed. "I didn't say it left the city. It has found a new host."

"You mean Asher," Mim said. "How is that possible?"

"I would imagine it would involve sexual intercourse," Dr. Duke muttered. "You know, when a man loves a woman."

"Not what I meant." Mim's face fell flat at Dr. Duke's words.

Dr. Duke ignored her and paced like a nervous cat. He had to figure out this turn of events quickly. He couldn't handle two unrelated major events at one time. Of course, they never happened by themselves. Suddenly, he paused stared off in a direction as if something caught his attention. He sniffed the air with quick intent. Without a word, he marched into Tracy's hospital room. Mim followed quickly on Dr. Duke's boot heels. Lastly, was Stephen who had resigned to rejoin the war and followed his mother and the old mage. Asher stood up watching them and then blinked. He hesitated only briefly before following them.

Asher paled taking in the eggshell white room as the party arranged themselves around the bed. His gaze then fell on his mother. Asher was taken aback by his mother's beauty. With twenty-some years and three kids ahead of her, she looked so young and calm. Her graying hair at that moment was a sunlit brown that hung in matted sheets. She looked exactly like Carin to Asher. Her eyes were trained on a small infant that rested in her arms. She looked up at the assembled party with a tired smile.

"Blessed be, Wise and Holy Crone," Tracy said quietly. "Dr. Duke, evening."

Rarer than evidence of Stephen existing were baby pictures of Asher. He never quite understood why his mother didn't have any of him from that early age. She had pictures of Jordan and Carin from minutes after their birth but none of his. For a long time, he had thought he was merely adopted. That the people around him were simply actors attempting to convince him otherwise like some form of the Truman Show without the insane argument against vaccination. This moment had confirmed the exact opposite of his beliefs. He had been born to his mother. Dr. Duke leaned down, inspecting the infant Asher. He scowled at the sleeping infant scrutinizing the child like a rare artifact.

"Well, I'll be damned," Dr. Duke said. "I'm right. The nexus is in the boy."

Asher wasn't quite sure what to think or say about the things he was witnessing. Their words and actions were very confusing to him. Everything sounded important even if it continued to sound like gibberish to him. It couldn't be real. No, it had to be real. Asher's view on a lot of things had changed since this morning, which did include the continuing viewing of this shadow play. As unrelated as it seemed, he thought, what a weird Thursday it had been. Tracy held the infant protectively close to her breast as her eyes flashed like lightning.

"That doesn't happen," she said coldly. "Magical entities don't possess infants."

"He's not possessed," Dr. Duke explained. "He'll be who you raise him to be. He'll just also be the vessel for the most powerful entity in all of creation. The nexus chose him as sort of the place to rest. Why him? I have no idea."

Well, that made even less sense, thought Asher. He had never felt like he didn't have a soul, which is what he understood those words to mean. He also didn't especially feel magical. As far as Asher knew, this was just a weird new age cult thing. He'd suspected that his mother was in one of those for ages now and this, this totally confirmed it. Though it bothered him that there was his whole family that seemed to be a part of it. He wondered if Brady knew. Even if he didn't, this whole thing felt like some sort of farce. Mim leaned forward with a critical stare at her grandson. The infant opened his eyes with a soft yawn before going back to sleep. She blinked twice as she turned back to the men.

"Normally, I wouldn't listen to the mage, either," Mim said. "But this time, he's right. Little Asher is housing a lot of magic. Oh, I knew this would happen when a mage entered into a union."

"Mother," Stephen said sharply. "This isn't the time to start that nonsense. Right now we have to get that thing out of our son."

"We can't," Dr. Duke responded. "Once a nexus chooses its resting place it cannot and will not be unmoved without its consent and then that could be very dangerous for Asher. No, at this point we need to keep him protected from the parasites and keep the nexus from completely taking over his physical body."

"You aren't taking my baby from me," Tracy said, holding her child protectively.

"And I wasn't planning to," Dr. Duke said. "He's safer with you than with us anyway."

"How old does he have to be for us to bind him to his magical source?" Stephen asked clinically.

In a split second, Asher hated a man he never met. Was he even Stephen Stone's son? The fact that he had been was rooted in this madness he barely understood, though a decision being made by this man he didn't know made him feel like the answer to that was no.

"You are definitely not scarring my son with your barbaric rituals," Tracy snapped at the mages. The room shook as the lights flickered their debate of staying on to watch this fight. For an instance, Mim looked almost proud of her daughter-in-law.

"Tracy please," Stephen said in his most soothing tone. "It's a common ritual for young magi. I went through it at my Awakening and I wasn't too much older than Asher."

"I'd be a bad mother if I didn't give him the choice," she said.

"Tracy, you'll be a great mother. You're the most powerful witch I know," Mim narrowed her eyes at Stephen's words. "But that can only go so far."

The assembled party got very quiet as a nurse entered the room. The dark haired nurse leaned down for the bundle of infant. Tracy flushed pink with embarrassment as she handed the little Asher up to the nurse. The older Asher squinted. Something looked off about the nurse. It was her eyes. The nurse had weirdly familiar depthless black eyes. She looked and felt off with those eyes. The party in the hospital room had the same unsettling feeling. Moving uncharacteristically fast for their respective ages, Mim and Dr. Duke moved to block the door while Stephen walked around the nurse in a defensive pace. The nurse turned her head to the side pleasantly.

"Gentlemen, Lady," the nurse said in an unsettlingly pleasant tone. "I need to get your little miracle to the nursery for his nap."

Stephen purposely stepped closer to the nurse. His warm skin tinted to a dark gray as his cold hands wrapped protectively around his son. His face became hard.

"Fairy," he commanded with a voice as cold as an ice storm, "give me my son."

"Sir," retorted the nurse, "I don't appreciate your tone."

"Fairy," he commanded again. "Give me my son."

"Sir," the nurse started getting a little more harried. "Please..."

The nurse's face contorted as her painted lips twisted into a jagged smile. Her face relaxed into a familiar masculine face before snapping back to the pretty face. Asher stole a breath as he watched. He knew that face but that couldn't be right. Iggy was his age.

"Back off mage," Asher's heart rate quickened when he heard the all too familiar voice depart the lips of the nurse. "This one is mine."

Asher felt ill, still not quite understanding the things he saw. This was like being plunged into murky brown water. He was cold and things felt dirty and the longer he stared, river weed got in his eyes. The more he saw the less he understood. Stephen sneered at the nurse.

"Oh for the love of Gaia," Mim growled. She opened her

purse and dug through the carpet bag. She grinned secretly as she placed her hand on something at the bottom of her bag. "Make all the pronouncements you want but fairies only understand physical action."

In a cartoony flash, Mim dropped her purse to reveal a long iron poker. The nurse's eyes widened. Stephen gripped his child as Mim swung back with the poker. Asher flinched as the poker connected with a sickening thud on the nurse's crown. The nurse let out a scream as her disguise dropped fully. Asher's body went stiff as his throat seized air and breath from his chest. In the middle of the floor laid a familiar pink haired figure.

"Iggy," Asher spoke barely in a whisper, "but how?"

Iago pulled himself up to his hands and knees. Calculatedly, his eyes darted around the room. Today wasn't the day to push. At that moment, Iago knew better. One day, that baby would be his, but right now he had to run. Iago bared his teeth and let out a loud hiss. His clawed fingers gripped into the linoleum floor. Reality ripped open like a threadbare pair of jeans giving way at the crotch. As the hole closed, the assembled party stared at each other in silence.

"So," Tracy asked, breaking the silence. "We can get him bound when he's how old?"

"Seven days," Dr. Duke replied. "You know it won't protect him from the parasites. It just binds the nexus to himself...safely."

"And fairies won't be the only thing out there," Tracy said. "I just want him strong enough to stand up to the rest."

The figures of this play froze mid-chapter. Asher looked around in confusion. Surely, this wasn't it. Not everything he needed to know was there, it couldn't be. This wasn't right.

"Seen what you needed to see?" Exposition Jones asked, appearing out of nowhere.

"No," Asher said. "It was confusing and didn't tell me anything about who I'm supposed to be."

"Knowing who you are ain't got nothing to do with your path in life. The past will always be confusing," Exposition Jones said. "It's supposed to give you an understanding to move forward, not to explain everything. You ready to go?"

"No, not really," Asher responded. "I'd like to see more."

"Yu-up." Exposition Jones drew out. "They all do, but we can't. Time to go."

"Is there a way to bring me out of this without braining me with the guitar?"

"Probably," Exposition Jones conceded as he raised his guitar over Asher's head. He swung down onto our hero with a bone crushing clang. Asher fell out of the vision and into darkness.

XX. Glass, Concrete and Stone

Iago was descended from fae royalty which meant little to the fae. If you ask any fairy, they are more royal than anyone. So much like Irish kings, everyone has royalty. That and a cracker gets you a cracker. Iago was different. He was the higher rank of royalty than most. He'd been off the path like the rest of his family however, like many fae, he had inherited some basic talents from his noble home that made him very dangerous. One skill was the ability to make potent and fine mead. His father, Loki; the Trickster King and the great Deceiver, was the finest brewer in the land of Arcadia. Iago wasn't as quite as skilled as his father, but his brew was quite intoxicating to both fae and human.

Iago could also craft words for his own personal use. This is nothing new. All fairies have this skill and, typically, are very good at this. Iago, however, was better than most. It's very dangerous to enter an agreement with a fairy. There are very few outcomes resulting from a fairy contract that end well for the mundane. Their trickery knows no bounds and can lead to permanent damage to the other party in ways that have yet to be discovered. In Iago's heyday, he had been deadly with his words. His body count was now almost into the millions with the use of simple words. That was, of course, before Iago had been banished from the Dream and his confidence damaged when it came to his craft. It had been generations before this moment when he had been punished by King Oberon, Lord of all Fae, with his madness or alleged madness. Iago had never figured out if he was mad or not. He seemed to think he was just fine. Part of the nightmare was that Iago felt he was rather sensible and sane in all of this. It had been before he spent his days in the mundane world where those skills were less needed. His word-smithing had fallen to the wayside. He had other skills that he'd had to rely on more than the ones which he should have kept up.

The finest skill Iago had mastered and still used on a regular basis was shape shifting. In general, Fae alter the masque they wear to blend in with the mundane world. They do this for two reasons. One, it is the law in the mundane world or at the very least in the New World which was run by the Department of the Arcane. Undue exposure of the mundane to magic was a deporting offense and generally fairies enjoy going into the paper world. After all, humans could be downright hilarious when poked just right and fairies will always attempt to do what they think is funny. This leads to reason number two that fairies comply with this rule and use a masque. It is extremely hilarious to the fair folk to deceive the mundane which was the whole point of creating a masque. It wasn't outright lying to the mundane, that almost never happened, but word trickery was a form of amusement that was perversely delightful to the fair folk. This was not Iago's forte. No, Iago was adept at physically altering his mass into a different form. He could literally change his shape and face without using a masque. This shouldn't come as a surprise since all the descendants of Loki were more adept at altering their appearance than most of their fae brethren. Iago just happened to also be better than most of his siblings. He had to be good at this. He was the Prince of Lies.

As Iago marched through the apartment complex, he held on to Asher's scent. This wasn't a difficult task. The nexus had a sweetly pungent aroma and the scent it left was easy to spot for any magic user. It was that sweet smell that one finds in a bakery that you can't quite place. Olfactory memory played an important role in altering Iago's masque. It was the easiest to recall. As he turned a corner, his body altered easily into Asher's lanky frame. His jagged smile tugged into a pained sneer as his body became scarred with lines of ink that ran down his new body. Just as he reached Asher's door, he blinked twice hiding his hollow eyes behind a shield of cold gray. The eyes were most important part of a false masque. You had to get that right or it would otherwise fall apart. It had happened in the past. He'd let his plans become a victim of his own vanity. This wasn't the night to let that happen. Iago couldn't afford for it fall apart.

He breathed in, letting his voice settle into Asher's register. He placed his hands on the door frame.

"Open up to me and grant more knowledge of the secrets that you hold," he whispered to the wood of the door.

The wood groaned gently as it relaxed, permitting the request of the imposter Asher. He passed easily through the door into the apartment. Iago turned an ear towards the interior of the apartment. Quiet, he thought, that's a bonus. People who were alone felt safe. He knew that made things easy for him to do what he needed. He distastefully snorted in the feminine odor of the apartment. Clearly, Natalie had decorated this nightmare, but Asher wasn't there. That made things even easier for him. He was confused for a moment as he listened to a hum from a distant corner of the two bedroom apartment. Iago cast a warning glance to Bag of Bones. The frail cat picked up its head and then passively went back to sleep. This wasn't really important to the cat unless it somehow affected the food. Then, she was going to be very, very upset.

"Babe," Iago lied. "I'm home."

Natalie ran on light feet to the door. Her smile radiated through the room as she threw her arms around his neck. Iago indulged in her warm familiar kiss greedily. He wouldn't lower himself to sleep with her, but that didn't mean he wasn't going to enjoy touching Asher's things. She hugged him gently as her body ached with want for his touch. That's when she noticed it. Something felt off about him and she knew. She withdrew from the hug as she took a step back looking for that thing that she wasn't sure was there. Her medical mind analyzed his face. She shook her head.

"You're not hurting?" she asked, confused. "Ribs and all?"

"No," Iago said. Privately, he realized that he'd made a fatal mistake. How could he have forgotten about Asher's injuries? Now, he had to change the plan.

"Are you high?" she asked disappointedly. That was the only reason he wasn't hurting in her opinion. That had to be the reason.

"Natalie, I care the whole world for you," Iago said sweetly. That had to be the right level of corniness for Asher's line. Asher was somehow always corny. He'd blame that on the hero complex. Most accidental heroes were corny on some level. "Why would I be high?"

"You just feel...off," she said with hardening compassion. "Like, it's not you. I feel like I'm hugging a pod person."

Now, he knew that he had to change the plan. The longer the lie went on, the more she'd be aware that he wasn't Asher. Then he had a risk of it all falling apart. She'd fight and scream and call her cat for protection. While it might not seem like a big deal, having Natalie in the Hedge was very important to his plan. He knew he had to keep being Asher. This was vital to do what he needed. Betraying someone's trust to lead to them into the Hedge was a time honored tradition of the fae. With their guidance people had been lost for lifetimes in the maze that separated this world from the land of dreams. However, blind confusion sometimes worked just as well.

Resolve came to him as the notion of successfully being Asher dropped from his plan. He smiled at her as his hands gripped her shoulders harshly. Natalie let out a whimper at the pressure and pain of his predator's grip digging into her flesh. He licked his lips as he smelled her fear. Ah, cruelty, how could he have forgotten how good that felt?

"There's a reason for that," he paused for dramatic effect as his jagged smile became more malicious. "I'm not Asher."

Her lips parted to counter his confession with protest. Talon fingers hushed that notion with a skin gashing tear in her shoulders digging into her collar bone. Natalie yelped as he shoved her against the wall closest to the window, pinning her in place. Her legs kicked at him in worthless defense from his brutality. His deceptively powerful frame kept her pressed against her cream colored walls, letting his hot snarl settle on her cheek. His hand came down over her trembling lips to suffocate any pleading wails for help. He looked her over with a sadistically impish gaze.

"Look, Buzz Kill Barbie," he hissed in a distorted voice. "You are about to be in the center of a plan that has been eons in the making. Everything in this paper world is going to be ripped apart and you get to help. That makes you special, sort of. What I need you to do is to scream. You may want to scream soon."

His hand that was over her mouth pushed her head violently against the wall. With his free hand, Iago punched the wall beside her head with a reality shattering slam. Natalie let out a terrified convulsion as the apartment shook around them and the lines started to break between two very different worlds. Behind her, a cold unnatural light bled through the cracking wall and filled the apartment and the space between them. In the other worldly light, Natalie saw Iago's true face. Her eyes were transfixed on the carved features of his jade black face horrifyingly accented by the white jagged smile. It was something that she expected to see from a nightmare. Deftly, dark tendrils reached out from the void and curled around her. As the tendrils tightened, Iago eased his weight off of her.

"She's all yours, boys," he announced eagerly.

Natalie screamed as the tendrils pulled her down into a burning through dusk-filled sky into the Hedge. Her body fell down a twisting spiral of celestial confusion. She watched helplessly as her apartment and reality faded into a starless sky. Her limbs jerked for liberation from her ethereal bounds. Tears started streaming down her face as her body became overwhelmed by a hollow terror.

Eventually, she hit the bottom with a concrete thump. Her eyes searched the blank gray sky for a clue to the events of the day or at least what had happened in the last few minutes. Gracefully, she sat up with blurred confusion. Her surgical fingers searched through her messy hair for blood and bruises. Good, she told herself no blood or cerebral fluid. Skull and spine feel intact. There was no pain, though nerve damage wouldn't be obvious if she'd fallen into shock. That notion fell out of her head and made a small stain on her pants. Of course, if she was in shock she wouldn't be this rational. She wouldn't have been aware of looking for the signs of trauma. She looked up again as the cityscape closed its high peaks around her blocking out the paper white sky. Natalie's face fell into a state of confusion. This wasn't her neighborhood either. She and Asher lived in the Harris House apartments located downtown. This claustrophobic street looked and felt like Old Gaiman. There was no way she'd fallen into Old Gaiman. It didn't even look like Old Gaiman, the more she looked around at it. More importantly, it didn't even make physical sense. She fell here. People didn't fall out of downtown apartments and land on the other side of town.

She did fall, right?

Her mind drifted through her memory like a Walt Whitman poem chasing the path of her fall. It had just happened literally what seemed like moments ago. It had to. She could remember the fall out a window but the harder she thought about it, the further away her apartment and her fall felt from her and her living memory.

She stood up slowly, waiting for a dullness of pain. Carefully, Natalie took in her new surroundings. The stagnated daylight highlighted the jagged urban skyline that belonged in a Lang film. She was lost in a place she didn't know. How she got there was now more or less unimportant at that given moment. Right now she had to get back home and out of the unfamiliarity of where she was. She surely couldn't be in this ominous landscape much longer before getting mugged or raped or worse. She had to figure out how to get help. She couldn't call for help. Her cell phone was in the apartment. Who would she call anyway? Well, she could call Asher. Why would she call him? She had the car and he didn't like to drive anyway.

Asher?

She placed her fingers at her exhaustion-covered temple as far off memories hit her with a mind shattering force. His ink scarred hands pressing on her chest. Her eyes trapped in his cold indifferent gaze like she was a dead piece of flesh. He pushed her through the wall. *That isn't humanly possible,* she thought; *basic physics indicated that it wasn't. He must have pushed me through the window. He had me against the wall with the window. In the struggle he must have just pushed me through the window when I wasn't paying attention.* She shook her head trying to get the feeling of cold out of her system. There was something not right about him though. No, he hadn't been right when he walked into the apartment. His embrace was that of a stranger. He even looked weird to her. Perhaps it was the grip of terror but he looked like a monster in that moment.

Natalie pressed her fingers against her side. How was she not hurt? If she fell out of a window then she would have major fractures in her ribs, legs, and back and yet she felt fine. Well, fine enough to walk. Even if, by some strange miracle, she had escaped unscathed, where was everyone? Their neighborhood was never this quiet. Did no one see her? Instead of helping, they hid from this, locking themselves away like this was the land of the dreaded sundown? A sick realization snuck up on her shoulders. There was a very simple reason no one was around. She had died and this was hell.

Asher.

It was the only conclusion that she had to come to in this isolation. Asher had murdered her with that push out of the window and now she was in the afterlife. That thought clung to her frame like a slightly shrunken sweater. It fit but was very uncomfortable right around the bust. Asher was never mean to her, so him killing her in cold blood seemed very out of character for him. She immediately dismissed that thought. After all, some monster wearing Asher's face had to have done this to her. She tried to work through that however, monsters weren't real. Maybe it was someone pretending to be Asher who had tried to kill her. That horrible visage was a product of a traumatic event. Then it dawned on her that wasn't right either. The only thing that made sense was that the man that she loved, the man she fought so hard to get clean, pushed her out a window to her death. Natalie began to cry.

The feeling that Asher had betrayed her and now she was dead was more than she could stand. She sniffed back hurt as she tried to collect herself. She had eternity to hate Asher and feel sorry for herself, however she wasn't going to stand on a street corner and wait for Doomsday. Her mother and father hadn't raised her to be that kind of person. No, she was going to make the best of a stupid situation. Once she figured out where she was, she was going to march right up to whoever was in charge and tell them what the deal was. The afterlife was about to get a little more organized.

She picked a direction and purposefully walked down a twisting sidewalk. The eerily still city creaked and cracked under her flip flops. Each turn felt like the last as the path became more confused. All the streets were identical to the last. Within a matter of seconds, the young doctor got lost in the concrete maze. The world grew darker as the city closed around her, tightly blocking out the bright cold sky. She heard the low hiss of a predator choosing a cute little blonde mouse to eat under her feet and behind her. Natalie quickened her step to a panicked pace as she glanced behind herself looking for her stalker.

Then, she stopped.

Natalie hit something warm that smelled of damn. She cringed at the uncomfortable smell of wet fur. Why would someone leave a fur coat in the middle of the street, she thought, the material is cheap but it's so big. Her body then stiffened when she felt it breathe. Natalie slowly pulled her body back from the beast. As the creature came into focus, her mouth opened in terror choking out fear.

Natalie had always been afraid of rats. When she was a little girl her parents lived next to a river. Every time it rained, their house would be infested with big nasty river rats. Having woken up many a time to see the large aggressive vermin staring back at her from the foot of her bed had trained her to be more than terrified of the creatures. So, when she came face to snout with a rat that was the size of and was about as attractive as a PT Cruiser, she was gripped with a terror she thought she'd forgotten about in her years of moving up North. The Great Rat locked its small red eyes with Natalie. It bared its salted fangs in a fur vibrating hiss. She tried her best to back away from its pending assault. The Great Rat swung its sword sharp claws at her retreating body. She let out a pained scream as the claws ripped into her flesh. Natalie fell backwards hitting the cracked ground. She could feel the warm liquid cooling on her skin in the dead air. She could bleed. She could feel pain.

Whether or not she was dead, this was **real**. She may or may not be alive. Good to know.

The Great Rat pressed its Ginsu Paws onto her heaving chest, trapping her in a supine position. Its long muzzle opened hungrily as saliva dripped off its needlelike teeth. She knew that her sudden realization about her mortality was about to be a moot point. That was until she saw a great purple blur streak across her vision and land on the large vermin. The rat squealed painfully as the blur sank its teeth and pearly claws into its back. The rat's paws lifted off Natalie's chest in a feral panic. Natalie scurried back against the wall, watching the blur fight off the rat. The rat threw the blur off its back and retreated into the dark shadows. The blur licked a paw before padding over to the terrified Natalie. It lay down beside her putting its soft head in her lap. Natalie reluctantly started to stroke the blur's head.

"Bag of Bones?" she whispered. The blur started to purr. Natalie let out a sigh of relief. "Can you take me home?"

The blur stood up and started down an allyway slowly. Natalie stood up quickly. She followed it with a great sense of calm. The blur led her down a set of stairs that led to a large platinum gate. The beast down beside the gate looked up at her. Natalie smiled as she pushed the gate open. She was finally going home. Her new found hope was dashed when a great light filled her face.

"Oh, what fresh hell is this?" She whispered.

XXI. Gift Shopping in Old Gaiman

The Spring sky grew dark with cold moist air as the clouds grew thicker and swelled with rain. The air was washed clean as the curtains of rain opened to give relief to the waiting world below. It would close soon enough, shutting off the memory of a warm March day. The loud cracking roll of thunder was proof of that fact as another storm rolled into the city. Iago pulled the collar of his jacket closer to his neck, brushing his ear lobes as he shivered with cold. Impending chaos always gave him a cold chill that ran up his spine and stirred his blood. He knew he was on the right path when the chill hit him. He felt his jagged grin curl into a fiendishly manic smile zig zagging across his face. He'd seen his plan come together beautifully. He would have to come up with a distraction for the Department of the Arcane to give him enough time to set up the final act. It wouldn't have to be too much time, but everything had to be perfect. This was a good day. The omens and signs were all lined up perfectly to tell him it was going to be a good day. It even came with the bonus of watching Natalie fall into the Hedge. He felt his shoulder blades rise as he vividly recalled the look of fear in her big blue eyes as she stared at him. His ears twitched recalling the scream as she fell. He licked his lips and let out a lustful growl at this recent memory. If he could, he would have sex with this moment and have several little moments with that one big moment. Nothing had felt better than this moment; he felt it rise up in blissful goose bumps on his skin. The impending reign of terror felt positively erotic. Iago wasn't beyond feeling human emotions. In fact, it was the exact opposite. Iago felt emotions more intensely than humans, as do most of the fairies. Fairies, however, do feel differently than humans.

There was one thing he felt more intensely than other emotions -- the pain of others that twisted out of betrayal. He loved that feeling as some people would enjoy a kiss. He would never need to get high on drugs. He could always depend on that pain forever. Iago stopped in the middle of the street and let out a soft shudder. Today was going to be a good day for him.

Iago turned his eyes towards the blackening sky. The clouds pulled together like a thick blanket wrapping around the world to keep it safe from the sunlight. He smiled as the wind tore through the trees and thunder bounced off the rain-swollen clouds that scraped the spires of the abandoned churches of Old Gaiman. He watched as a flash of white lightning split the sky in half. Iago's face fell only slightly as he watched a violent storm roll in from Butcher Bay. Normally, he would have loved this. Set design played a big role in the creation of his work. Nothing caused more panic like an impending and violent storm. However, if the thunder became too loud, no one would bear witness to his great final act. If this was going to be like the birth of the nexus, it was going to be loud and bright and violent much like the storm blowing in from the sea. If there was going to be a storm, how would anyone notice the end until it was over? That wasn't a part of his plan.

Iago watched the sky carefully, trying to will the rain to his bidding. The pregnant clouds rapidly blew towards Warrior's Mountain. It seemed like the storm was going to clear off and a pretty day was going to come through perfectly. Iago was thrilled to see that he had some manner of magical skill to control the weather. He smiled as he started walking again. His feet turned down the broken asphalt, stepping on the corner of Gray Street and Lakey Avenue. He hummed while his boots clicked on the breaking brick as he crossed into the old city from West Gaiman.

Slowly, the landscape turned from the dirty urban cityscape

to the dust filled abandoned fronts of Old Gaiman stores and buildings. Iago methodically examined the crumbling structures, carefully looking for something very, very important. His eyes searched through the abandoned store windows and closed up bars for The Crucial Address. He stopped in front of a long abandoned storefront church. His fingers traced over the bleaching image of a flaming sword painted on the glass that flaked at each blow of the steady wind. His grin grew wider.

Iago had found what he was looking for. Now came the hard part.

There are few people that Iago couldn't handle on a regular basis. Generally, people had a very hard time dealing with Iago. The owners of the church that Iago was seeking were those people. Clans of hunters are not a group of people that one wants to be associated with in Gaiman Heights, regardless of what group you are affiliated with normally. They are almost as hated at the Marked and have a tendency to preach to you about the coming war. Iago hated them. Hunters are notoriously hard to work with or around. They are far too serious and, therefore, far too closed off to work well with others. However, this clan had what he needed. Iago stopped at the plastic-covered doorway. He looked down at the man who was sleeping in the doorway. He a rolled his eyes as he poked the man with the toe of his boot.

"Arise loyal gatekeeper," Iago commanded. "I have business with thy kinsmen."

The gatekeeper opened his good eye irately. He stood up looking at the fae through a curtain of mangled hair. Iago smiled at he looked over him with his scarred eyes, vigilantly trying to figure out who this visitor was. Once the fairy's identity registered with the gatekeeper, he sneered in irritation at the fairy. An angry growl slithered through yellowed teeth. Iago rolled his eyes again. He truly disliked the hunters. Some of them were so isolated and territorial; it was easier to deal with a rabid wolverine. You could occasionally cuddle with the wolverine.

"Thou hast no business here, fairy," said the gatekeeper. "Leave this place."

"Do you know who I am?" Iago felt offended that this hunter had the audacity to try and tell him what to do.

"Thou art Iago; Prince of Lies; the child born into the union of Loki and Morganne. Yes, I know who you are."

Iago's nose flared violently as he leaned forward, his jaw clinched like a steel trap as he looked back at the old man in anger. The gatekeeper stared back at Iago with an expressionless face. This was a dangerous place for someone to be, as a fae's wrath was not to be taken lightly. The Gatekeeper wasn't afraid of Iago. There was nothing to be scared of in this world when you have God. He was right. More importantly, he had God on his side. Iago let out a predatory growl.

"Look here, you over-evolved ape." Iago sneered again. "I'm the reason you idiots have a temple. I made you! Now, let me into thy stronghold."

"That may be the case," said the gatekeeper. "But thou art not my kinsmen. Thou art the Deceiver and not welcome in this holy place."

"I built this holy place," Iago yelled. "I will ask you one more time, grant me access."

"And I shall say it again then. No, trickster fairy. Leave this pace."

Iago looked down at the gatekeeper, searching for a chink in the metaphorical armor. The Gatekeeper looked back unfased by

Iago's demands. Iago scowled at the gatekeeper before he let out a rueful scoff. If threats weren't going to work, then they had to try something else. He was going to be using a different angle. He had a mission. Iago smiled at the Gatekeeper.

"Look," he said in a cooling tone. "There is no reason for you to get all hot and bothered. I loaned your kinsmen a few things a very long time ago. I am in need of those now. Give me what is mine. I really would hate to be violent over a few simple trinkets."

"Art thou threatening us, fairy?" asked the Gatekeeper.

"Threatening?" Iago asked, slyly batting his long lashes at the Gatekeeper. "No, telling you my desires? Totally. Can I have my things?"

The Gatekeeper shut his eyes and let out a soft sigh. His pupils moved rapidly as if reaching for something. Carefully, he looked back at Iago with the unimpressed look of disdain.

"There is no record of this agreement," said the Gatekeeper. "I shall ask you to depart from this place for the last time."

Iago pursed his lips as he contemplated his next move. There wasn't a lot of ways this ended the way he wanted. He could continue on his path without the tools, but could he then secure the ending he desired? The answer to this was no. Iago squared his shoulders. His black eyes remained trained on the Gatekeeper. His right hand reached behind him as he whispered a small prayer.

"Where there is a need and a will, guide my vengeance with indifferent steel."

Within seconds, there was a long metal spike in the fairy's sweaty hands. The Gatekeeper's eyes bugged out of their sockets for the briefest of seconds as there was a pressured sound of piercing. In a fluid and swift movement, the spike went into the Gatekeeper's skull. He didn't have time to react to the assault. Iago twisted the spike sharply before the Gatekeeper's corpse dropped to the ground with a heavy thud on the concrete. Iago looked down and let out a rueful laugh before he caught a glance of his shirt. He groaned at the dark red spots on his clean t-shirt. The one thing that he didn't want to happen in all this mess had indeed happened. He'd gotten blood on his shirt.

Iago stepped over the Gatekeeper with a lamenting sigh. He ripped off the plastic and started at the heavy oak door. He glanced back to the street for a moment. Old Gaiman was quiet during the day. No one important came out during the hours of sunlight that washed over the city. That meant the clan would be in their mundane skins for now. He rolled his fingers around the carved emblem of a flaming sword on the veneered wood. He narrowed his eyes as he thought about his next move. He couldn't use fae magic. Hunters, despite the fact that they will lie to you about it, use basic wards to keep the doors of their strongholds locked. Magic used to break through wards will just repel the wielder. Some of my finest work, he thought. His fingers traced a cross over the sword before he knocked three times at each point of the cross. The door lurched open with an archaic groan. Iago smiled quietly. He liked religious zealots. They were so predictable.

Iago started into the innocuous stronghold. It could be said that hunter strongholds are deceptively big. There is a simpler way of describing it. However a simpler description has long been associated with a very popular British Science Fiction television show. While I am a fan of this show, I'd rather not be sued by the makers of said TV show. I will simply say that strongholds are bigger on the inside. Iago started down the middle of a great long hall. He paused as he looked around the semi-dark rooms. Normally, when one breaks into a hunter's stronghold, the best place to go is the armory. Armories have the best toys. The second best place to go is the treasury. If there is a way to make a quick buck, it's ripping off the treasury. Iago wasn't looking for money or weapons though. He was looking for something far more private. What Iago was owed was more important. Iago was looking for their temple.

He spun on his heels and walked in a direction that he believed was facing Bethlehem. His eyes searched the stronghold quietly as he walked down a darker hallway. He finally came to a gilded door. Iago pushed the door open as his grin widened.

Hunter's temples are very consistent. There is always a large crucifix over a stone altar. There is also typically an icon of St. George, the patron saint of soldiers and the slayer of dragons, on the right in the Medieval finery and St. Sebastian -- also a soldier and a martyr -- on the left. In the center of this altar was a large clay urn with a small wooden box in front of it. Iago smiled as he sauntered into the room. He paused as he reached for the box. A soft whisper dancing in his ears murmuring with gentle words attempted to convince him to stop and to touch the urn instead. Iago found his eyes watering as he stopped in his tracks while the whispering invaded his ears. He looked up with his eyes wide as the writing on the urn glowed. He opened his mouth in terror.

"Knock it off!" Iago finally yelled. "Do you really think that I'm one of those monkeys you can trick into letting you out of that cute little Sumerian bento box?"

The urn stopped glowing as the whisper receded away from his ears and things suddenly became quiet. Iago clutched the box to his chest looking at the urn, shaking his head in disappointment at its occupant. He grinned.

"I know things suck for you in there," he said casually to the urn. "But don't worry; it'll be all over soon."

The urn pulsed in protest of Iago's pronouncement. Iago

snorted as he turned to exit. Then, for a second, He was hit by the sound of ten thousand screams as columns of flames flashed in his vision. He grinned as a pleasurable shiver went down his spine. Things were on the right track. Now he was off to have tea with an old friend. Iago walked down the street with a happy tune on his lips. Yea, this was a good day.

XXII. Midnight in the Garden

When Asher woke up, he felt the cool evening air blowing across his face coaxing him from his dark slumber. For a second the thought of being in a dumpster occurred to him again. He stared up at the light-scarred night sky passing over the high tree tops which eased the fears that he was indeed dead or at least in a dumpster. He felt the damp cold of descending dew soak into his jeans and t-shirt, chilling him gently enough to make his life uncomfortable. His brow furrowed as the night air blew onto his moist skin, making it harder to lie on his back and stare at the sky. Asher let out a groan as his head swam in the painful sea forced upon him by repeated blows from a National Guitar. Deftly, and with great effort, he rolled to his side. That was when he was greeted by a red-brown form. Asher blinked in confusion as the figure licked his face, happily welcoming him back to the waking world. He scratched behind the figure's ears with a weak smile.

"Hey, Yoshi," he said hoarsely. "Good to see you weren't eaten. Where's mom?"

Yoshi yapped excitedly before standing up on his short legs and waiting for Asher to join him. Asher stood up on more than wobbly legs as his stomach spun, forcing a pressure that almost contracted the muscles in his throat. The small dog trotted with great purpose through the well-manicured grass and ferns leading Asher through what seemed to be for all intents and purposes an urban Eden towards the ultimate goal. Yoshi stopped in the middle of a round clearing that formed a ring around a small sanctuary. Asher's eyes fell on the earthen altar adorned with bright green leaves sprouting from young branches within the leavenings of clay and grass.

Then, he saw his mother.

His mother was indeed there. She stood facing the altar intentionally focused on chants that were barely breathed in noiseless prayer. Her middle-aged frame hovered about six inches above the ground as her arms hung out-stretched embracing an unseen force that pulsed through her. Around her glowed a powerful white light incasing her and quietly protecting her from anything and everything that could attack her while in a vulnerable state. Below her shoeless feet, flowers and new grass sprung free from the ground and the altar without restraint. Yoshi trotted to the altar and sat beside his witch. He yapped at Asher loudly over the golden hum. He swallowed quietly before approaching the altar.

"Mom?" Asher quietly asked, afraid that he was interrupting something important but too confused to worry about it being the case.

Tracy turned gracefully to greet her son. The sad soft smile that scrolled across her lips put him ill at ease. Something bad had always followed that smile. Something terrible must have happened while he was out. Or, perhaps, he was about to take another ride on the madness train and she knew it. He took another swallow as he steeled himself for round...round...he'd lost count of where he was. She departed from the light and walked towards him with her familiar in tow.

"Sorry about that," she said breathlessly. "I haven't communed in the Garden in a long time. It's nice to still feel a spirit in this place. Did you learn anything on your Awakening?"

"Maybe?" Asher shook his head as he tried to muddle over images that he had a hard time trying to hold on to. He shook his head. "I don't know. It's all very confusing."

"I'm not surprised," she responded. "I don't think anyone learns anything from mage rituals. From what I gathered, confusion is pretty common. I don't know the specifics about your father's Awakening. I don't think he could remember his much either. He just told me that it felt like it was directed by David Lynch."

"Did you go through this, too?" Asher asked. "The vision thing?"

"No, honey," she said. "I'm a witch. Witches are visited by the Crone or, at least, a vision of her when we are called to the sisterhood. Your grandmother is a fascinating and scary woman."

"You knew Grandma Mimi before you married dad?" Asher puzzled. "And you still married him?"

She chuckled quietly.

"I didn't know she was your grandmother then. I found out when your father introduced us. If I had known, I might not have married him." She turned away with a nostalgic glaze to her watering eyes. "He proposed to me here. He knew that I loved gardens and this was the nicest one in the city. He'd just started working for the Department and I was finishing up at McKean State. We came here to picnic one Saturday. During dessert he asked me to marry him. Of course, I said yes. Then we..."

She caught herself mid-story as her skin burned a bright pink.

"Never mind."

"What is this place?" Asher asked, carefully ignoring the fact that he was standing on the spot where he was conceived.

"This is where the nexus rested before it chose you as its vessel," she explained with a wilting sigh. "I'm really sorry for not telling you sooner. I really thought it would give you a normal life not knowing what you really are."

"Yea," he said coldly. "That didn't work out so great. What am I exactly?"

"I don't really know how to explain it," she said, walking in a westerly direction. "The nexus is the final resting place for all magic. When a magical being leaves a physical form, it leaves most of its earthly magic behind. When enough of that comes together it creates a nexus for the magic to rest. It chooses a vessel and remains for all time. That is you, dear. You are that vessel. Other than that? You are who you've always been. You are Asher Pennywise Stone. You are my son. You are Jordan's and Carin's brother. Nothing, now or forever, will change that."

"Why not tell me?" The information hadn't quite sunk into Asher's beaten head just yet.

"We thought it was for the best." Regret from her actions bled through on each syllable of her words. "Your father wanted to tell you when you were old enough. It's the responsibility of the elder order member to educate an apprentice, doubly so if it's a descendant. When he died, I sought the advice of the Crone. She said that you were safer as a veiled human. I was going to defy the Crone when you turned sixteen but then I met Brady and things got complex."

"Brady doesn't know about magic." Reality finally sank in from her words, opening irrational gashes through which seeped through pure rage. "How can he not know about magic?"

"Because he's a normal person," she said. "You just can't tell a normal person about magic."

"Why not?" asked an enraged Asher. This wasn't only about the fact that everything about him was a lie. It was the conspiracy of silence that surrounded him to create this lie that made him angry. "Seems like it would be less of a headache if people didn't lie to each other. Do you really think I won't tell Natalie?"

"That isn't your call," she said sharply. The ground shook lightly under their feet. "Our job is to protect the mundane world from us. That means limiting the exposure and not shoving them into our world."

"And not telling me did what?" Fury flew off Asher's lips in clear wet drops. "I've had a weird-ass day and then I find out not only that magic is real, but I'm also some sort of Messiah which, by the way, is a lot of pressure. Now you're telling me I can't mention that to anyone? Bull shit!!! You give me one good god damn reason not to share this with the world!"

"Very simple," she said in an even measured tone, over-enunciating her words. "You haven't seen what being unveiled can do to an average person. It can and has driven people completely insane. Asher, before you go off and play Deep Throat about a world that you barely understand, ask yourself one question; can you live with yourself when Natalie spends the rest of her life in Twillingast Asylum?"

Asher tensed as he thought about Natalie. Her gentle frame sitting in the corner of a padded room hugging herself trying to keep the filth and madness away from herself to hold on to sanity. Her eyes darting terrified at imaginary specters that floated around her head whispering nightmarish songs and accusing her of sins that were less terrible than she'd believed. Her knees brought up to her chest, trying to protect her fear aching heart. He could see her lips move noiselessly begging for mercy between screams. She'd hate it in there even if she wasn't crazy but she would be crazy and hurting. He couldn't do that to her. His body eased reluctantly as Tracy stepped closer.

"I know you're upset," she said quietly. "I don't blame you for being upset but don't let that impair your judgment. Think calmly like your father or mother would have done. Now, more than ever, do what you have to in order to keep your loved ones safe."

"And I do that how exactly?" he asked, calming down.

"Asher," she said softly. "You have all the natural skills and spells to be a great mage. Even if you don't fine tune your abilities, you're a force to be reckoned with and that's what you do. You defend yourself and your family like you did with the manticore."

"I killed that manticore with your katana," he told her stupidly. "Like I was a Zatoichi."

"That's not surprising either," she said. "When your father was finishing his apprenticeship, his elder gave him that katana. According to Kaito Yahakara, it's a Masamunse blade. He called the blade the Sekken or, in English, the Stone Sword. They say that Masamunse crafted swords that could only be wielded for good causes and held by honorable men. I don't know if that's true about Sekken, but I do know one thing; that sword can be wielded by two men; you and your father. Half of the spell is on the sword and the rest is on your wrist. Stephen insisted on it."

"Mom?" Asher asked hesitantly.

"No, Asher, we're still not in Back to the Future: Part Two."

"No, not that, but thanks for the reassurance. It was a concern of mine," he responded. "But how do you know that I'm not evil?"

"Truthfully?" she said quietly. "I was worried about that myself when you were born. Pure magic and very powerful beings are easily corrupted by human frailty. I've seen too many good witches turn to black magic because of their craving for power. I used to think it was power that corrupted. Asher, *mon petite*, I can tell you that it's not power that corrupts but how a person uses that power. You use power for evil and it will corrupt your soul. I'd like to think my oldest son is a good person who will do the right thing with whatever he's given."

Asher sighed as he looked up at the starless night sky. He rubbed the back of his neck.

"Mom," he said quietly after a long pause, "I'm scared."

"We all are," Tracy said as her pale hand settled on his cheek. "But, *mon petite*, please keep that fear. It'll keep you human, but don't let it rule you. The one thing that'll end you quicker than anything is being choked by fear."

"Mom, what if I fail?" he asked.

"It's better to die on your feet than to live on your knees, *mon petite*." Her voice trembled with pride. "Failing while giving 100% isn't really failure. Asher, I have nothing but faith in you. You are destined for great things."

"Can I go home?" Apprehension melted into his words. "I want to make sure Natalie is all right."

"I don't see why not," she said. "It would be good for you to reconnect to normalcy. I'll get Karl and Norvita to drive you home. You know he's been looking for you all day."

"I had no idea," Asher said, feeling lightly guilty.

"Yes, dear," she said. "You're kind of a big deal."

XXIII. On the Origins of Magic

The existence of beings with supernatural powers is simply part of the fabric of reality and has always existed whether you want to believe it or not. It hasn't, as the skeptics want to think, dwindled in an atomic age of reason nor was it born out of superstition from long ago. It is the unexplained, intangible part of being alive that has been woven into every atom of our being whether you believe it is there or not. Magic has existed long before you, I or even Mim, can remember. As best as anyone could tell, as long as there have been people there has been magic. This does not mean that magical beings know the origins of their species so to speak. Like mundane humans, the question of "why are we here?" has plagued magical beings for generations. Well, not every magical creature is concerned with this question. The more primal creatures, i.e. ogres, trolls, and the like have never questioned their existence. This isn't a sign of unintelligence in the primal creatures. In fact, it's quite the opposite. They just fail to see the purpose of worrying about a question that they aren't able to answer. Many see this as a sign that the less cultivated beings are far smarter than everyone else combined. However, the higher societal creatures, vampires, witches, and magi find themselves more domesticated and, therefore, having more free time. They find themselves preoccupied with the question that has haunted philosophers and theologians for generations. Each race has their own idea of where they came from. Despite the differences of the species, these views are somewhat similar to each other.

If there is one species that finds themselves obsessed with their origins, it's the vampires. It is widely believed that the crux of this obsession comes from the very nature of the vampiric condition.

Vampires aren't born, despite what the media and Stephanie Meyers books will tell you. Vampires are created from the human clay in a violent manner. Because of their mortal heritage, they are burdened by the question of Why that all children of Adam are burdened with from birth. Then that humanity is ripped away from them in a highly ritualized murder. The final step of this is the once human being who wanted to know why is transformed into something less than human. They become a monster born out of death who callously feeds on the blood of living.

For a sane person, this transformation would be traumatic and raise a variety of questions. Of course, no one said that vampires were sane people before their fall. Most vampires were damaged long before they succumbed to the cold embrace. Even if that isn't the case, vampires are some of the least-liked creatures in the supernatural world -- not as disliked as say, The Marked, or even worse, hunters -- because of how they are created. By and large the resurrection of the dead is very uncomfortable for the living. The only exception was a nice Jewish carpenter who, a couple of thousand years ago, said some very nice things. Despite his rising from the dead, many people seemed happy to see him alive and mostly well after his ordeal. However, most resurrections, excluding that Jewish carpenter, are often done through dark magic or mad science. The birth of a vampire is highly ritualized and reeks of blood magic, a very dangerous form of black magic, which makes everyone uncomfortable. The pariah status begs the vampire question of why.

This is why many elder vampires are obsessed with tracing their lineage, from offspring to progenitor, for generations in an effort to find the very first, or alpha, vampire. But who was the first vampire? No one knows. Many have speculated, but their conclusions vary, depending on the age and nationality of the vampire. Vampires have always existed in every culture. In Southeast Asia and China, vampires believe that they are descended from the jiang shi or the hopping corpses. The Asian vampires believe they are relics of the wizard's curse that created the jiang shi. Middle Eastern vampires have a similar creation story. They believe that they are descended from Ninkasi, the goddess of wine. It is believed that the wizard Enki created Ninkasi to feed him life wine, or blood, to cure his failing mouth. This is not a popular idea in the west. Many believe that this is due to the fact that many western vampires would rather not owe a wizard a damn thing.

Another factor is age. Older vampires cling to the cults, but those are vampires older than two-thousand-years old. Those vampires are extremely rare. Younger and, therefore, westernized vampires believe less in ancient wizards. Many of them belong to the Catholic sect called the Iscariotites. The Iscariotites believe that when the nice Jewish carpenter, while he was talking to his Father about something that he wasn't quite sure he wanted to do, was in a garden he was betrayed by a kiss. The person who did this was paid back with the curse for his troubles. Some will tell you that they are the children of a loan Roman Centurian who was given a raw deal because of that poor Jewish carpenter. Younger European Jewish Vampires and a few radical non-Jewish vampires will claim a heritage from Ham, or Cain, or even Lilith

With the dawn of the modern era, the dependence on Biblical reference for support of the condition decreased. Many vampires under the age of six hundred believe that the vampiric condition is less of a curse, but more of a disease. It made sense to believe that it was illness after a long period of time. The Black Death was an illness and was once believed to be a curse, so why couldn't the vampiric condition be the same? The younger or more educated vampires change their views of the condition based on the changing field of science. For example, in 1859 the <u>Origin of Species</u> was published. This caused many vampires to believe that they are an evolutionary offshoot of Humanity.

Witches, on the other hand, believe that they are simply extensions of the ancient religions that have been long forgotten by people. Their powers were once shared with archaic priestesses which is why many witches hold themselves to rituals to focus their powers. They will tell you that magic comes from the Crone in a weird birth myth. Once that magic was given to the world, it was broken up into three houses of power: earth -- elemental magic tied to the use of natural elements; white -- power used to combat evil and for healing; and black, which is evil magic. The Crone will tell you that all of this is true. This is a lie. The Crone, in reality, doesn't know where her abilities came from either. All she does know is that she was different and she was going to be very powerful.

Witches believe that they are ordinary people who have found a way to tap into elemental magic through focusing on rituals and tapping into the natural energy that flows through reality itself. Once a witch first taps into that power, they are visited by a vision of the Crone who welcomes them into the sisterhood. Then, they are sent out on their merry way to craft the prayers that'll give them power. The existence of humanity and why we are here becomes less important to comprehend than the understanding of how to manage their powers and serve the path they have chosen to walk.

Mages have a different view of the origins of magic. Mages believe that there is a spark in the human soul that powers magical abilities. Every person, it is speculated, has these gifts. This accounts for the soothsayers, the psychics, and the like. Mages are said to have an extra spark that they have honed through careful study, turning the focus inward as opposed to witches who focus their abilities outward through ritual.

Unlike witches, mages study ancient tomes to hone their craft. They believe that knowledge is the key to the magic they wield. Of course, knowledge doesn't necessarily have to be learned from tomes. In many tribal societies, mages pass their knowledge of inner study through oral tradition from elder to apprentice.

With this wealth of knowledge, you would think the magi would have the most knowledge of any about we are here. They don't. In fact, the magi are the most clueless about where people come from and why. This is because mages that are in charge of finding those answers have yet to find an answer. Once they do, then the magi will tell you what they think.

It would be incorrect and rude to assume that the fairies don't find themselves preoccupied with this question. Usually such thoughts pass off like a belch and they move on. What fairies are more concerned with is how other creatures came to be in the world. Fairies know they'll never understand where they came from and if they did, they wouldn't want to know. No one is quite sure why this would be the case but the speculation is simply that the truth wouldn't compare to the stories, then why bother trying to compete? They are more interested in inserting themselves into humanity's creation story. The proof, they say, is the existence of organized religion. The idea of worshiping a being with super powers is clearly a fae construct. Many devout people have lost their minds and their faith listening to the claims of the fae. The fae are, of course, lying. The truth is that the fae have no clue as to where we came from or why we are here. Not only that, they don't care. All fairies really want is to watch people squirm.

The only group who know everything about it are the angelic or the demonic. Being around since the dawn of time gives them that kind of insight about these things. Convincing them to tell you is another story. Demons won't tell you. They'll tell you they will, but ultimately, they won't. Angels, on the other hand, will tell you everything but only as a incomprehensible parable that no one will understand.

My suggestion? Just keep wondering, it's much safer.

XXIV. And It Fell Apart.

Phase one was complete. He'd shoved Natalie off to her fate in the thick of the Hedge, thus starting the descent towards the final stages of his perfectly crafted plan. She was, he believed, probably dinner for a naga by now. Iago didn't care if she was alive or dead. It was irrelevant to him. Her purpose had been served and Asher would follow her into the Hedge.

He had his tools; check.

Now, came phase two. That was where Puck came into his master plan. Puck wasn't aware of his role yet, but he would know soon enough. Puck should have known by this point without Iago telling him what his role was, nothing had changed in the time that they'd been together. They had been co-conspirators for eons and long before time had been counted by rational thought. Iago had always dragged Puck through his scenes with the intent of them sharing in every moment of chaos that could come forth from him. Puck would be resistant to his plan at first, then he'd be convinced pretty easily. It was how it worked; their dance towards the end goal. However, it was getting harder to convince Puck since they'd been in exile. The longer they stayed in the mundane world, the softer he'd become and the more stubborn Puck became. It was a humiliating experience for them. Puck seemed more affected by the loss than he let on. If Iago didn't know better he would have said that Puck felt remorse for their crimes. He needed to stop that. Puck was being dangerously cautious these days.

Iago paced while waiting in Puck's office for his long-term friend. He was bracing for a fight. He had to prepare for this. This fight was going to be an uphill battle for him. Puck had said that he was going to think about it. The more time that he had after the proposal not being convinced, the more likely he was going to come up with a reason to not do it. Iago had come too far to not go through with this plan. He stopped mid-pace when the bell from a Prohibition Era elevator cut through his thoughts. He turned to see a green door and it's occupant who skipped out of the elevator quietly. Amaya smiled at Iago. He smiled back, carefully calculating this moment for his next option.

"Hiya, Iago," she said loudly, being as friendly as she had ever been. "Have you seen Puck?"

"Hiya Amaya," Iago replied, attempting to mask his vicious plans. "I haven't. I was waiting on him."

"Oh." She made a hesitating face. Her bare toe ground into the concrete floor trying to control herself. "Hey, Iago. You know your plan? The one to unite home with this super boring place?"

"I sure do!" Iago said confidently. "It's my best to plan to date."

"I'm sure it is, except, well," Amaya wavered lightly as she decided whether or not to break Iago's heart. She twirled a strand of her blue purple hair around her finger. "Breaking open the vessel at a thin spot on the Hedge would cause an explosion that'll destroy both worlds and all marshmallow peeps. They've been separated for way too long. It'll be bad; like really, really, really bad."

Iago leaned in, putting his face inches away from the water nymph's face, narrowing his eyes at her. His sparkling black eyes bored his irritation into her skull, trying to rip her soul apart for questioning him about this plan. Amaya knew what he knew or had hoped he knew. This meant that Puck would know or he already knew. That did not bode well for the rest of the day. No matter, Iago would do what he needed to do move forward. This had been the theme of his day, finding a problem and then fixing it by any means necessary. He forgot how good he was at this. *Shame,* he thought, *I have to do this again. Oh well. A better need is being served.* Slowly, his jagged smirk transformed into a malicious tooth-lined grin. His hands secretly went into his jacket pockets as he snorted at her.

"Really, Amaya?" he asked as his demeanor changed rapidly to dark designs. Ears were perked listening for frailty. Tails were coiled with a violent rattle. He was about to strike.

"Yea huh, Iago," Amaya said, nodding firmly and oblivious to the sudden change. Being trusting would be her downfall one of these days. "The Elders said so. They also said you were there at the time of the split. Maybe you forgot because it was a really long time ago. I mean wow Iago, you're super old, like dawn of time old."

While Amya rambled about Iago's age, Iago thought about how this could all go. He already knew the ending of this play. I do too, but I wrote the story so don't worry. I have no intention of giving any spoilers. But it's ok -- we're at Chapter Twenty Four; we're pretty close to the end anyway. Hey, thanks for reading this far. It means a lot to me that you have.

He also knew that he wanted his best friend there with him at the end of things. He wanted to look at Puck's face as they marveled at his handiwork just before the end of things. For that to happen, the final act had to be played out as he'd written it. He had to remove some outlying factors. There was no hesitation now. Amaya normally might not let the secret spill if he promised to give her something, but Marshmallow Peeps were in danger. He knew what had to be done. Iago slowly pulled his hands from his pockets, encased in a pair of thin leather gloves. Smiling, he reached behind him.

Much later, Amaya would rest gently in Puck's arms. She'd

look up sweetly at him and ask him why he had an iron poker in his office. He'd run his fingers through her beautiful hair and tell her it was just in case Iago went crazy. He knew that at some point he'd have to use it on him. She would then ask him how well did that work out? He'd kiss her forehead and tell her how very sorry he was for everything that had happened.

Iago swung the poker with a cracking blow into Amaya's doll like face. He all but took her jaw off with the second crushing swing. She recoiled from the blows, spilling into Puck's desk and holding on for support as her legs gave out from under her. An Arctic blast of pain radiated through her skull and neck from the repeated assault. Iago swung again hitting the back of her head with a freezing thwack that forced her to lose her grasp on reality. She collapsed on the concrete floor as her blue glittering blood exploded from her hair and dripped down her neck. It stained the collar of her tunic and it formed a puddle around her body. Her shock-spasming body writhed towards the exit, attempting to escape as she tried hard to focus on a door, any door. It came out jumbled on her lips as they stopped working the way she wanted them to. She was met with another bone-breaking cold strike to her spine that gave out a stomach turning snap. She suddenly fell into stiffness on the floor of the office. The imprinted patterns on her skin drained to a lifeless gray as her blood ran quickly from her lips and nose and formed sickly sweet puddles under her face as she gasped for air. Iago rolled the battered water nymph to her back admiring his handiwork while she convulsed and tried to hold on to life. *Hmm,* he thought, *I made a mistake.*

Next time, I should do this near a vampire nest. There would be nothing left.

He pressed the heel of his boot into her chest as he jabbed the pointed edge of the poker into the pallid flesh of her throat. She gasped with panicked breaths as her vocal cords and windpipe froze. Her river stone blue eyes begged Iago for mercy or at least for a reason for this assault. She wanted to know why.

"Don't look so hurt, nymph," he said as cold as the poker twisting against her trachea. "This plan has been a very long time coming and now you're in the way, but you're right. I should have known about the effects of that kind of explosion. I killed the first vessel when I ripped the two worlds apart. Don't worry, I'll fix it, but I don't need you stopping me by running your mouth. I need you do something very important though. Amaya, I need you to die for me."

Iago raised the poker above her helpless body dramatically. He plunged the penetrating edge of the poker into her smooth stomach. A freezing pain shook her body as big drops of horror rolled down her cheeks. Iago pulled out the poker with satisfied grunt. He lifted the poker higher preparing for the second erotic blow.

"Iago!" Puck yelled in surprised horror as he walked in to discover the grizzly scene. Iago looked up from his hunched position as he backed away. Puck rushed on the wings of angels to his nymph's side. His hands played over her dying features. "Why?"

"Because usually, she likes rough penetration," Iago quipped darkly. Puck sneered at the callous words. Iago rolled his eyes at Puck's indignation. "Oh don't act all surprised. That little slut had it coming."

"This wasn't part of your plan," Puck said. His voice broke in disjointed grief. "Iago, if she dies, I don't want to go home...ever."

"Oh I wouldn't' worry about us going home," Iago said nonchalantly. "I gave up on that a long time ago."

"But you said..."

"That breaking down the Hedge would merge the two

worlds," Iago cut in. "That is true. Of course, as I expected, and Amaya confirmed, the resulting explosion will destroy both worlds."

Iago paused for dramatic effect. He let out an overly fake sigh as a part of his act.

"She was going to tell you that I wanted you to help me at the end of things, so I tried to kill her. It would have worked until you walked in." Iago shrugged. "Oh well. In retrospect, I guess I should have let sleeping dogs lie. The outcome would be the same. Come or not. At this point there's not much you can do to stop me at this time."

"You're going to destroy all of existence -- for what, Iago?" Puck yelled. "Because you have a grudge?"

"Yes!" Iago said quickly. He then thought about his answer for a moment. "Well, that and it'll be the last great act of Chaos. No one will do it better than me!"

"Iago," Puck shook his head, "This is madness."

In a predatorily swift swoop, Iago came inches away from Puck. His hot breath wreathed down along Puck's face in a violent snarl. Puck jumped back with a startled bleat as he stumbled on to his knees. His eyes widened as if he was staring down the maw of a hungry jackal.

"Go on. Be cliché," Iago barked through his terrible fangs. "Say something else about how I won't get away with it. Tell me how you will stop me. Because right now you can't. At this point, no one can."

"No, I know I can't." Puck snarled defiantly. "But the mages can and will."

Iago snorted as he slunk back. His feet placed one right in front of the other as he leaned forward stalking his prey. Slowly a squealing howl of a laugh escaped his lips.

"At this point, Puck, I don't even think the mages could stop me. I assume they don't know." Iago laughed. "What the hell, let's make this more interesting. Go tell them, I dare you."

If you want to convince a fairy to do something, dare them to do it. When you dare a fairy they assume cannot do it. Out of pure spite, the fairy will attempt to complete the dare. Case in point, Iago didn't think Puck could do it, so Puck had to prove Iago wrong.

Puck stood up braced with defiance. Then, he looked down at Amaya's gray and still body. If he didn't act on his defiance, he'd lose her in a rare feat. He gave Iago a stern look as he scooped up the fading water nymph in his arms protectively. The couple vanished in a puff of blue purple smoke. Iago sighed disapprovingly as the smoke dissipated from the office. Puck had made a poor choice. Even if Puck told the mages, they could try to thwart his plans. They could try, but they wouldn't succeed. Puck really should have cast his lot with the winning team. It was most disappointing that he hadn't. Iago shrugged. He could always use the extra diversion. There was nothing left for them to interfere with at this point. The parts had been cast. The stage had been set. All that was left was to wait for the audience to take their seats and the curtain to go up. Iago grinned. This was going to be a great show and he knew where to find the best seat in the house.

XXV. Land of Confusion

Natalie felt her breath rush back to her lungs as her eyes watched the purple sky convulse with life as it draped over the blue-green trees and fire-red mountains. Her feet sank into the soft shag carpeted ground as she stepped forward into this new world. If I am dead, she thought, at least hell is pretty. She felt her shoulders tighten as a wave of apprehension jerked through her body and she looked around trying to recognize something. Her hands pulled at each other as she walked along a path attempting to make what she was seeing fit into her understanding of the world. Beside her, walking in close step with her timid steps, was the purple blur. Its tail switched protectively close to the back of Natalie's legs. She knew it had a tail; she knew it was purple, but looking directly at it was like trying to see through those fuzzy censorship boxes they put over genitals or witnesses' faces on prime time TV. She blinked as a frightened shudder went through her body, telling her that nothing was right to her. The blur nuzzled into her calf trying to calm this dread. The blur could smell the fear off the doctor. Natalie's fingers reached down and stroked the soft fur of the blur. The big cat thing let out a heavy purr, approving of the attention. At least she had a friend in all of this.

Natalie yawned tiredly. She felt like she had been awake for thousands of years and the day was pulling on her like hot sweat. Tiredness threatened to claim her legs and body pull her into a fatigued slumber. Her eyes searched the growing forest of ninety-foot peace lilies and orchids that formed a floral canopy over her head. She wrinkled her nose at the warm sweet smell of flowers turning her stomach.

"Curiouser and curiouser," she muttered

When she was a little girl, her mother would read her <u>Alice in Wonderland </u>before she'd fall asleep. Now, as she walked on, she wondered if Alice felt tired through her adventures with the March Hare and chasing the White Rabbit. Of course not, she told herself. Alice was a child and children would never get tired of silly things. They would skip through and find this a wondrous place. So, either she was in hell or in Wonderland. What would Alice do if she found herself here? She'd find a smiling cat or a hookah-smoking caterpillar to give her some guidance. She did have a cat, but it didn't seem to talk or smile. It was simply a cat. OK, a huge purple cat, but still. There wasn't a caterpillar, just more large flowers hanging over her head. At least the flowers weren't telling her she was an ugly weed. That was her least favorite part of Alice's story. She wavered lightly before she stopped moving her feet. Natalie collapsed to her knees from exhaustion, unable to keep walking any more. She slumped forward and let out a tired yawn. The blur lay down beside her offering his back as a pillow. Natalie rested her head on the beast and buried her face into the soft fur. Finally, Natalie shut her eyes.

She didn't notice it at first. Sleep was heavy on her and it was so gentle. She wasn't sure about what it was on her arm. She thought maybe it was Bag of Bones cleaning himself next to where she'd fallen asleep on the couch. Despite his age, the cat was quite affectionate towards her. Then, it occurred to Natalie that this wasn't her home. The reality of her situation was slowly settling in around her. She had fallen asleep in a foreign place. Slowly, she opened her eyes. Natalie was met by a chin as a tongue slid down her nose. Natalie naturally did what any confused person would do. She let out a terrible scream.

The figure also let out a scream as it backed off of Natalie.

She sat up as the blur rose and slinked between the two protectively. The figure looked back at Natalie through a curtain of curly brown coppery hair. Natalie blinked quietly. Clearly, this wasn't a wild beast. This woman wasn't too much older than her. She couldn't be. Natalie leaned forward over the blur. The figure leaned forward also, staring at Natalie.

"H-H-Hello?" Natalie said in a shaking voice. She hugged against the blur. This was a new thing for her and she'd worked the night shift in the E.R. "Are you lost here too?"

The girl pushed her hair out of her face as she crawled towards the blur and Natalie. She carefully inspected Natalie before shaking her head with a fervent no. Natalie nodded, getting somewhere or at least so she thought.

"Okay..." Natalie said slowly. "Do you know where we are?"

The girl nodded her head happily in a yes. Natalie blinked slowly.

"I...see." Natalie was starting to get tired again. "Can I ask you where we are?"

The girl nodded yes again. Natalie let out an exasperated huff at the girl.

"You don't talk do you?"

"Oh no, I can," said the girl cheerfully. "You didn't ask me if I wanted to talk."

Natalie blinked stupidly at the words coming from the girl. The next thing she did was laugh. A stunned laugh pushed through her throat as tears stung her cheeks. Her nose wrinkled as she let out a sob. One sob turned into another and then another. Natalie buried her face into the blur's fur letting out a loud wail. The girl crawled under the blur. She then wrapped her arms around Natalie in a comforting hug.

"Oh, God," Natalie wailed. "I'm in hell."

"Nope and nope," said the girl as she continued to hug Natalie.

"What?"

"You're not in hell and I'm not God," replied the girl.

"Then, where am I?" Natalie asked for the first time that day.

"Arcadia," said the girl. "It's not hell. Nothing smells that bad. I hear Hell has a better jazz bar though. We're working on that. I mean who ever heard of Hell having a better jazz bar than us!"

At this juncture, Natalie was no longer convinced she was dead. No matter what transgression she'd committed in this life, it just didn't warrant this kind of punishment. This place was beyond anyone's construct. What it felt like was she was slipping away from sanity. It had finally happened. Her time with Asher had finally broken her. She was probably on the carpet of their apartment babbling about the pretty colors. That made perfectly good sense. The confounding girl, the large purple cat and even Asher being a demon could easily be explained by a psychotic break. She knew that when the hallucinations subsided, she was going to find herself in the middle of Twillingast Asylum.

Oh God, she thought, I've become one of them. Natalie had worked in the E.R. when the crazy ones came in to the Hospital. Didn't they babble about the things they saw before them? It was always about the bright colors and lights. That's why they all talked about the white light in the hospital. They'd talk about that in the same breath as the monsters on the street. Natalie had gotten to the point where she ignored the insane ramblings of her patients. Again, typical residents of Gaiman Heights generally ignored what they didn't understand. Natalie didn't understand and she didn't want to understand. She was happy enough going through the routine that she went through every day and becoming numb to the madness. It was easy when it was the same voices and the same stories again and again. As of late, though, that had become more difficult. On Asher's last birthday, she'd gotten his name tattooed on her wrist. It was fine work -- even Evil Edward said so. The weird thing was the recent comments. More than one person had commented on the blue light radiating off of the tattoo. She wondered if there was something in the ink that caused madness. No wonder Asher was always weird and that she had followed him into the abyss. The things that she did for Asher.

Asher?

Everything was fuzzy. Her apartment, the fall, what she had for lunch were just a distant memory. Even the time she spent walking in the Hedge was far away. With all that was drifting away from her, Asher remained vivid in her mind's eyes. Every time she thought about him, she could feel him smiling into her neck. She felt herself smile. When that happened somehow, she knew she was safe. She looked back at the girl and the blur. She nodded quietly as she stood up.

"Okay," Natalie said quietly. "Where is Arcadia in relation to Gaiman Heights?"

"It's not nowhere near Gaiman Heights," said the girl. "Puck lives in Gaiman Heights and he lives far away from here so it's far away."

"I...see," Natalie said, not really caring who Puck was. "And where is Arcadia?"

"Here," the girl said. Natalie sighed. Then, the girl blurted out. "Are you a mage?"

"What?"

"You're dumb and you smell funny," the girl replied. "Are you a mage?"

"Are you always this rude?" Natalie asked.

"Oh, always," said the girl. "But you started it, mage, you insulted my home."

"What's a mage?"

The girl turned her head to one side and blinked. *Silly blonde girl that tastes like magic and doesn't know what she is,* the girl thought, *that's silly.* For a moment, she wondered if stupidity cursed mages. She blinked again.

"Do you still use the word wizard?" asked the girl. "Are you a wizard, mage?"

"No," Natalie said. "I'm not a mage."

"Well, you smell like one."

"Do you ever stop talking?"

"Nu uh," said the girl. "I have a lot to say."

"A lot to say?" Natalie fumed. "You haven't said a word that was useful!"

"Not my fault," said the girl. "You haven't asked for help."

"Fine!" Natalie conceded through gritted teeth. "What's your name?"

"My name is Penny," Penny said. "Changeling and the very best friend of Amaya: Princess of the Midnight Rain and the daughter of the Queen of the Wild River. Betrothed and bound to the Fourteenth son of Pan; Puck."

"Right, my name is Natalie. Penny will you help me?"

"Yea, I will."

"Great." Natalie let out a sigh of relief. "Can you help me out of here?"

Penny nodded as she stood up gingerly. She offered her hand to the lost doctor. Natalie smiled quietly as she took Penny's hand. She swallowed as she looked forward. The blur rose up with a soft purr. Without warning, Penny skipped off in a direction. Natalie stumbled as she followed Penny. The blur followed Natalie. She looked around as they walked deeper into the thick floral jungle. The giant leaves started to obscure the Impressionist-painted sky. Natalie swallowed a she saw eyes flickering in the shadows. She squeezed Penny's hand tightly as they skipped along. The jungle vibrated with a wild animal calls out of the greenery. Natalie jumped when she heard a second one. She furrowed her brow, listening closer to the calls settled into a familiar rhythm of song. She was right. The animals were crying you in the night to the tune of Toto's Africa. The blur padded behind the pair quietly.

The assembled party reached outside of the forest just as a lemon yellow sun painted a purple sky to pink and yellow with dawn's first light. For a moment, Natalie thought she was home. With the light beaming down, it almost looked like the Winterfell Mountains that lay due west of Gaiman Heights. That was until light fell onto a bone colored castle carved out of the side of the mountain. Natalie's jaw fell slack as she let out a pained squeak. Penny looked back and smiled.

"This isn't Gaiman Heights," Natalie stammered angrily. "You said you'd get me out of here!"

"I said I'd get you out of the forest," Penny corrected, "and I did."

"But I wanted to go home!" Natalie squealed angrily. She was reaching her wit's end.

"You didn't say that," Penny said. "Whose fault is that?"

Natalie let out an exasperated gasp before screaming a series of incoherent consonants that spat out in an angry pattern from her lips. She wanted to hit Penny, but that didn't seem right to her. She had to make the best of this and that didn't mean hitting a well-meaning and annoying little girl. She didn't wait for a reaction from Penny. Instead she turned on her heels and marched towards the Ivory Tower. By this time, you know that when Natalie has had enough of insanity she becomes determined to makes things better.

Of course, you also know that at this point in our tale that she was often oblivious to mortal danger.

In her defense, this danger hadn't been liberated from his stone sheath until Natalie stood before it. Once it was awakened, the beast strode towards the doctor with his double edged axe in his hands. His neck forcefully popped causing the careful inlayed silver of his Brahma horns to dance in the glittering sun. Natalie jerked to a halt in terror.

Despite the plethora of things that had happened today, a Minotaur was the last thing she expected to be running into physically. She took a shuddering step back as the great Minotaur lowered its head to meet Natalie's gaze in a greatly aggravated manner. She felt a scream choke out of her throat as the Minotaur's nostrils flared with each heavy snort. Her choked scream came out louder when she transfixed her gaze on the dancing gold ring swaying in his septum with each heavy snort. As if on cue, the blur leapt over Natalie's shoulders and towards the Minotaur. The Minotaur raised its large hands and battled at the large cat much like one swats at a fly. Natalie found herself crystallizing with terror as her only ally crumpled to the ground. She glanced back looking for Penny. Natalie's hapless guide to this new world had disappeared. Natalie thought this was a wise idea and decided to follow Penny's lead. Just as she turned, the Minotaur snatched Natalie's messy ponytail. She screamed as he lifted her up by her hair.

"What do you think you're doing, mage?" the Minotaur gravely bellowed.

Natalie opened her mouth, letting an arid vowel sound escape her lips. Her feet kicked in the futile protest. She wasn't sure why she thought that would work. It hadn't before; there was no indication that it would work now. The words of her defense were stuck in mucusy lumps hanging on the sides of her throat, stopping anything that could save her. No, she wasn't a mage. She was a doctor who was lost. She didn't know how she got there, not really. She could guess. She was tired, scared and all alone. All she wanted was to go home and back to her bed. Think Natalie, she told herself, what would Alice do? She would talk her way out of this. Natalie wasn't that good at talking her way out of things. She wasn't Asher. Asher had a perfectly silver tongue that would have been perfect at these times.

Asher.

Natalie licked her lips as she squared her dangling shoulders with determination. Her quivering body stared back at the Minotaur in terror. She breathed in confidence as she mustered the will to speak. Her protested remarks came out as a squeak. The Minotaur roared at her.

"Thou refusest to speak to me," he roared. "Brianus of Crete! The sworn protector of the Ivory Palace, home of our great king Oberon and his fair Lady Titania. If thou wilt not speak to me then I will hand thee over to our Great King for Judgement."

"But," she finally mustered.

"Silence, Mage!" the Minotaur bellowed.

The Minotaur turned quickly towards the palace dragging Natalie behind him. Natalie watched frantically as the world passed around her. The gold and gem encrusted door opened carefully for them. The Minotaur continued to drag the doctor down a long blue hallway. Natalie's eyes watched as the frescos whirled above her. If she wasn't so terrified she would have found this beautiful. She felt the Minotaur stop. Quickly, he tossed Natalie onto a set of stairs with brutal force. She cast her glance up the stairs with apprehension. In this situation, she expected to see a large throne. Instead, there was a solid gold tub before her. Her eyes watched as the purple bubbles rose then popped, letting out light scents. A slender golden-haired figure peered over the edge of the tub to watch her. Natalie quivered as the blond man looked her over.

"Brian!" said the man disappointedly, "That isn't the rubber ducky I requested. I guess I could play with her in the bath though. Toss her in."

Brian nodded before picking up Natalie. He carefully dropped the young doctor into the bath water. For a moment, Natalie sank into the warm water and hit the bottom of the tub. She paused to enjoy the refreshing current before she rose up again. She resurfaced in enough time to watch the curly haired man wave off the Minotaur who, surprisingly to her, departed. Natalie watched as the blond man plucked out the floating flip flops from the tub. He nonchalantly tossed them on to the ground with a wet thump. Natalie shivered watching him.

"I would have gotten you out of those clothes first, but whatever," he said with a sigh. "I love your nail color. Is that natural?"

"I-I-I'm not a mage," Natalie said quickly.

"I know that," King Oberon said. "If you were a mage that awful smell wouldn't be coming off you so easily. Your feet are already starting to smell better. Who's Asher?"

Natalie looked back him with her pretty eyes wide. Had she almost forgotten about him in the bath? How could she have forgotten his name? More importantly, how did this man know who he was? She rubbed her tattooed wrist carefully. Oh.

"He's, he's my boyfriend," she whispered.

"Oh, well, then you're single and here forever," said the king. "Ever thought about getting married?"

"Not recently…no."

"I know!" squealed the Great King clapping his hands. "You could marry me! I haven't had a new wife in ages."

"Wait, what?" Natalie said hastily. This didn't ring right to her. She wasn't looking to marry someone she'd just met.

"Wouldn't this be just grand?" He hugged Natalie's foot in his excitement about a wedding. "Oh I just love this idea!"

"What' if I don't want to get married?" Natalie said quickly. She had to think fast.

"You can offer me a bargain, something in trade," said the king with a lascivious leer. "Maybe a game of chance, you know, like chess or marbles. I might be considerate about not doing something that might tip the odds."

"Cards," she said quickly. "I'm really good at cards."

"Ooooh, that's a new one. Let's play cards."

XXVI. No More Stones

She stared at Asher eagerly as she perched her arms and head like a parrot on the headrest of the passenger seat as if she were eyeing a tasty-looking treat. Asher blinked and looked back at the exotic looking girl feeling like a caged oddity. Norvita was pretty, but the longer she stared at him, the more uncomfortable Asher felt. No one likes being looked at for a very long time. He fidgeted in the back seat as she continued to stare at him eagerly. Finally, he smiled back at her. Norvita let out a soft seductive giggle. The passenger side door opened suddenly. Within seconds, she was in the back seat with him and firmly placed on Asher's very confused lap. Asher tried to back himself into a corner with a nervous smile plastered on his face. The smell of want and pheromones wafted under his nose.

"You're really pretty," she said in a sweet husky voice as her body pushed against his, eagerly coaxing a sexual moment..

"Thanks," he said hesitantly. "So are you."

"I want you inside me," she said, gripping his shirt and putting her lips just below his.

"What?" he asked, brow quirked.

She sat up on his lap throwing her legs on either side of his thighs as she prepared to ride him. The passing rain clouds of Asher's eyes picked up their pace as he watched her nubile body rise above him in a euphoric grind. Eventually his gaze fell to her haltered breasts as they heaved excited breaths begging to be touched by his eager fingers. Her fingers fell like feathers on his chest with purple sparks igniting on to his shirt. She let out a soft moan as her frame spasmed coaxing a pale blue light out of his chest. An orgasmic moan pulled through her writhing body as her hips ground against Asher's perplexed lap. His eyes looked back at her in a state of awkward sexual arousal. As he was new to his own abilities, Asher wasn't sure what made him desirable to people. This had been the fourth time today that he'd been in an oddly sexual situation. Was it because of the nexus? That thought terrified him. Was this what he had to look forward to? A series of supernatural rape? His thought pattern was interrupted by an urgent knocking on the window. Asher jumped in surprise. He threw Norvita back into the front seat, twitching with embarrassment. Norvita let out an oomphed grunt as she struggled to regain her balance with a light swear in a language that Asher didn't speak. He cringed as his skin started to itch. There was a second knock. The two of them turned their attention to the voyeur of their awkwardness and naughty fun adventures. Norvita covered her mouth in horrified shock. A heart-broken Puck looked in on the pair, his jaw twitching to either hold back a scream or a wave of tears. He hugged the mostly static water nymph in his arms. He knelt as his body let out a heaving sigh while her half open eyes glanced lifelessly at the occupants of the car. Asher cringed at the blue blood staining her dead face.

"Help?" is all Puck said.

Finding help for Amaya wasn't difficult. From earlier in this novel, you know that the Department uses healing magic in their infirmary so I don't feel the need to elaborate on it more than we already have. I'm plenty loquacious as it is. I will say this though, healing magic works just as well on fairies as it does on humans and mages. It just happens to be slower because you are trying to counter a different type of damage.

As for the turn of events for Puck, that is a different story. He'd been ushered into a dark room with Karl and Norvita with not another word spoken. Since these good people were Asher's ride home, he did what any bewildered human being does, he followed them to this interrogation room. He blinked at the mundane use of one-sided glass. It had seemed to him that you'd use something far more advanced than a trick he'd seen over a billion times in a cop movie or TV show. He wasn't exactly sure, but with everyone he'd encountered at the department of the Arcane, he expected a medieval torture rack or something. Not a room that looked like Lenny Briscoe and the guy from Rent would be sitting in. He leaned forward as he watched the scene unfolding on the other side of the glass. Puck sat facing the glass with his head buried deeply in his shaking blue-stained hands. Karl slowly sank into the chair across from Puck. He sat rigidly up with his head tilted to one side in a concerned glance. Asher, for a moment, wondered what Karl did before he came to the Department, assuming the Department did recruit and that Karl wasn't some sort of magic born being. He'd guess cop and we know he is right. Asher didn't know he was right. Like I said, Dramatic Irony. I told you it would be back. Norvita stood beside Asher. Her fingers twisted a strand of hair into a tight-knitted braid around her index finger. Asher glanced at her heatedly, waiting for her to pounce on him again. She blushed as she kept her eyes forward, knowing that if her control slipped an once she would do what he was thinking.

"Karl likes to do the cop thing alone," she said quietly. See, now Asher knows he's right. "He says in this situation, I'm too distracting to magical creatures."

"Yea, you are."

Norvita licked her lips as her skin turned a bright red under the brown. Asher gasped in bitter realization of his words. He felt his heart pump quickly as he started to be embarrassed at his presumption. He quickly changed the subject. "I've seen that guy before. He's Rob Goodfellow. He runs Goodfellow Comics, that hipster comic shop in Old Gaiman. Iggy and I used to go there all the time."

"His true name is Puck," Norvita explained. "He's a tricky bastard, that one."

"Mage or witch?" Asher asked,expecting the answer to be one of those two.

"Fairy," Norvita said without twitching.

"Huh," Asher said with a soft blink. "I didn't realize he was gay."

"No," Norvita said, aghast at Asher's faux pas. "Like a pixie. Puck's that kind of fairy."

"Oh I didn't think..."

"That's sooo racist. I'd never say something like that about gay people or fairies! I'm Facebook friends with George Takei! For a super powerful being you're really pretty stupid."

"I just found out that I was a super powerful!" Asher responded.

"Not an excuse." Norvita rolled her eyes. "Noob."

Asher turned his attention away from <u>Gossip Girl</u> and back to <u>Law and Order</u>. Karl set his bifocals on the metal table and leaned back casually. Puck peeked at Karl through his stiff and coppery fingers. His mossy green eyes danced in pools of deep sorrow.

"He tried to kill my wife and you don't believe me?" Puck said somberly.

You know, for those of us who were more interested in George Takei than what was going on in the other scene.

"Puck, you know the drill," Karl said in his detective voice. "It's not that I don't' trust or believe you, but Puck, for the record I need you to do it."

"That's racist!"

"Puck, it's not racism," Karl said with a tired sigh. He heard this argument more than he cared to. "But it's a known fact that the fae lie to humans without being aware that they are lying. So I need you to do it."

"I'm not going to do that..." Puck was irritated. "You're really going to make me do this?" he asked

Karl said nothing. Instead, he gave Puck his somber, parental look. Puck fidgeted in silence. He looked around before leaning forward.

"Free from deceit and vice, my words and actions are true. I swear it trice." Puck said quickly.

"Good." Karl said. "Now, Puck, what's going on?"

"Iago has gone nuts," Puck said quickly. Too much time had already been wasted. "He's always been odd, but he's officially dangerous."

"Puck, Iago has always been dangerous," Karl countered. Asher wondered when someone was going to tell him this. "But his plans always backfire. We assumed that's a part of his curse. What's different this time around?"

"He's lucid," Puck. said "It's rare, but when it happens, like every couple hundred years or so, he's sane for seven years. I must have missed it the last time he came out again. We don't talk much since the nexus got sober. Then, today, jeeze it's like the fates were smiling on Iago. He's dangerous now, though. Last time Iago was like this, he started a war."

"This time," Karl said. "What's his plan?"

Puck sighed as he tried to smooth out his curly hair and steady himself to reveal the truth. He brought his gaze up to the mirror.

"Total reality destruction," Puck said gravely. "He and I can never go home. I know that. Iago's last prank in Arcadia assured it. I won't tell you what we did, but it was awful. We killed the first nexus."

The inside of Asher's mouth dried up like the Nile River in July as his heart rate climbed. A latent memory that wasn't his flashed in his brain and made him feel very uncomfortable. He could handle being popular, but the idea that people wanted him dead? That scared him.

"It was a mistake," Puck continued. "I always thought it was an accidental part that it separated us from you. I thought that Iago had never meant to kill her and that what happened was just not supposed to have happened. When the dust settled, literally, our Gracious King banished us here. Iago went back once and that ended with the curse."

"Yes, Puck, we all know the story," Karl said. We knew the story a bit. I don't think it's ever fully explained. One day I will elaborate, but that won't be today. Asher didn't know it at all and wanted to know. Someone would let him know later. I sent an email. "But we need to get to the point of the visit.

"How is Iago going to end the world?"

"If you break the vessel of the nexus on the weakest spot in the Hedge, it'll tear down the wall. He knows it's a living being again. He's planning on killing it."

"He knows the nexus is human again?" Karl asked. "Well, we can prevent it from getting hurt."

Asher didn't know what irritated him more; the fact that he was being called an "it" or that his best friend planned to kill him. He should have been more upset at the elaborate conspiracy of silence, but that was something that had already happened. The man who was his best friend was trying to kill him. He was going to be upset about that, but really? He was being called an "it". He wasn't too surprised about Iago. Iago was homicide in a pink package.

"Iago knew before the magi." Puck said. "He smelled the human frailty when the nexus chose its new host. He's got a plan to lure him into the hedge. What it is, I don't know."

Karl put the bifocals back on his face as he rose from the chair. He nodded for Puck to follow him. They walked noiselessly out into the hall where Asher and Norvita were watching. Karl gave Norvita a knowing look about what I suspect had been going on in the back of his Crown Victoria. She became embarrassed again and glanced away as she blushed quietly. Asher watched Karl and Puck with a jaw made of marble sawing back and forward. He was starting to become very annoyed with the situation again. Do you blame him? People were lying to him and not telling him about it. You'd be irritated in his shoes too.

"Well, this seems pretty easy," Karl said plainly. "We keep the vessel under lock and key and away from the homicidal pixie, then reality will be safe."

"I have a name!" Asher said through clenched teeth. "And I don't belong in a cage."

"No one is putting you in a cage," Norvita said. "Calm down."

"Don't tell me to calm down!" Asher yelled. "He's trying to kill me. My best friend is going to kill me."

"He isn't going to kill you," Karl reassured. "No magic born of ill will can penetrate the walls of this fortress."

"What about Mom and Carin?" Asher asked. "He could go after them."

"Your family has been here all afternoon. They're safe." Karl countered. "Your sister and Norvita are, apparently, super best friends now."

"Totally!" Norvita said. "I'm going to get her into my sorority next year!"

"What about Natalie?" Asher asked. "She doesn't know about this."

Karl looked at Asher with a critical eye. He took in Asher's concerned expression. He knew that look. He'd been in that kind of love before, a very long time ago. While Karl wasn't an all-powerful being, he knew what he'd do to anyone who threatened Monica before she fell out of love with him. Hell, he knew what he'd do if Annie or Nora were in trouble.

He'd rip the bastard apart.

In a flash, Karl formulated a plan.

"Right," Karl said as he channeled General Patton. "Norvita and I will go and collect Natalie and bring her back here. Puck are you still bound in vow?"

"Do you really think I want to end the world before this season of Idol?" Puck asked, brow quirked skeptically.

"Right," Karl said. "Puck, you stay and guard the vessel no matter what. Asher, don't die."

"That's it?" Asher asked angrily. "Stay here with the women?"

Karl turned on his heel and sped down the hallway with Norvita in tow. Asher drew his mouth into a thin line. Karl had marginalized him in a plan that was about him. That made him feel just a tad bit worthless. He looked at Puck almost bitterly. He didn't want a babysitter. He didn't need a babysitter. They stood in awkward silence.

Quietly, a cell phone cut through the uncomfortable stillness with a soft melody. In all of today's confusion, Asher had forgotten he was carrying a cell phone. He pulled the ringing phone from his pocket. He breathed a sigh of relief as Natalie's name popped on the caller I.D. screen. At least one thing went right.

"Hello?" he said quickly as relief sank in. "Nat?"

"Hey, Asher honey." That voice wasn't Natalie. The melodious voice that crept through the phone was familiar but it wasn't Natalie. "How are you doing, buddy?"

"Iggy," Asher hissed into the phone. "I know your plan. Where's Natalie?"

"Good," Iago's grin snaked into Asher's ears through the phone. "I can save everyone a huge amount time. Natalie's here with me. Hang on, let me see if she wants to say 'hi' -- Natalie?"

Suddenly, there was the sound of static that comes from setting down the phone. Then out of nowhere, came a loud scream to stab at Asher's soul. He shut his eyes as a heartbreaking pain stabbed his chest. He definitely knew that scream. That was Natalie. She was in pain and it broke his heart.

"Iggy, please," Asher begged, barely speaking. "Leave her alone."

"No," Iago said indignantly. "You guys want me; you can come here and stop me. If you are going to though you should hurry. Pretty blonde girls don't' last long in here."

Asher's hands shook and sparked blue in anger. Quickly, Puck knocked the phone out of his hands.

"It's a trap," Puck yelled. "Iago is the Prince of Lies! He's trying to goad you into making a mistake."

Asher relaxed his hands, trying to regain composure. Puck was right. Iago was trying to make him screw up. This would be unhelpful to Natalie. Iago probably didn't have Natalie. She was at home reading a book with that old cat next to her. Then, Asher's mind flashed with a grizzly image. He could see Iggy standing over Natalie's bruised and beaten body. In stark detail, he could see every unspeakable act that he performed on her helpless body. Asher's fists gave off a cold blue light again. He glowed brighter as Natalie's screams echoed in his ears. His body stiffened in terror for Natalie. That's when Iago's words came back to him.

Pretty blonde girls don't last very long in here.

Asher's luminous fingers curled into a tight fist. With an anguished scream, his fist collided with the nearest wall. With a resonating boom, the wall that Asher punched split wide and a cold gray light poured in from the crack. Puck knew that light and it scared him. Mages couldn't enter the Hedge like that -- only fairies. Asher stared apprehensively at the light. All his instincts told him to run. However, he knew that Natalie was in there. She was trapped in there.

He had to save her.

Without a second thought, Asher ran into the crack. Puck stood at the precipice of the opening and wavered about walking into the light. Getting that close to the Dream was risky to his life. Being that close would make him want to cross back to his home. Puck backed away until he felt the pull of the vow dragging him towards the crack. With great apprehension, Puck dove in after Asher.

XXVIII. Tribute

She walked through the Old Gaiman Street shaking the tiredness of the mundane world from her fiery braided mane that had three days' worth of grime and grease caked into it from under an unwashed toboggan. She paused when she came to a decaying dumpster overlooking the parking lot of the Church of St. Cecilia. No one went to St. Cecilia anymore. It wasn't the spirits that languished there. Many wanted to believe it was the lack of trust in Holy Mother Church after the sins of some men who should never have been working with children came to grizzly light. But simply, it was the mundane had moved out of Old Gaiman and into the suburbs. It was pretty sad really. It wasn't a bad neighborhood, but now it had fallen to abandoned ruins when the wealthy fled to build identical houses outside of town or somewhere else when this city became was no longer interesting to them.

The church itself was a work of art. Built by craftsmen from the old world in a style that used to be very, very popular with the reboot of a gothic style in America. There was glass that once was bright yellows and blues painting the night with their soft glow, but had been cracked and broken from time and good-hearted vandalism. The chipped gargoyles still stood in silent vigil for the day when St. Cecilia's children would come home. She sighed as she pushed the dumpster to one side. She was never a fan of when things were pushed off to the side so callously. She empathized with such neglected as she wandered through this world of excess. She awaited her entrance back into a more welcoming land, wrapping herself in the hand-me-down jacket as a gateway slowly opened up before her. The cold bright gray light embraced her like a lover welcoming her into his bedroom after a long journey. She breathed in the air of her home as she walked into the light. She liked walking in the mundane world but it wasn't this place. Her place had been where it always was. Not in the mundane world and never in Arcadia and never in Heaven or Hell but in all of them and none of them all at the same time. She extended her hands forwards as her tattered rags burned away to a Kelly green velvet robe that was entwined with delicate knotted patterns. Her ruddy face lightened to freckles speckling her rosy cheeks.

It felt good to be home.

She walked on the ever-changing path that led to the heart of the Hedge and to her grand palace. In her time ruling this land, it had evolved to keep itself safe. In days before concrete palaces and the world being covered with smog, her home was a heavy green forest of briars and sharp leaves that tore away at a poor lost soul's very being. The foul creatures that preyed on that innocent flesh were vicious and violent, but nothing you wouldn't see anywhere else. The Hedge evolved with the times, matching its tall branches to those found in the world of a nightmare of glass, concrete, and stone. Even her beloved wild beasts had changed from snakes and rabbits to vile looking crocodiles and 8 foot rats. Despite the changes, her palace remained the same as it always had. She kept it that way for sentimental reasons. Long ago, her palace had been built to offer her tribute in exchange for bringing a good harvest or healthy children by people who thought she had some manner of sway over that sort of thing. She'd live in that quiet place and listen and offer the blessings she could. Her palace hadn't changed because she liked humans. They were such funny creatures who were so afraid of the natural world. They were so scared they would worship alleged old gods for anything. She knew one old god who asked for cow tongues to make it rain. Humans didn't do that kind of worship anymore, but they were still funny in her estimations. She still liked them even if they weren't as needed as they used to be. She missed those days.

At one time, they had worshipped her as a goddess. In return she brought them the blessings of song and bountiful harvests. There were some who still worshipped her and her kind enough to make trade with them. She'd give them a blessing for a tribute which meant nothing really except what they believed it meant. The world changed, but she knew people still paid tributes to her. Instead of offerings and sacrifices they named daughters and prayed to her. St. Patrick and the Roman Catholic Church made her a saint. *That feckin' Roman pirate*, she thought bitterly, *he changed my name.*

She hadn't really cared. There were many of her kind that no one would remember. In a changing world, she was happy to be remembered -- even if it was incorrectly for a magic trick that she didn't perform. She sat in her high throne overlooking a great hall with a tired sigh. Her fingers dug through a satchel, pulling out her latest prize. Her fingers rolled a large cat's eye marble between thumb and forefinger inspecting the trinket as carefully as one would inspect a large diamond. She had traded for it with an adorable little girl who bore her Romanized name for a blessing. The little girl didn't know who she had traded the marble with, but she would soon enough. The little girl was going to get the blessing of song. She was too caught up in the marble to hear her great doors open and shut until she heard the slam of the doors. Her powerful hazel eyes searched the halls.

"Who doth go there?" she bellowed broughishly.

The figure of a pink-haired man danced up to the Great Throne as if to a song that no one else could hear. She eyed him carefully as he humbly knelt before her with great apprehension. Slowly, he brought his eyes up to greet her as he tried to control the jagged smirk on his face.

"Greetings and blessings to you, Fair Brigid," he said. "Daughter of Dagda, mother of Radothan, beloved in his life by Kind Braid. Mother of Inspiration and sworn Protector of the Hedge. Tis I, Iago. Born of the union of Loki, the Trickster King, and Morriganne, Goddess of Deceit. Prince of Lies."

Brigid inspected Iago carefully with a critical scowl on her Hibernian face. She leaned back attempting to summon the darkest forces she could muster to repel the fairy from her sight.

"Thou are not welcome in my sanctuary, pookha," she said disdainfully. "Be gone with thee before I hasten the end of thy life."

"But, Great Lady," Iago said with a seductive purr. He found himself trying to make his smile handsome. It was working poorly for him. "I bear thee tribute."

Brigid's cold face warmed at Iago and his words. The best way to calm an ancient one's temper and beeline towards their hearts is always a gift. This is true for most fairies but more so for ancient ones. Gods and Goddesses always like people to remember they are important enough to give a gift to. She rose from the throne and gently glided to the kneeling Iago. She peered down at him with great interest.

"What didst thou bring me?" she asked.

Iago smiled as he reached into his jacket. He took two items out of his pockets and offered them up to her as his pink head remained bowed carefully down. The first was a large red stone that he held in the palm of his hand. Brigid's eyes stood transfixed on an orange fire dancing inside the gem beckoning her to come and see. The other gift was a shining crescent shaped dagger etched with an unrecognizable language on the blade. She was far more interested in the stone than the blade. This was obvious by the way she picked up the stone. She turned it over in her hands eagerly inspecting its properties.

"So pretty," she whispered to herself as she felt the fire lick the insides of her brain. "What is it called?"

"It is called the Eye of Shiva, my lady," Iago explained. His voice subtly worked around in her mental bodice unlacing her insecurities about him being there. "It is said that it was given to Asoka by Lord Ganesh to signify his great reign over the Hindu people. It is also said that when he wore it attached to his sash he was able to claim the souls of his enemies and their power if they had any within them. The yogi I acquired it from tells me it is quite a powerful totem. The blade may seem ordinary, but it's enchanted with the unspeakable tongue; the alleged language of the angels. Something that can cause madness in the mundane if they try to understand it. I know for a fact that the blade can kill anything. Combined with the Eye of Shiva, it could make one unstoppable."

"Why would I ever want that?" she questioned slowly, still entranced with the gem.

"Because, Great Lady," Iago said smoothly. "They are for your tribute."

"If this isn't my tribute, then what is?"

In a flash, Iago gripped the blade while shoving the great ruby into her forehead violently. Brigid stood frozen in terror as the light blade pierced the pale skin of her chest opening up a large hole. The orange fire within the stone sparkled as it grew brighter. Gold dust poured from the open wound. Brigid felt a processing coldness come over her body. Her hands and feet lost feeling as they turned to a dark limestone. As the last fleck spilled out of her Celtic frame, she froze into lifeless stone. Iago stepped back admiring his handiwork as his fingers curled around the Eye of Shiva. He shrugged off his jacket as he stared at the stone corpse. With the blade, he cut a deep wound that opened his shirt and masque. His fingers pushed the gem into his chest. He let out a grunt as his masque flickered. His fingers convulsed as a bolt of power pulled though him. He cracked his neck as he grinned.

"My gift to thee, Great Lady," Iago whispered for dramatic effect. "To make thy temple for the nursery for the end. I give thee a release of death before the coming storm."

Iago laughed callously as he strutted to the throne. He settled into the throne and cast a glance down the Great Hall. The easy part was over. The next installment would be harder. Well, half hard. Puck would be easy. Asher, on the other hand, was the problem. There was too much strength there that he couldn't control easily. He'd have to convert his powers to the important parts of his body to be able to compete. It would be hard, but he'd be powerful enough. He grinned. His goal was in sight. Now, all he had to do was to wait.

He hummed a Boomtown Rats song to himself.

XXVIII. Into the Hedge

Asher stumbled over his feet and into the middle of a decaying city street as he came through the crack in the wall. His eyes looked around the urban wasteland with peaked interest. This place wasn't his home or the Department. He was in a weird place. Teleporting was a new event for him. *Well,* he thought, *being a god-like figure comes with some super cool X-men like powers. I should learn how to enjoy them.* He looked around as his eyes were stung by the brightness. He shielded his brow and squinted in the harsh gray light. Natalie was here somewhere. He knew he had to find her. His feet tried to remain stable as the ever changing ground before him shifted with each passing second. His steps felt uncertain as he soldiered on through the maze of the Hedge. He couldn't stop even if he wanted to at this point. He had to find her. Iggy had her. Iggy was hurting her. He would find them. He would make them pay.

Asher straightened his shoulders and picked a direction that he thought would be acceptable for his mission. He marched off into that chosen direction with the purpose he'd shown in chapter one. Did he know where he was? No. Did he know what he was going to do? No. That wasn't going to stop him. Natalie was more important than being right in any given setting. She'd saved him from himself, it was time to return the favor. Besides, this wasn't the weirdest thing that happened to him on this particular day. In fact, statistically speaking, there was a better chance of him finding her by choosing a random direction than by standing still. With his luck, he'd find her. He was almost hoping for an odd video game or epic hero situation. That would score him major points with her. He was growing confident in his confusion. He had no choice; the only thing that stayed constant with him in this was his confusion. He knew if all else failed he had his confusion. It was like a long standing hurt, it meant that he could know that this was the real world. More importantly, he knew he'd find them in this madness. He could feel a pull towards her every time he thought about her and her scared face. He felt that his life was going to be fixed through doing what he had to do. This is what his mother had told him to do. Protect the ones you love with the skills you have developed. He wasn't sure what skills he had but he could teleport and he could fight. That was better than nothing.

Asher came to an awkwardly-high chain link fence that crossed his path almost ominously. Asher found himself climbing over the fence that closed off a large field with profound determination. He looked over the long leaves of grass swaying in the dead breeze. He cleared his throat as he stared down at the urban Serengeti. It started to increase in length along the horizon. It reminded him of his childhood. Walking home from the pool or a baseball game across the vacant lots that felt like heavy tundra always took forever. The vacant lots always seemed bigger back then. Sure enough, the field expanded by a mile and it kept growing. Asher sighed hopelessly. It seemed that the fates -- or at least the Hedge -- were conspiring against him.

"Hey! Asher!" called a distantly familiar voice. "Wait up!"

Asher turned almost angrily towards the voice. He really didn't want or need a distraction right now from his own goal. Asher couldn't afford to be slowed down, not when Natalie was in danger. He's not very bright for a hero, if I may say so. I really will try harder next time. I mean it's my first novel. You ever read people's first novel? They aren't the strongest tellings.

In a reluctant contrast to what he wanted, Asher waited for

the owner of the voice. He watched a head of muddy brown hair bob up and down as it skipped along in the tall grass. No, not skipping, that isn't the right word. He was trotting on what looked like goat legs. Asher squinted. Under the coarse hair and long curved horns was Puck. He stopped beside Asher, breathing hard.

"Puck?" Asher said. "The hell?"

"It's dangerous to go alone," Puck heaved out in gasped breaths. "Take me."

"What?"

"You can't just go stampeding off into the Hedge," Puck said. "Even if this isn't a trap, the Hedge feeds off the amplified confusion of magical beings. Considering the amount of magic you have coursing through you it's going to try very hard to keep you here. No doubt by this point something or someone has your scent. Can't be hard -- you smell odd."

Puck stopped looking around. He bent his head down.

"But there's something not right though. It's far too quiet. It's like the animals are scared of something."

"It looks like an M.C. Escher nightmare." Asher said. "What is this place?"

"Seriously? Are you retarded or just deaf? I just told you. This is the Hedge," Puck explained. He started to walk off in a direction that wasn't the one Asher had chosen. Asher followed him anyway. Who was going to argue with a goat man who knew where he was? "I thought I made that clear. It's the land between Arcadia and the mundane world. You know, the border land. I wish I could say my kind planted it here, but we didn't; it grew up wildly out of necessity. There was a gap in the worlds and something needed to fill it in so we have the Hedge."

"Funny," Asher replied bitterly. "When you say "hedge" I

don't think urban wasteland. I think of shrubbery."

"The Hedge is like every other old being in existence. It evolves and changes to survive." Puck shrugged. "Someone walks into a throng of bushes in this day and age and it's jarring. The Hedge would be conspicuous and that would be counterproductive and others would then know everything. It changes when it needs to change. I'm surprised though. Its shakes unstably when a very powerful creature enters the Hedge. It's pretty stable right now with you in it. That's...awkward."

Puck scratched his beard. "Weird, but maybe it's because you're special."

"Lucky me," Asher muttered.

"Yea, I know it kind of sucks being a Messiah figure. That doesn't mean you get to be heroic and completely stupid," Puck said. "This isn't a place you can run into safely. It's bad enough the landscape changes every second, but it also has creatures that'll eat you alive with a bit of ketchup and cheese. That's why you won't find her alive...not alone anyway."

"I don't care," Asher said sharply. "He's hurting her and I can't let him do that."

"I understand that. Trust me, I do, but you have to be smart about it," Puck said. "You need me to get through the Hedge. I've spent more time here than you."

Asher stopped in his tracks and looked at the fae flatly. "Fine," he grumbled. "Then, what exactly do we do?"

"Well," Puck said. "We're in the Hedge. If Iago and your woman are still here, then I know who we need to chat with. We need to see Brigid."

"Brigid?" Asher asked. "Who's Brigid?"

"Goddess of wisdom and fertility. She's also the protector and ruler of the Hedge."

"So, in addition to mages, witches and fairies, there are gods and goddesses?"

"Not really," Puck said. "The majority of fae claimed those titles a long time ago. Before you apes got science to explain everything, we took credit for it. Don't get me wrong, not all gods are us, but most are probably a fairy."

"Which ones?" Asher asked.

"Honestly?" Puck said. "I don't know. I suspect half of the so-called gods are my people, but don't know whether or not they are telling the truth. Oh, hey, that reminds me. What do you have on you?"

"My wallet, some keys, a pack of gum, my phone." Asher then thought about it. "Why?"

"When we get to Brigid's palace, we have to pay her tribute. You know, a small trinket or something." Puck randomly changed direction. "Gum is more than enough. Let me do the talking though. The fae customs are stupid complex."

Puck led Asher out of the field just as the grass shook with a score of cute rabbit demons that hopped somewhere else unrelated to this plot. They turned on to a desolate street. The buildings closed around them, making the field a distant memory. In fact, Asher found himself not being able to remember the field or even the adorable bunny demons that had made a brief cameo. Asher shook his head and walked on the path. Puck trotted along the street, attempting to keep up with Asher's long steps, his hooves clattering along the sidewalk like the hard pounding of rain. His head bobbed and weaved trying to remember his way through the maze of streets. Asher wondered if he ever get tired of listening to the clip clop of hooves.

"So," Asher said. "What are you...besides a fairy?"

"What do you mean?"

"There are different types of people in the normal world -- I just thought there were different types of fairies. Wait, are you going to tell me that's racist?"

"Nope, in fact it's the first intelligent question you've asked all day," Puck said. "I'm a satyr. Descended from Pan. We're sort of like elves, except less dickish. We spent most of our time hanging out with nymphs and playing flutes. I can play like Jethro Tull, man. You know we're into the same thing really, us and nymphs. Partying, dancing around in nature -- things that would make you blush. Amaya and I have been bound together for almost 6000 years."

"Wow, that's impressive. How do you make it work?"

"We fuck a lot."

"Oh..." Asher probably should have realized. "And what is Iggy? Is he also a satyr?"

"Iago's a pookha," Puck said with a cringe and a bleat. Sharing this much information about the fae was never a good idea. Puck could claim later that Asher wasn't human so it was okay. That was assuming of course, they both survived.

"They're a race of dark fairies. Typically, they're shape-shifters and are always liars. Iago is the offspring of Loki and Morgainne. Not only a deceiver but prone to violence."

"I seem to recall you guys are really good friends. Why are you being so helpful?"

"I like people," Puck said. "Even before we were taken away from you, I liked people. You apes are just too funny. And I like living. I'm so not ready to kiss all that goodbye. I'd do this even if I hadn't sworn it thrice."

"That little poem you recited. Does Karl always make you do that?"

"Department policy when dealing with the fae." Puck rolled his eyes in irritation. "Totally racial profiling, but apparently the fae can't be trusted so we swear things thrice to be truthful. Pain in my....oop we're here."

As they reached the end of the desolate street, an ornate cathedral sprung out of the asphalt like a great out-of-place tree. It wasn't just the gorgeous medieval cathedral in the middle of the urban wasteland that was confusing, though for any American it might be. I suspect Europeans are more like, yea and so what? It was what the cathedral was made of that perplexed Asher. The green limestone structure pulsed with a low hum that would have made anyone concerned. Asher furrowed his brow as he stared at the scary sky line. Maybe it was the culture shock but he thought the black clouds by the spires were far too ominous. He watched the clouds curl into a funnel as Puck pulled the door open. A rush of cold wind hit them like a violent storm warning telling them to go back. Puck ignored the warning and trotted into the cathedral. Asher followed behind him. The pair wandered down a long hallway towards the Great Throne. Once they reached the Great Throne, Puck humbly knelt pulling Asher down beside him.

"Greetings, Great Lady," Puck said with his tail wagging nervously. "Tis I, Puck...."

"Fourteenth Son of Pan," hissed a voice from the throne. A voice that wasn't Brigid's, but was far too familiar. The kind of familiarity that causes one to cringe when the realization of who it is dawns on one. "And thou hast brought me a great tribute. Present thy neck, Vessel of the Nexus. It now belongs to me."

Puck recognized that hiss far too late. He knew it wasn't the voice of the mother goddess who lived in the Thorns. He knew the whisper better than he wanted to and it moved him to tears. It was the whisper that licked your ears and told you to do bad things. Puck swallowed his terror as he cast his eyes upwards to the throne. Sitting in the throne was a large black-green beast casting his solid black eyes down at the pair with wrathful indignation. He looked like the dark paintings of the krumpus that Asher had seen in some of Brady's books. A twisted and grinning nightmare from some dark altar with stone white fangs, accenting a horned dog beast of black jade radiating tentacles that would have scared H.P. Lovecraft. An orange light pulsed from its chest. Asher's knees went weak as he tried to stand up. His eyes were frozen in horror on the ominously swaying tendrils. Asher never wanted to run so much in his life. He wanted every bit of his body to turn and leave but couldn't find the strength to do so.

"You're not Brigid," Puck said dumbly. He knew it wasn't Brigid. In fact, Puck knew exactly who it was. He hadn't seen that horrible face in a very long time. He couldn't remember the last time he saw that face. He was truthfully terrified as would anyone else who knew that this face was around again. No wonder there wasn't any activity in the Hedge. Iago had gone black. That was enough to cause the vilest of creature to go underground and hide from the light. Puck fought to find something else to say apart from his stupidly obvious words but he was frozen into a speechless state.

"No, I'm not," hissed the Monster through perfectly white and sharp teeth. A sinister chuckle came behind that laugh. That was more than enough for Asher to recognize the form. Behind that terrifying mask was an all too familiar voice that crept into his waking mind.

"Iago," he whispered to himself.

"No, not anymore," Iago announced. "Now, I am the Keeper of the Hedge. Present thy tribute."

Puck turned back to Asher with the most somber gaze. This was his fault. He had tried to get Asher out safely and it led right into the trap that had been created. If Iago had been in his right mind he would have enjoyed the fact that he'd gotten what he wanted; his best friend with him at the end of things. In fact, Iago did enjoy it for a moment. It wasn't the part he'd written, but it was good enough for what he wanted. Puck took a moment to realize his role in everything. If Iago hadn't beaten Amaya, he would have led Asher to that lonesome hill whether he wanted to or not. Iago would have made it that way. He was always going to play the role of sending the lamb to the slaughter. He'd played his role regardless. He rose to his hooves defeated. Iago grinned as his tentacles waved victoriously around him. Puck literally had no choice in the matter. He had to accept the part that was written for him. Begrudgingly, Puck gripped Asher's shoulders as he dragged him before the throne. Parts had been cast in this terrible drama. Puck knew what he had to do.

"Run," Puck whispered.

Before Asher could utter a word of protest, Puck threw Asher down the hall towards the exit. He rolled down the aisle before tripping over his feet and finally landing on his back. He sat up in just enough to time watch Puck doing what he would later call stupid heroics. Puck lowered his head angling his body parallel to the ground. He led with his horns charging at Iago aiming for his chest. It was a solid plan really until Puck was swatted away like a piece of fluff from a dinner jacket with a tentacle. Puck hit the smooth wall with a consciousness-losing thunk. Asher struggled to make his legs work for an escape. He had to get out. He had to save Natalie from whatever fate she was suffering. He couldn't let Iago kill him in this strange place.

He couldn't get up.

As much as he wanted to, Asher found himself stuck in place like being caught in a large vat of molasses. The harder he struggled the more stuck he became to the ground. Iago glided with a swagger towards Asher's collapsed form with the quiet dignity of victory. The tentacles twitched and felt the ground with a suctioning pop. Iago turned his head to the side admiring his victim. A tentacle gripped the blade of his magical knife and one by one the tentacle passed the blade towards his hands. Iago sighed, taking in the panic on Asher's face.

"I'm sorry Asher, buddy," Iago said. "You know, I'm going to miss you."

Iago straddled his victim, whispering a small prayer in a language that Asher didn't recognize. He raised the blade dramatically over Asher's chest. With a loud scream, Iago plunged the blade into Asher's chest with all the strength he had to move heaven and earth. Asher jerked forward as the blade impaled his heart and it gave out a final beat. His last living thought before dying came out as a wordless scream of protest that released the last bit of air in his lungs. Iago laughed as he twisted the knife before pulling it out. The cathedral shook as Asher's death rattle cracked the walls and moved the foundation. Iago smiled to himself. The end would be soon.

XXIX. Lamb to the Slaughter

There was a thunderous crack that shook the shifting earth under the cathedral as it ruptured the very foundation of the Hedge. Iago grinned as a destructive vibration hummed through his jaded frame, telling him that all of his hard work was mere seconds away from finally paying off. To his own very great amusement his hackneyed plan created in the span of five hours had come together perfectly and ended successfully. This was something new for Iago. He was almost sad that his first perfectly-executed plan was going to end reality. He felt like he had more in him at this point. *Well, no crying over spilled milk,* he told himself. He commanded one of his tentacles to pick up Puck by his ankle. He drew the limp satyr towards him. Iago took a moment to admire his handiwork as the end of time of spilled into the cathedral through the crumbling walls. If Puck was awake, he would be begging to be laid down flat with his face to the floor. He'd never wanted to see Doomsday.

No one did.

Then the shaking suddenly stopped as the light hung at a perilous angle, threatening to overtake Iago, the Cathedral, and everyone else and then someone hit pause. A cold white blue light started to bleed out of Asher's chest wound, covering his slowly dying body. His body stiffened as the cells that composed it debated intensely on whether or not they were going to die today. While the cells entered a filibuster on the subject, something else made a choice. After eons of collecting the powers and pure magical essence of the dead supernatural creatures, the nexus had developed a taste for a few things. It had started to develop a taste for human comforts like those who made up the nexus once shared. The comforts of humans were so wonderful. For example, the nexus liked barbeque chips and smooth jazz. Having spent so much time buried in the ground, it liked having a live host again. They were cozy and added a little extra protection. Being tread upon wasn't comfortable even for an intangible ball of magic. All of these things needed to continue to exist. There wasn't anything that didn't like existing. Its host wasn't doing a good job of existing right now. He needed a little extra help to stop the person that was threatening to end them and had already harmed them. The nexus wasn't going to let it kill them.

It liked Asher.

Asher slipped away from reality and was tucked away safely somewhere else in the back of the body. What it would do to save them would be a little too much for him. He wasn't exactly ready for all their secrets and he could easily use the rest. In time, the nexus would teach him how to wield their powers better. That wasn't today. Today they needed to heal their body. The nexus flickered for a moment as it channeled white magic to the frayed bone and tissue in its chest. It breathed out of Asher's chest. It wasn't time for him to use their body. It was time for the Nexus to do so. Iago checked his watch. Reality should have ended and yet he was still here checking his watch. He looked down just as the Nexus opened Asher's eyes. What would have normally been the stormy gray eyes of Asher were replaced with a powerful bright light radiating out like some manner of superhero. Iago found himself staring into the heart of the blue light. He stopped. As Iago looked down at the Nexus, he felt it bore into his soul. Iago was bombarded by every nasty thing he had ever done over the span of time. He crept back from the entity as he tried to steal a breath between the reading off of his crimes. Iago's eyes twitched in pain. Slowly the Nexus rose up with an expressionless face, noiselessly judging their attacker. Iago cleared his throat looking back at him.

"Huh," Iago said finally with a twitch. "I didn't see that coming."

"Pity that you didn't," said the nexus with a rush of soft voices ranging from deep male voices to soft feminine ones falling from their lips. Iago found himself trying to not shake in fear that he'd never felt before. "Then you would have known better than to incur my wrath."

Iago had never liked being threatened even if it was by a super powerful being. He wasn't going to be the small child that got pushed aside. In a fit of rage, he lunged at the Nexus with an agitated growl. He swung the blade fatally at the Nexus trying hard to land a blow. No one ruined his plans unless it was himself or maybe Puck. The Nexus let out a soft sigh as the blade passed through it like it was simply nothing. With an almost ethereal quickness, the Nexus reached into Iago's chest. It ripped the Eye of Shiva from its tomb with a bone crushing pain that Iago tried very hard to shrug off effortlessly. It looked down at the sparking gem before it crushed the thing in their hand. Iago dropped to his knees, letting out a pained scream as his body slowed down. It looked down passively at the pookha before pulling Iago back to a standing position by the throat. Iago looked back into the wells of unimaginable power and trembled in terror. He felt the guilt of a thousand crimes he'd committed visited upon him yet again. Iago found himself gripped by an emotion that he'd never felt before. Iago felt remorse.

"Asher, buddy, please," Iago begged as crystal tears rolled down his cheeks breaking on the ground. "Don't let it kill me."

"Kill you?" asked the Nexus. "Pookha, I do not kill. I merely claim."

Before he could beg again for his own safety, Iago felt his body become stiff as a board. The blue energy of the Nexus pushed spikes into the jaded flesh of his throat. Iago felt a painful suction pulling energy from his body. His crawling skin illuminated the palace with a dark green light as it was absorbed by the Nexus until it was gone. A shock of green flickered once over the Nexus and disappeared. The Nexus gently let go of Iago, who slumped to his knees just as the weight of mortality sat on his shoulders holding him still. He felt his body slow to a boring pace. His ears couldn't feel the vibrations of a reality that sang a maddening song. Quickly, Iago looked down at his hands. They were pink and had thin lines in them. His lower lip quivered.

Iago's greatest fear was realized. He was human.

Iago let out an anguished cry towards the heavens. The Nexus looked down at Iago pitilessly as he screamed in agony. It reached down and gripped Iago's faux-hawk. With a ground shaking grunt, it swung Iago in a circle and then tossed him as hard as it could. Iago went soaring off into the bright light through shattered holes in the cathedral and towards the beyond. The Nexus watched confidently as Iago went off into the sky and back into the mundane world. If the aim was right he would land back in the garden. The Nexus cringed feeling something added to their form. It looked down at its hands as they sparked with undigested magic. A blink came over the Nexus. Contrary to popular belief, the Nexus has no real affiliation with either good or evil. To have that, the Nexus would have to think in a human way about what it does and its actions. It did not believe such things. It simply existed and did what it did. For example, it saw orange sparks dancing on its hand. The thing it would normally do was to simply take that into its collective and things would move on with its day. That didn't happen this time. This time, there was a voice that told it to stop. Things weren't right and it was their job to fix that. They couldn't let mother down.

The Nexus didn't want to listen, but it knew that the voice

was right. The vessel was always right.

The Nexus let out a sigh as it retreated back into the vessel. Asher blinked as he reclaimed himself back from the brink of his own loss of humanity. He stumbled forward cautiously on weak legs. For a moment, Asher hadn't been sure that he survived or not as he looked around at the destruction that they wrought. He swallowed for a moment before a calm voice, the voice that had always been there talking to him, whispered directions to him. He was fine, it told him, he was alive. They had saved everyone from what could have been a nightmare. He needed to listen calmly to himself and they'd be okay. Asher nodded, focusing for a moment on the fire dancing on his hands. He was having a hard time believing that he was very much alive. He had found that he couldn't recall much of the turn of events. *It's okay*, whispered the Nexus, *just watch the fire. We need to find its owner.* Asher looked around again at the destroyed cathedral. Iago was gone. Isn't that where they got it? *No,* it said, *it's not Iago. This is older and higher magic than what you'd get from a fairy.* Asher cast his eyes towards a stone statue with terror painted on its face. Asher swallowed as he walked closer.

Asher nudged the blade that Iago had stabbed him with with his foot. He then reached down for it as he carefully tried to shift the flame to the free hand. After the day he'd had, Asher wasn't going to take any chances. If this thing so much as looked at him in the wrong way, he was going to stab it in the face. *She won't,* said the Nexus. "I don't care," said Asher, "I'm not taking any chances." Asher tucked the blade into a pant loop inhaling a brave breath. He placed his hands on her face. Asher leaned forward with his lips guiding towards her open horrified mouth. He breathed an orange fire on to the stone releasing it from them. Slowly, he felt stone starting to thin, letting a form come through the body. He could feel the living heartbeat pulse at hidden veins within her body as it started stirring under his touch. She inhaled with a sharp gasp. She tumbled forward into resurrection. Asher swiftly reached out and caught her. She looked up at him as her cheeks went rosy pink.

"Hi, you must be Brigid, Keeper of the Hedge," he said. "My name is Asher. I'm looking for someone who is lost in here. Her name is Natalie. She's young and blonde and got put out here. Puck said you could help."

Brigid rocked back on her feet, dumbfounded at the turn of events. Goddesses rarely died and very few of them were brought back by a mage. She stared wildly at Asher's patent-pending smile. She should verbally berate Asher for being rude to her. However, that was going to wait for another day. She was far too weak and he was being far too kind to her. He helped her into her throne. He stepped back with a soft swallow waiting for any news.

"No, I haven't seen thy woman," she said in the throes of confusion.

"No, I imagine not," Asher said calmly. "You have been busy with Iago. Do you know where I should look then?"

There was a crumpled figured that pulled itself out of from under rock and dust. Brigid froze as she waited for the second attack. Asher turned gripping the blade as he crouched down. Puck slumped on a wall regaining his bearings. The pair eased as Puck waved while grimacing in pain.

"Birgie," he called between pants. "You're alive!"

"Puck!" she called back happily. "What are you doing here?"

Puck stumbled before the throne. He grinned at her, feeling better than he had in years. He was hurting but it felt good. It felt noble. He also knew that it was because he was this close to Arcadia. He knew that kind of happy.

"I swore an oath to aid the Nexus here," Puck said. "Right

into Iago's trap. Speaking of which where is he?"

"Gone," Asher said as frigid as a February wind. "I don't know where, but he won't be hurting anyone again."

"O...kay...." Puck said slowly. "Did he say where Natalie is?"

"I can't remember if he did or not," Asher said. "Brigid says she isn't here though."

"I did say that. She'd be in Arcadia, perhaps," Brigid said quietly. Her fingers inspected the hole in her robe. "I do thank thee both for restoring my life. I have nothing to repay my debt to thee."

Asher thought about Brigid's words carefully. He'd never had anyone who owed him a favor before. Well, he did, but not on the grand scale of owing someone their life. He wasn't quite sure how to react. Maybe Puck had first dibs. He glanced over at Puck for guidance. Puck's face had a blank expression. He knew what he wanted. He also knew that he couldn't ask for it. Fortunately for him, Asher had gotten his own idea finally. He smiled brightly at Brigid.

"Oh, I can think of something," Asher said confidently. Brigid stiffened as she waited. No one wanted to be in debt to a powerful being. Puck looked at Asher with peaked interest. "I don't know how to get to Arcadia. Even if I did, I'd still need a guide there. I need to get Natalie back home without being eaten by anything."

"I could help," Puck interjected. "But I'm still banished."

"I know, Puck. I was paying attention," Asher said. He knelt before the throne humbly. He glanced up quietly. "Brigid, is it possible for you to guide me through your Hedge to Arcadia?"

"My good sir," Brigid said sweetly. "Thou that safeguarded my hidden home and returned me to the world of the living. I am grateful, however thou hast great power. I fear that in a weakened state, thou presentest a great temptation to me and I cannot hinder thy quest for true love with my selfish needs. The best I can do for thee is grant my protection. By my grace, no harm shall come to thee whilst thou travel in the Hedge."

"That's great," Puck said sarcastically. "I still can't go into Arcadia."

Brigid's bright green eyes danced as she looked down at Puck. Her gentle fingers searched into a pocket of her green robe. Within seconds, she produced a solitary purple rose glazed with a silver light. She beckoned Puck closer to her. With a nervous tremble he took his place kneeling beside Asher. She leaned down to a fix the flower to one of his horns.

"Go and tell them how you protected all of us, Son of Pan," Brigid commanded. "Thy bravery shall absolve thy sins. If thy Great King harms thee, he shall deal with my wrath. I do ask one more favor. There is a blackness surrounding that blade. I wish for it to be far away from me. Take it with thee."

"No problem," Asher said. "I'm sure the Department has a place for something like this. Thank you so much my lady."

They exchanged heartfelt goodbyes before Brigid led them to the back exit. The door led down a row of steps to the bottom of a dark hall. The pair walked down a twisting path. The natural light dissipated as blackness crept behind them. Puck looked back at Asher in silence.

"So," Puck said when the quiet became too much for him. "Did you explode or what?"

"I honestly don't know," Asher admitted. "It was like watching it unfold on TV in a dream at the bottom of a well. It was so far away. I couldn't concentrate on it. I know I felt like I vibrated for a little bit. Maybe I did explode."

"You know, you're taking this all pretty well," Puck said.

"Yea, I know," Asher said thoughtfully. "Hell, a few hours ago killing Iago and resurrecting an old god would have damaged my calm so badly, I would be jonesing for a big slice of heroin pie."

"They make it into a pie now?"

"I would find a way, damn it. But Puck, I had a lot of time to think while being possessed. I could run away from my destiny and be Asher the junkie or I can be Asher the hero. I kind of sucked at being Asher the junkie."

"You could just be Asher the guy, you know."

"Yea, I don't think I can."

"At least you picked a cool profession for you. You killing all the magic in Iago was pretty bad ass," Puck conceded. "I guess you really didn't need me in all of this."

"I don't know," Asher said quietly. "Everyone needs some help to be a hero."

Puck rolled his eyes at the cliché. The pair took the last step off the sidewalk towards a long hallway in utter silence. Asher felt a pang of guilt in the pit of his stomach. He knew that he wouldn't have made it this far without Puck. Now, Puck was feeling useless. That made Asher feel guilty. He hated feeling like a tool.

"So," Asher said casually. "You're going to do all the talking in Arcadia, right?"

"Seriously?" Puck said as he choked out a disbelieving laugh.

"Yes, I'm serious!" Asher said. "I've been a mage for all of six hours. I don't know any of these customs. I'll say the wrong thing and they'll turn me into a purple walrus or something."

"We can't have that," Puck chuckled. "I'll get you in and out safely."

As they reached the end of the hall, a gold and platinum door rose up before them. Asher squinted, looking at the elaborate inlay depicting bright pictures of animals that Asher didn't recognize with their fanged mouths open. This might have been the most beautiful door he'd ever seen. Puck smiled a sweet nostalgic smile. How long had it been since he stood at this gate? It had been eons now when the world was new and green and everything had seemed all right. His heart swelled with joy as his fingers touched the complex inlay. His tail wagged as big tears rolled down his cheeks.

"Puck, are you okay?" Asher said, concerned at the tears.

"Yea," Puck whispered. "I'm just coming home again."

Slowly, Puck opened the door.

XXX. The Comedown

When the door opened, Asher let out a soft gasp of surprise as he looked upon the other side of the Hedge. Before them stretched a thick forest of lush greens and deep purples that spanned further than Asher cared to look. A soft melody whispered through the flowers the size of trees that to a person paying more attention would have been Toto's Africa. Apparently the Arcadia really rather enjoyed that song. A large purple cat padded by Puck and Asher not giving them a second look as it retreated into the thick of forest. An orange monkey swayed from a leaf, watching him with large iridescent eyes. Asher stood in awe of the deep colors of this world. They had been in the Hedge for so long with its grey-lined haze that anything different would have seemed bright, but it was like this world was created specifically for high definition. It seemed almost too real to Asher. Before he stepped in, Asher took a concerned look back at Puck. The satyr trembled excitedly at the sight of the sweet land of Arcadia. Joy and fear spread through him so deeply that he wasn't sure he was ready to return home. Part of him wanted to run and hide under a desk or someone's skirt. The conflicting emotions sent a quiver through Puck's fur. Asher felt bad again for Puck. He was charging through a desperate rescue mission with an unwitting hostage. He really didn't want to inflict more pain on Puck.

"Look," Asher said gently. "You've done plenty, Puck. If you're scared, it's fine. I can make it from here."

"No," Puck said hesitantly. "I made it this far, I can go further. What's the worst that could happen?"

Puck knew the answer to that question. He also knew the ramifications that could come from asking that question out loud. He would rather not think about the potential consequences of his actions. It made things easier as they stepped into the lush world of the Dream. Asher stopped as a surge of euphoria rushed through him. His eyes went wide and his pupils dilated in a pleasant relaxation that worked through each firing neuron of his brain. He knew that feeling all too well and this was so much better than what he usually felt. This was the best high he'd ever had in his life. Asher stumbled into Puck as he was distracted by the feeling that he loved far too much. Puck didn't care about the clumsiness of Asher. Puck let out a soft moan as he looked around the place he once called home. His heartbeat quickened in his chest as he was wrapped in the blanket that made him feel safe. Puck literally couldn't remember the last time he was this happy.

"It's beautiful," Asher euphorically whispered.

"I know," Puck replied.

They had taken two steps inside the forest when two great big trees sprung to life. Asher felt his knees give way as the trees clamped their branches down on their shoulders. Asher let out a weak sigh. He just wasn't that terrified anymore. Diverting the end of the world made the animated trees less jarring. At this point of this day, this was all too familiar to him. Puck, on the other hand, was terrified. Quick-responding guards meant only one thing; the Great King knew he was there. He let out a bleat of protest in fear. Puck knew this was the end of his life.

"Fourteenth son of Pan," the guards said in the unison of a hard breeze. "Thou must report to Our Great King. As for the Vessel, thy presence is requested by Lady Natalia post haste."

Asher watched as Puck was dragged away by the oak guards, lamenting the impending death of his new friend and now savior. He resolved to ask Lady Natalia, whomever this was, to help Puck out of this predicament. He had helped save the world from destruction, he deserved better than his fate. Asher spun on heels and watched as the curtain of foliage parted, revealing a path out of the jungle. He blinked for a moment before walking down this path. It wasn't even remotely the weirdest thing that had happened to him today, so Asher naturally followed the path towards another goal. He didn't really see what else to do in this matter. Besides he had a good feeling about this Lady Natalia. He walked down the twisting path to the end of the forest that led out into an open field of golden grain. That was when he saw a white palace looming over the forest. Asher blinked and somehow found himself in another throne room. Throne rooms and hospitals, that's what he was getting tired of today. He really needed hobbies that didn't involve either, he decided. He turned with irritation on his face and with a tirade of anger on his lips. Well, until he looked up at the woman sitting on the throne. His heart thumped hard against his chest as he looked into her soft blue eyes that cradled him lovingly. The large purple cat padded past Asher and then settled down at her feet. It looked at Asher passively before curling into a massive purple ball and falling asleep at its lady's feet. Asher was far too busy to make a connection to the creature that had first encountered them as they entered Arcadia. He was busy being smitten with the lovely fairy queen who was keeping his attention. She was stunning. Perfectly stunning, he thought. He watched as her elegant fingers played with a braided strand of her white blonde hair, wrapping it around her ring finger. She rose quietly, letting a purple velvet gown fall elegantly over her shoeless feet as her breasts heaved with an inrush of breath. Asher tried to kneel but found himself instead watching her as she leapt off her throne. He felt her arms around his neck hugging him with familiarity. When their lips locked in a soft kiss, he knew who his fairy queen was. Believe it or not, people kiss differently. No two people kiss the same way. This was the kiss of someone who pulled him out of perdition and cleaned him up. It was a kiss that woke him in the morning and welcomed him home at night. He had found her.

Clichéd...I know. It'll be better next time around.

"Hi, to you too," he said when their kiss broke.

"Asher," she said, clinging tightly to him. "I never thought I'd see you again. It's been so long since I've seen you."

"Natalie," Asher said, confused. "I've been gone for most of an afternoon. It's not been that long."

"Time passes differently here, dear," she said. "I maybe have been here for an afternoon in our world; but here, I've ruled Bluesong and the Changlings who live here for over forty years."

"Yea, kudos on being a noble. Who did you kill to get that?"

"Oh, no one," Natalie said. "I married Our Great King."

"Oh," Asher said, crestfallen. He came all this way to find out she'd moved on without him. Maybe that's not so clichéd. A part of his heart chipped away. "You fell in love with someone else."

"What? No," Natalie said, shocked at Asher. "I don't even like Our Great King. I won the marriage in a card game. For an old fairy, he sucks at card games. Then again, I play Gin Rummy with the kids in the Peds ward. Those cancer kids are card sharks."

"So, you still love me?"

"I was so angry at you for so long here," she admitted shamefully. She looked away sadly. "I blamed you for banishing me here. You took me away from my safe place and threw me here. I thought I was dead for almost ten years."

"I didn't do it," he said hurriedly. "Iago..."

"I know all about it Asher. News travels fast here. Brigid let me know before you came here." She placed her pale hand on his face. "I even know how pretty you really are now which begs the question, why are you here?"

"I came to save you and take you home," Asher said, feeling a little stupid. "Not doing a really good job with it so far."

"Home?" she said, confused. "Oh, I don't know, Asher. I have so many questions about returning to the paper world. Could I get my job back? Will the mundane world be enough for me? Can I pretend that things are normal ever again?"

"Will you marry me?" Asher said softly.

"It's a question I ask myself every day."

"No, I'm asking you, my lady." Asher let go of her hands and knelt before her. He looked up at her, holding on to her hand and smiling. "Natalia Campbell. Ruler of Bluesong. Will you marry me?"

"Yes," she whispered into his lips.

Meanwhile...

Puck felt the warm rush of immersion as he splashed into warm bath water. His dripping mane carefully rose to the surface as he looked around. Puck swallowed the familiar scent of bath salts and lavender as he gasped for air. He shivered in terror as a cool breeze wisped around his horns. The Royal bath tub was never a friendly place to find yourself dumped into, well, not if you were banished from Arcadia eons ago. He leaned over the edge of the golden tub trying to hold back bleats and any and all attempts to expel his fear orally. He wasn't dead. Puck knew he wasn't dead...not yet anyway. That wasn't right. Wasn't he promised that? Return home and die a slow and painful death as opposed to bath time. Then it occurred to him. If he wasn't going to die then his fate had to be that of Iago's madness. He didn't want to go insane like Iago. He'd rather be dead. Puck tried to desperately escape the tub in a panic.

"Pucky Ducky Quack Quack!" said a giddy voice. Puck's ears laid flat against his head as a bleat escaped his lips. "Lovely to see you!"

Puck glanced up reluctantly. He swallowed as he turned to the youthful blond man who sat at the other side of the tub. Puck nervously sank into the water. This was it. This was the end of things for him.

"'Sup, King Oberon Kenobi," Puck said cautiously. "Still bathing, I see."

"Well, Brian did draw fresh water back in 1955, so of course I had to oblige," said their Great King. "Someone has yet to bring me a rubber ducky as I requested. Instead I keep getting bath mates who reek of magi. You are less pretty than my last one, but you smell just as bad."

"I can explain," Puck whispered.

"I should hope so," said the Great King. "I would think that whole 'I'll kill you' thing was going to keep you out for, like, ever."

"Iago tried to kill Amaya and end the world," Puck said. "I couldn't let that happen, so I aligned with the nexus and the mages."

"Will the nymph be all right?" asked the Great King.

"Yea," Puck said with a soft sigh. "I hope so. I didn't think we could be killed so easily."

"Oh, we can," said the Great King. "Immortal doesn't mean impenetrable. If you try long enough, you can kill anything. Puck, we can die in ways I haven't begun to understand."

"Obi," asked Puck. "am I going to die?"

"No, Pucky Ducky Quack Quack," said the Great King. "I won't kill you today; although I will make sure you get what you deserve."

XXXI: Several Weeks Later

Asher hummed a happy tune as he wiped the very last of the excess shaving cream from his now clean-shaven chin. He gave his excessively cheery face a onceover in the bathroom mirror for the twentieth time that morning, making sure that everything was perfect. He then gave his reflection that patent-pending, charismatic smile as he loaded his toothbrush up with more toothpaste, almost taken aback by his own charm. He brushed his teeth in a gingered rhythm with more joy than anyone should reasonably have for brushing their teeth. Today was going to be a good day for him. He could taste it.

Asher practically danced into the bedroom, allowing the song in his head to direct his movement for a moment. He paused at a neatly pressed suit on the corner of his bed. It had the slightly frayed edges of a once worn suit that had been discarded in the used pile of life. Natalie had always hated when he wore thrift store clothing. She knew that he was more than that and he should start dressing like it. He was better than the seven dollar suits that he tried to wear. But Asher liked looking a little shabby. There was something comforting about wearing broken in clothes. He picked up the suit jacket, rolling it around in his hand and smiled to himself. The scent of sandalwood wafted off of it. That meant his slightly worn navy suit came from Pandora's Thrift Shop in Old Gaiman. She had gone into Old Gaiman for a new used suit. This was true love.

She'd become more accepting of his quirks since that day in May. He could find himself telling her about the things that he saw and she'd nod and understand. It was liberating for him to have someone to share this with. Asher was more than excited to move into this new phase of their lives. This new understanding came with an added bonus to his life. It had brought peace between her and his mother. They were now finding themselves becoming more cohesive and safe. He was thrilled to have Natalie finally liking his family. None of these things compared to what he had personally gained, however. The peace between his family had helped him accept his fate in this hidden world. With Natalie supporting him and understanding what his life was going through, he could ease into his new life.

They hadn't come to the conclusion of working for the Department easily. Asher and Natalie had talked for weeks after leaving Arcadia. They had even brought it up to his mother who was almost against it until they came to one conclusion. Asher was too powerful to be hanging around quietly working a normal job. That meant that he could be left sitting on the sidelines. This was equally unacceptable -- the wealth of power living in him and the sense of right and wrong that had been instilled in him demanded action. After discussing it with his mother for the last time, Asher asked to be a part of the Department of the Arcane. He knew that this was his destiny.

Embracing his fate wasn't as easy for him as he thought would be. Namely, he had to let go of his job at Thunderstrikes. It was the job that had turned him around and got him back on his feet. He'd grown quite attached to his place of work. They were sad to see him go, but it was inevitable. No one works a minimum wage job forever. Torg Olsen had known it was only a matter of time before Asher left anyway. No one stays hidden from their place in the universe forever. It still made Asher feel bad.

"Asher," Mr. Olsen said on his last day working for the old man. "It's fine for you to move on. You grew up in two years. You've changed, now move on."

Asher had changed. He had cleaned up and gotten with Natalie. He was starting to be the man who he was supposed to be before he went down the wrong path. It wasn't just that he had gotten clean. In the span of twenty-four hours in the spring, he went from being a recovering junkie to a heroic figure. It was daunting, yes but it gave him a sense of peace. For the first time in twenty-seven years, things made sense.

He insisted on going through the hiring process at the Department. They told him that he didn't need to do such a mundane task. He refused that logic. Asher knew that being handed things would make him lazy. That was the first step into backsliding. Asher made a vow to never ever backslide again.

"What is wrong with you?" Klog the HR Troll asked. "You are the source of all magic. Even if you weren't the nexus, you're the son of Stephen Stone. You don't have to interview. We'll just give you a job."

"I know," he said confidently. "But that's not fair to the other people and too much for me to live up to that legacy. I want the job on my own merit."

He still wasn't sure if he had gotten the job on his own merit or not.

Asher straightened his fresh purple tie before walking out of the bedroom into the foyer. Natalie and his mother sat together on their secondhand blue and white striped couch. An endless library of wedding magazines and planning books claimed the living room and were seeping into his dreams. His mother had chosen to remain in Gaiman Heights after that day back in the Spring. The dig in Mexico would be over in a few short weeks and then Jordan and Brady would be home. Tracy didn't see the point in going back. She had more important things to worry about. She had the house construction to oversee and a wedding to plan.

With her home being in an unbelievable state of disrepair, his mother had made a temporary home with Asher and Natalie. This had spawned an uneasy peace in the house that was often associated with coastlines before a hurricane. While Natalie had become more accepting -- if not more understanding -- of a world she could not explain, she was still leery of her future mother-in-law. Not hateful, just leery. Fairies would always be leery of mages and witches and vice versa. It was a natural thing to have happened and it was going to have to be acceptable for now. Natalie was working through that rather well. Asher secretly hated this turn of events. Something about his future wife and his mother unifying their neuroses made his skin pucker up into sharp goose bumps and shiver uncontrollably. It would only be a matter of time until their intensity started to focus on him.

Asher became distracted by a small auburn blur trotting past his feet in a playful stride. Getting his mother meant also housing Yoshi. Asher wasn't sure he'd let the familiar leave once his mother moved back into her own home. It was nice having a semi-active pet in the house. Yoshi attempted to make everyone else feel better. At this point as he trotted by, Bag of Bones gave chase at his aged pace. After a moment the old cat let out a small sickly meow before going back to sleep.

"Oh, that would lovely on you," Tracy said, pointing to a low cut sleeveless Vera Wang number in one of the books. "It would really rather frame that long neck of yours. Have you decided where you guys are going to go for your honeymoon?"

"Arcadia," Natalie replied matter of factly.

"Oh I bet it's pretty this time of year."

"It's pretty every time of year," Natalie said.

Asher cleared his throat to break the idle chit chat. The women in his life looked up at him gently.

"Well," he said, making a small model turn and then smiled. "How do I look?"

"You look handsome," Natalie said. "I just wish we could do something about those neck tattoos."

"His father had the gnarliest-looking neck tattoos," Tracy said, looking over her son. A proud grin crossed her face. "You look like you mean business, although it's missing something."

Tracy stood up gracefully as her hands reached behind the couch. Before Asher could say anything his eyes fell on the black scabbard of the manticore-killing katana. He felt a pang of heartache as his hands gripped the ancient blade. This was a big day, he knew that. It was like sending your child off to kindergarten. After twenty-seven years of not being a part of this world, he was officially joining the community that he'd long belonged to. He had spent his life waiting for everything to feel like it was going to fit together. Now, as he stood in his living room holding the blade that had protected him and had kept his father safe, things finally fell into place. Asher was home and his life had meaning. He looked back at his mother.

"Asher, House of Stone, Son of Stephen, vessel and protector of the Nexus," Tracy said formally. "I give you the Masamune Sekken with the blessing of your ancestors. Honor them and walk in truth and light. Please...just be careful out there."

"I always am," he said coolly. His gaze turned to his fiancé. "Nat, I'm leaving."

She paused before leaping to her feet. She radiated a warm glow as she wrapped her arms around him. Her nimble fingers placed a light silver necklace around his neck. He smiled as he looked down at the overly complex design on the pendant looking back at her.

"I know you don't need the added protection but that has some spirits attached for safety," she said. "So it makes me feel better."

"Knowing you want me home safe," he said, taking her hand and placing it on his chest, "is all the protection I need."

"Oh, Asher," she said dreamily. "That's like, the cheesiest thing you've ever said to me."

"I could try ha...." he stammered.

"Is there a class they make you take to say things like that?"

"Well, I..."

"That was pretty corny, honey. Like Hugh Grant movie corny," Tracy interjected.

"I could..."

"You should go," Natalie said. "We can't have you late on your first day."

Asher gave Natalie a light kiss before quickly leaving the apartment. He found himself skipping down the steps like a child heading off to his first day of kindergarten filled with excitement and terror. He couldn't be happier to be stepping out onto the dusky street to go to work. He glanced down the street and its dwindling population. The mundane were going to crawl into their warmly lit homes. His people would start to claim the city soon. The Crown Vic was nowhere in sight. It would seem that Karl himself was running late. This didn't bother Asher. Nothing could ruin his fantastic mood.

For the first time in a long time, Asher was content.

Asher smiled again as he watched the sun surrender to the

summer night sky and sink behind the skyline of buildings and trees. That was when Asher was hit by a coarse brown ball of fuzz colliding violently with him. Asher fell backwards towards the concrete helplessly as he let out a started scream. He panicked for a moment as he felt pressure on his chest before his eyes were able to focus on the fuzzy ball on his chest.

"Puck!" Asher said excitedly. "I haven't seen you since me and Natalie left Arcadia. I thought you were dead. How are things?"

"Great!" Puck said brightly. "Because I totally helped you defeat Iago, they paroled me from my sentence, so I get to come home more often and when I want. AND Amaya and me are going to have a baby. We're thinking of naming it Poptart."

"That's, that's great," Asher wasn't sure if Poptart was a good or appropriate name for a baby. Then again it was the child born of fairies. "I'm really happy for you. Congrats."

"Thanks man. Oh hey." Puck slapped Asher's chest. "Congrats to you too, Penny and Amaya are super busy trying to get the guest cottage overlooking the lake ready for you both."

"Who's Penny?" asked Asher apprehensively.

"Amaya's very best friend in the whole world. That reminds me." Puck sat up, straddling Asher's chest. He reached into one of many pockets on his gray army surplus vest. He produced a smooth round stone and placed it on Asher's forehead.

"This is for you and Lady Natalia from us."

Asher picked up the stone from his forehead and blinked. He turned the dark brown stone, examining the rock with a quirked brow.

"If I take this," he asked carefully. "what do I owe you?"

"Nothing, it's a gift," Puck said, slightly offended. "Nothing harmful in giving a gift. It's our way of saying thank you for not exploding and ending all existence."

"Oh," Asher said. "What is it?"

"A gargoyle egg."

"Wait what?"

"Chill out. They are the easiest things in the world to take care of. It protects your home and eats rocks."

Just as Asher opened his mouth to either curse or thank Puck, an old Crown Vic pulled up to the curb. Puck pouted as he recognized the vehicle. He knew that the modern mage had few options. That didn't mean he had to like it. Cool people like Asher didn't need to be cops.

Of course, Asher wasn't really a mage in his estimation.

"Later Asher," Puck said as he got off his chest. "Don't let them turn you into a total dick."

As Puck finally trotted off into the night. Asher stood up slowly shaking his head. He brushed the gravelly dust and city filth from his suit as he climbed into the passenger seat of the Crown Vic. Karl watched Asher adjust himself in the seat. Asher normally would have been irritated with the whole display of everything and doubly so with hanging out with Karl except for Karl's face. Karl's stony expression looked almost as happy as he was.

It must be a good day, thought Asher, even Karl's in a good mood.

"Sorry, I'm late," Karl apologized. "My daughter Annie called. She got the part of Guinevere in her school's play. I've been begging barrowing and stealing to get the night off to be there."

"It's cool." Asher said as he fastened his safety belt. "I take it she's excited."

Karl chuckled.

"According to her mother, Annie is a little mad. She wanted the role of Sir Gawain. She kicked Bobby McCray when he wouldn't switch with her." Karl shook his head. "She's going to be hell on wheels when she's a teenager."

"At least you're getting some practice with Norvita." Asher looked around suspiciously. "Where is she anyway?"

"Norvita is with Agents Dira and Aguirre." Karl merged onto the overpass smoothly and without fanfare. "They needed a psychic to question a very difficult suspect. And I figured that your first night on the job should be free from nonconsensual dry humping. Speaking of which, I found what is up with that blade you brought back from the Hedge."

"That has nothing to do with what happened," Asher said. "but what is it?"

"Well," Karl's expression changed quickly. "It's too light to be a fae or human weapon. Judging by the scythe-like curve in the blade and the inscription on it, I'd say it's ethereal in origin, more likely angelic. If it's an angelic blade, that opens up a whole host of questions. Angels are hard to catch and they're known for their precision weapons that can kill pretty much anything, normally. You shouldn't have survived a swing from it."

"I'm not normal," Asher muttered.

"Yea, that's true. I'm not going to start that unique and special snowflake crap. Hell, the abyssal scholars are perplexed by your existence, which means you're different." Karl shrugged. "Luckily, it does narrow down the owner's list. Ethereal weapons are impossible to get ahold of in the mortal realm so they're rare to say the least, but once we get the demonologist to look it over we'll know where it comes from and who it belongs to."

"Is that where we're going?" Asher asked as he looked out the window. He didn't recognize this part of the city.

"Nope." Karl cringed as the car scraped along a pothole. "Asher, what do you know about vampires?"

Asher thought about spouting the things he'd learned in movies about vampires and then thought better of it. This was a learning experience for him in a new world and he was going to be respectful. Besides, movies never, ever got it right.

"Probably not as much as you do," Asher conceded.

"Well, I do have an encyclopedic knowledge of the occult," Karl said. "But you're about to learn firsthand."

The Crown Vic stopped in front of an ancient bar in what Asher guessed was South Gaiman.

"Pitch's?" he mouthed to himself

Meanwhile...

Norvita knew that this assignment was going to suck and not in the fun way. First off Aguirre and Dira wouldn't let her play with the radio in their SUV. Karl would have let her play with the radio. At least Karl would have talked to her. They didn't talk to her at all. They didn't talk to each other either. Just because golems didn't know how to interact with people didn't mean that they could be rude. Then they took her to Twillingast Asylum. Norvita hated being around crazy people. Their thoughts would worm into her head, making a life little harder. When you hear thoughts that are convincing and slightly insane it wears on one's psyche. It was like losing one's mind in drips.

Someone was going to buy her a very stiff drink after this.

She fidgeted nervously as madness swam threateningly around her ears like swarming piranhas. The clay-molded agents escorted her to an iron-barred room. Her pretty eyes watched a huddled figure in dirty gray pajamas. His shaking body curled into a ball in a corner. His dry elbows rested on his knees hiding his terrified face. Norvita swallowed as she watched his ghostly fingers pull his hair into greasy spikes trying to feel his way back to being what he was. Iago does looks frail, thought Norvita, I almost feel bad for him.

Almost.

"According to staff," they said in unison, "our suspect has only said two words since his incarceration."

"No music," Norvita whispered.

"Yes," they continued. "As you know, there are unresolved elements to this case. Miss Patel, if you can tell us anything, we'd appreciate it."

Norvita leaned forward and squinted her eyes. She breathed in the stifling air as she turned her head to one side, listening to Iago's thoughts. Something else cut through the voices of mad whispers. It hit her with a violent push that froze her body as rigid as if she'd been hit with blunt force trauma. Her mouth opened trying to release the painful scream seizing her mind. With another psychic hit her eyes opened. Just as quickly as the vision had taken her, it let go. She'd had visions before. Not everyone thought in words. Sometimes things would come through in pictures. They weren't harmful, just simple pictures, it meant she had visions.

This wasn't one of those times.

This vision hurt her in places she wasn't sure she could feel. People's thoughts, no matter how evil or nasty, rarely hurt like this. She felt an indiscernible pain ripping heavy gashes into her soul. She saw fire that licked the night sky. Nothing specifically on fire, per say, just a lot of red and orange flames that were overpowering everything else. She then heard a loud screech of pain that ran through her ears and vibrated into her head. She swore it sounded like a pained scream. She looked back at the agents and smiled weakly.

"I'm not getting anything from him," she said hoarsely. "He doesn't have anything planned."

"Psychic," Iago said warmly. His hands craned up at her. Norvita flinched as she stared into his lifeless blue eyes. "You shouldn't worry about what I could be planning. You should worry about what I've done."

Norvita stopped breathing as his words hit her face and froze her blood cold. The screaming wail resonated in her ears painfully. Tomorrow, she'd call her grandfather and they would interpret her visions. That was for tomorrow. Tonight though, was a night for booze and angry sex with Carson.